Two Feet Press

UNDONE

An UNLIKELY SERIES Novel

Book 3

JB SCHROEDER

Two Feet Press

PO Box 351
Chatham, NJ 07928-9991

Undone © 2018 by JB Schroeder, LLC

www.jbschroederauthor.com

Cover photographs @studio77.bk.ru/depositphotos,
©belphnaque/depositphotos, and ©bradcalkins/depositphotos

Digital Edition 1.0

ISBN-10: 1-943561-07-9
ISBN-13: 978-1-943561-07-0

To Dad
With love

~

So grateful for your never-wavering support
So glad you opened my heart to NYC all those years ago

CHAPTER 1

MAXINE RICCI, a born and bred New Yorker, knew which subway lines connected where, which bodegas had fresh fruit at a reasonable price, which nail salons might give you fungus, when to smile at a cat call—and when to flip someone off. Her willowy, redheaded model Helena Castle, however, was brand-spanking new. The eighteen-year-old had recently been plucked from a mall in Nebraska by one of Max's best scouts. Helena was new to the Big Apple, new to modeling, and heck, still new at life in general.

Under Max's wing, though, she'd learn modeling *and* she'd learn to make her way in the world—whether it was New York or Milan. She had the look, the intangible one Max just knew would have photographers itching to shoot her.

Max had been doing this a long time, and there was nothing more gratifying than seeing someone's dreams come true. *Making* a star. But she also loved simply putting people to work; helping them use their assets, discover their strengths, and find their niche. She had a knack for it. And she was nearly always right.

Of course, it was yet to be determined if Helena truly had the drive. Modeling was a tough business, and not everyone was cut out to do the work. Luckily there were other types of modeling jobs—tiers relating to both fame and pay scale. If a model didn't cut it on the runway or in the fashion magazines, there were always other options: advertising, commercials, fit modeling, showroom modeling, part modeling. The list went on and on.

Max approached the corner where there was a gaggle of people waiting for the light to change. Even this early on a Saturday, this area of the city was crowded. She gripped the strap of her Coach bag tighter. Protecting against pickpockets was second nature. That was the price she paid for style—designer bags didn't often take into account security.

Max sucked in a deep breath of possibility as the light changed. She loved a fresh slate. Seeing Helena come into her own was going to be awesome.

Helena was staying in a fourth-floor walk-up near Port Authority. Not the most attractive location, but central to transportation, safe, and well-maintained. Max's company, Ivory Management, kept it year-round, but rent came out of the models' pay. The girls needed the camaraderie when they first arrived, they learned from one another, and face it—hardly anyone in New York could afford not to have a room-mate or two, or three.

Max pulled out her phone and texted *almost there* as soon as she crossed the sidewalk.

Helena had a hair appointment bright and early. Max had been using certain stylists for years, paying well, and in some cases making their careers. Keith Tomlin was one of those, so he'd graciously squeezed them in ahead of his first appointment. And thank God because Helena's hair, while a gorgeous color, had never had a decent cut, let alone one from a true artist. She grinned. This was going to be such fun. Exactly why she was escorting Helena to the appointment herself, rather than having her assistant Cameron Bender do it.

She had a key to the street level door and used it, then dumped it and her sunglasses in her bag as she started up the stairs. It felt more like August than early September. She was already too warm and had a feeling the climb would make her hair curl at the temples and nape.

Max knocked on the door of 4C and waited. The stairwell smelled like somebody had made brisket last night—somehow it always did. Being half Jewish, she knew her comfort foods. Of course, her Italian half was just as comfortable with a good Sunday sauce.

Max pursed her lips and knocked again—harder. She called, "Helena, you ready?"

The girl had better be ready. She'd talked to her just last night to remind her about this appointment, and they'd agreed to meet here at 6:45 a.m. on the dot. Sometimes, as eager as models were to start a new career, they were also excited to discover the New York party scene...

"Helena!"

Why wasn't anyone answering? With only one large bedroom with two sets of bunks, one dated bathroom, and one cramped living room–kitchen combo, the place wasn't very big. Surely they could hear her. *And where the hell were the others?* Max wondered, rooting in her bag again for the key. Oh yeah, Kristen was in L.A. on a shoot, and Catherine had jetted home because her dad had undergone unexpected bypass surgery. The fourth bed wasn't being used this month.

Max twisted the key but the deadbolt didn't turn—it was already open. She grabbed the knob and that turned without the key as well. Well crap, Helena needed a common-sense lesson in safety. Top priority. One did not leave doors open in New York, no matter how secure the building.

"Helena!" Max called again as she strode through the living room, dropping her purse on the coffee table on the way. No answer and no noise. The girl better not be asleep. Max shoved open the door to the bedroom—

And nothing. Unmade bed, clothes strewn all over the floor. Jammies hanging on the top corner of the bunk frame.

Max spun, huffing out a frustrated breath. Two steps and she was at the bathroom door. She yelled, "Helena," and pounded on the door with her fist.

It wasn't latched, so it swung open a few inches. That's when Max saw it.

A bare foot, size ten, with bubble-gum pink sparkly nail polish—the wrong color for a redhead—prone on the floor.

She gasped—had she fallen and hit her head on the tub, or had she passed out drunk after puking up her guts?

Max pushed at the door, but it hit something soft—Helena. Max stepped in as far as she could and peered around the door, only to rear back in horror at the scene before her.

Blood—everywhere.

———

The detective, Danny Iocavelli—a native New Yorker like Max from the accent, who looked like he should be nursing his troubles on a barstool in Dublin—wasn't exactly the comforting sort. That was okay, she thought, since she hated to be coddled. But she had no answers either, and the repetitive questioning was getting old.

She sat stiffly on the sofa in Helena's apartment, he faced her in the one remaining chair.

"What time did you talk to the victim last night?" Iocavelli asked.

"Her name is Helena."

He raised an eyebrow and she raised one right back. She reached for her cell phone on the coffee table. Perhaps if they played show and tell, he'd be satisfied. She hit recent calls and turned the screen to face him. "9:27 exactly, and the call lasted for 2 minutes and 48 seconds."

"Uh huh." He jotted it down in his little notebook.

Old school in a young body. Thirty tops, she thought.

"All right—"

Just then there was a commotion at the door. The officer posted there said, "Sorry, no entry."

A man attempted to get around him, placing his hand against the door and trying to squeeze through. "I'm here for Ms. Ricci."

It was Cam, Max's assistant.

"Sir!" the officer said sharply and blocked him with his body.

Max stood. "It's all right, he's with me."

Iocavelli rose too, tucking the pad and pen in an interior pocket of his well-worn leather jacket. "This is a crime scene. No one enters." He slid a glance toward Max. "But you can go. We'll be in touch with more questions."

Max nodded, she only wished she had something helpful to give him. "Thank you. Will you… keep me posted?"

Iocavelli gave a curt nod. Her shoulders slumped, taking that as a no. He probably wasn't allowed to tell her jack.

The detective barked at the other officer. "Who the hell is posted downstairs? And why isn't the crime scene tape up?"

"It is," Cam raised his chin. "I needed to get to Max."

She tuned them out. Max glanced toward the short hall between the living area and the bathroom where some crime scene techs worked—squeezed in yet working in perfect tandem. Much like the crew backstage during a fashion show. Something Helena would never see.

Max squeezed her eyes shut and breathed. When she

opened them, she reached for her purse, smoothed her hair away from her face, and walked out, eyes forward and shoulders back. Not quite strong and sure as usual, but better than the quaking knees and queasy stomach she'd had when the police had arrived.

Cam launched himself at her the minute she stepped into the hallway. She wore heels as always, which put them at an even height. He wrapped his arms around her and squeezed.

"What the hell, sweetie? Are you okay?"

Cam had been her dear friend and invaluable right-hand man ever since she'd opened her agency, Ivory, and before that, he'd been a colleague in the business. He'd started in makeup, and she'd started in casting. Homosexual and long out of the closet, he was one of the few men who never hit on her. While she appreciated that, what she really loved was Cam's astute nature and his loyalty to both her and Ivory. He knew what she needed almost before she did, and even when he didn't necessarily agree with her decisions—snarky comments and all—he still had her back.

He'd been the first one she'd called today—after 911 of course. Not only had she needed to tell someone, she'd needed him to get Helena's parents' contact information from the files for the police. They'd make the initial call, but she'd certainly talk with them as well. Tears welled in her eyes. What in God's name would she even say in a situation like this? She couldn't imagine anything this horrible—and yet, she'd seen it. With her very own eyes.

"Let's get you out of here," Cam said and ushered her down the stairs.

When they'd reached the street and Max had sucked some deep lungfuls of air, he said. "What do you want to do?"

"I have to call Keith. We missed the appointment."

"I called him. He's horrified."

"Oh, no. You shouldn't have told him the details. We can't let this get out. Her parents haven't even been told yet."

"I'm sure that officer will be calling them pronto if he hasn't already. And there is no way this isn't going to get out. Besides, I didn't know much to tell him."

Max clenched her jaw. He was right. Overall crime was down in the city, but something like this would make headlines, and fast. *Aspiring model new to city. Attacked in her own apartment. Fought hard to live.*

And she must have. The backs of her hands and arms bore slash marks. Maybe instead of raising her arms to fend off her attacker, she'd covered herself? Yet…she hadn't been naked. She'd been wearing a nubby pink robe…

It had gaped open, or maybe it had already been open, Max thought. She saw the scene all over again in her mind's eye. There had been numerous stab wounds in her abdomen. There was also a puncture wound on her neck. Blood had been everywhere—spray on the walls, the shower curtain, the sink, the mirror…pooled under her upper half where she lay.

But the worst part was the gel, a translucent yellow sheet similar to cellophane but stiffer that photographers sometimes used in the studio… A gel was simply a filter for light to shine through and could create some cool effects. Here though…

One had been placed over her stomach, taped down with a huge black X, blood smeared between Helena's skin and the gel. Another was taped over her face, nearly hairline to chin, in both directions.

Max shuddered, and then blinked as she suddenly realized that Cam was snapping his fingers in front of her face.

"You are *not* all right. We need to get you home," he said.

"No. Too quiet there. I'll go to work." Max looked around to get her bearings. Boy, she was really thrown if she couldn't even remember what corner she was on.

"Uh," Cam said, squinting his eyes at her, "it'll be rather quiet there, too, given that it's Saturday."

"But I can distract myself maybe."

"Okay, I'll come with you."

Max nodded and they turned south toward the fashion district.

"So," Cam said. "You want to tell me about it?"

Max told him the beginning, pressing her hand to her mouth when she remembered that she'd been annoyed, thinking Helena had forgotten or screwed up. But when she got to the bathroom part, she trailed off.

"What do you think happened? She was knifed you said? All—" he waved his hand over his front, "cut up?"

Max felt bile rising in her throat and halted. She really, really couldn't discuss this.

"Jeez," a woman complained as she barely avoided colliding with Max. Cam stopped, too, as people streamed around them.

Max swallowed. "I think I'd better go home after all. I'm not feeling very well." She stepped to the curb and stretched out her arm, then shrieked a whistle when she saw a yellow cab with his light on. The vehicle darted toward her and stopped on a dime. She wasted no time climbing in.

"Call me. I'm here if you need me," Cam said, and shut the door for her.

She nodded but didn't look at him. She gave the cabbie her address, then two blocks later changed her mind. She'd go see her best friend Miranda, who'd have hugs, a shoulder to fall apart on, and decent coffee—plus something to spike it with if she couldn't pull herself together.

She most definitely did not want to be alone.

CHAPTER 2

IT HADN'T HAPPENED like this before. Well, things had happened, but not like this, not exactly, not for a long time. He was both stunned at this new turn of events, and yet not surprised. How was that possible? The circumstances—yes, it had to be. This particular set of circumstances made it possible. Wrenching old wounds viciously forth from a place long buried.

It'd been a long time since he'd found himself avenged. But betrayals—especially purposeful ones, meant to deceive—were worthy of that, weren't they?

As soon as he caught wind of a major betrayal, there was no stopping him. He couldn't have, even if he'd wanted to.

He shook his head. It almost didn't matter. Helena was gone. Gone for good, and that was for the best. She wouldn't ruin that beautiful body with grotesqueness after all.

He'd remember her only as she'd been when they'd first met. So gorgeously unique. So fresh, so smooth, so delicate. Every curve absolute divinity. Meant to be viewed and adored. Meant to grace print and film, and maybe even the runway.

Well, there was a limit to her fame now. She'd never be more than she was. Never reach the pinnacle she could have. No use speculating on it. Yet, it hurt. It always hurt, so much, to say goodbye this way. Death, he well knew, was forever.

And he'd so desperately wanted her to live in his day, as

well as his night. These girls, these women were capable of that, he knew. They were royalty among the masses.

He'd have to return his focus to the others. Because there were others. He'd simply been distracted—so instantly taken with Helena.

He prayed that his favorites remained pure. He truly hoped they didn't disappoint him. He wanted them to soar, he wanted them to be big. He wanted to continue to watch them shine, to adore them, to help them reach their maximum potential.

Yes, another. An opposite to help him forget.

Inky black hair. So sleek and slim. Skin like gold. A natural grace. Dark eyes that spoke of secrets. Secrets he desperately wanted to know, to understand innately, to *feel*.

CHAPTER 3

SHANE O'ROURKE PUSHED open the door to the office of O'Rourke Security and groaned when he saw the light squeezing around his uncle's door. It was Saturday morning after a brutal night. Joseph O'Rourke, Shane's uncle, then mentor and now partner, had already been briefed about last night's loss—disaster, debacle, failure, shite show—but they hadn't spoken in person. Apparently they were about to commence round two.

Shane flipped on the overhead light in the common area where their receptionist usually sat and crossed the room. He paused at Joe's door and leaned his head against the doorframe. He stared at a spot where the paint had chipped off and tried to corral his swirling emotions. Regret, disappointment, fear, frustration, disgust.

"Don't just stand out there, come in," Joe called.

Shane snorted, and pushed open the door. "Can't give a man a minute?"

"Another minute's not gonna matter." Joe pointed to the wooden chair in front of his desk, then leaned back and crossed his arms loosely over his middle.

He was a big man, still in shape, early sixties, with a slightly ruddy complexion. Besides his Irish accent, normally Joe was somewhat nondescript—blending was important in their business—but recently he'd started to grow a beard. With more gray than black in his close-cropped dark hair and new beard still filling in, he looked like a scrappy, but well-fed dog.

Shane tossed his suit jacket over the chair and then slumped into it.

"How you holding up?" Joe's eyes had been taking in Shane's details since he'd come in. And Joe knew him probably better than anyone.

"Been better."

"Yeah, I can imagine." He reached for his coffee with a slight tremor in his fingers, and slurped, then pointed to the pot in the corner of his small office. "You want?"

Joe was a coffee fiend. That pot was on constant drip. Shane wondered if he should be cutting back now. Would it make any difference? The TV was also constantly on in the same corner, although thankfully the news was on mute. Someday the old outlets in this building would probably burst into flames—starting in that very corner.

Shane shook his head. He, himself, almost never needed it. He was constantly jazzed up. What he did need was some sort of export button instead. And today was worse. No sleep, constant briefings, the questions inside his head—feck, if he had caffeine he'd explode.

"It happens," Joe said.

"Not to me," Shane said.

"Yes to you, and to me, too," Joe said.

Shane scoffed. "You haven't lost an asset since I started working with you."

Joe grimaced. "1989. Karl Menke. Scientist. 1997: Sera Cachman. Victim of a stalker. 2004: Formula 256 at Tileon Labs. 2006: Fred Parse. Witness."

"Jaysus." Shane's own refrain started running through his head. *2018 Carrie Sorrelle. Witness. Twenty years old.* God willing his own list would stop there.

"Yeah," Joe said. "I remember every detail. And trust me, you'll second guess yourself until the day you meet your maker, but once in a while we do lose them despite our best efforts." He slurped again, then set the cup down as he leaned forward. "You gotta look at the overall track record. You know how many jobs I've taken over the years? Those, the successful ones, thankfully, I can't even count. So I've saved far, far more assets than I've lost, despite the fact that the bulk of them don't cooperate for shite."

Shane felt like there was a marble behind his Adam's apple, and he forced a hard swallow. Carrie Sorrelle had been one of those. She hadn't taken the threat seriously and had tried her best to elude him in every way possible. A witness to a drug deal, a major one, that was about to go to trial, she'd been convinced that with the dealer behind bars she'd been safe. But it wasn't some random street thug she was dealing with. This was a major organized crime ring. Shane and his team had warned and explained and pushed and cajoled. Her dad, who'd hired them, had even bribed her with a new car. But she was young, stupid, and shortsighted. She was into her partying, needed attention, craved action, and was a sneaky, creative little thing to boot.

"With all our prepping and planning and training, we still often only have seconds." Joe tapped his middle finger on the table twice. "Split seconds."

That had been drilled into Shane during training. In the U.S., most attacks are over and done with within five seconds. It had only taken a second for him to realize Carrie had managed to give him the slip, and although he'd been right behind her, bullets took far less time.

And once she lay there dying, despite his best efforts to staunch the bleeding, she looked even younger than her twenty years. He was filled with remorse, felt powerless, and his anger gained momentum fast—it always did when he started to feel out of control.

He flexed his hands, then cracked his knuckles, and then his neck. "How do you..." He shook his head. "How do you ever get past it?"

Joe looked him in the eye. "You don't. You learn from it. You add it to your experience base."

Shane swore. "I don't know. I don't have your background. Maybe—"

"Bull," Joe snapped at him. "You've proven yourself over and over, and you've definitely got what it takes. Besides, it's not all on your shoulders, not yet."

Thank God for that, because not only was he not ready for it, but this latest screw up couldn't help an already struggling bottom line.

Yet, it would be on his shoulders eventually. At Joe's insistence, Shane had been made full partner a couple of years ago and well ahead of official retirement, the older man had begun to step back. He no longer did security detail. Early signs of Parkinson's meant he didn't trust his trigger finger. Now he brought in business, advised, guided, and generally ordered everyone else around. Not that he hadn't already.

"Go to the gym," Joe said. "Beat something—or someone—up. You'll feel better."

Most of the time, yeah, boxing saved Shane's sanity. But this time? He doubted it. Still—it was the only thing he knew to do when life sucked this much.

He grabbed his jacket and was halfway out the door when Joe said, "Oh hey—you probably haven't seen the news yet."

"No." Even if he'd had time, he would have avoided it. He didn't want to know what they were saying about the Sorrelles, his failure, or the chances for the dealer in his upcoming trial. "What's up?"

"Your old agency, that modeling place, made headlines."

He was long gone from that world and good riddance, but he played along. "Ivory Management? What? Another skin treatment gone wrong?"

Joe hit a button. "Some young model bit it."

That world had serious pitfalls if you weren't careful. Shane asked, "Overdose? Party accident?"

"Murder."

"No way." Shane wondered if it was anyone he'd known. He focused on the screen. A reporter on the West Side. An officer guarded a doorway. Nothing seemed to be happening there now, but that never stopped the talking heads. Pictures of a model named Helena Castle flashed on the screen. One showed a fresh-faced, sweet young thing. The other was a headshot—professional enough, but not of the caliber that Ivory was known for. He should know. He'd landed a contract with them at age nineteen, after loads of odd jobs, one of which had brought him in contact with a beautiful leggy girl. He'd been bedding her off and on for a while when she landed her own modeling contract and hooked him up with an interview. He'd been bouncing around from couch to couch, often Joe's, generally working restaurant jobs with a few fights for side money thrown in. Modeling sounded as good as any other job. He'd been wrong. Harder work than he'd expected, but exhilarating and exciting, too. He'd been a natural, or so he'd been told, making more dough than he'd ever dreamed of. For a while, he'd thought, he'd had it made. Lights, camera, action.

The news station showed what must have been an earlier clip. Maxine Ricci, owner of Ivory, coming out of the building with her assistant, Cam. She looked stricken. Really upset. Pale, no lipstick, and the collar of her shirt was only half standing up.

Shane had never seen her like that. She was normally…
on. Totally together. Focused, commanding, stunning, sexy…

And oh yeah, don't forget, a stone-cold bitch.

Just then, Shane's cell phone vibrated in his pocket. He
looked at the display and told Joe, "It's Danny."

Joe smiled and waved a hand to indicate he should take
the call.

Danny Iocavelli was Shane's cousin. They'd grown up
together—in the summers anyway—each year when Danny
had come home to Ireland to stay with the Irish half of his
family.

They greeted each other warmly, and then Danny as was
often his way, cut straight to the point. "What can you tell me
about Maxine Ricci of Ivory Management?"

Shane stood up straighter. He hadn't seen that coming.
Danny must have landed this morning's case, and of course
he'd known that once upon a time, Shane had been an Ivory
Management model. What could he say?

"Well, there's a reason Ivory is one of the top agencies in
the business," Shane explained. "Max works like a fiend. And
she's really got an eye, an instinct. She's made a lot of careers."

"What else?" Danny asked.

"You want personal life? She churns through men—if
you've met her then you know why—but supposedly never
mixes pleasure with business."

Danny said, "I've met her. Go on."

"She's smart and tough, but…" Shane thought about how
to put it, "…somewhat ruthless."

"Ruthless, huh? Tell me more."

Shane sighed. Way back when he'd have thrown Max
under the bus without a second's thought. But he wasn't the
immature, bitter kid he'd been then. He'd moved on and had

no desire to revisit the past. Maybe if he gave Danny his bone, he'd slink off.

Shane said, "She treats her models well—when they are making money." Shane glanced at the TV screen, which still showed the Helena Castle story. Helena was new, she would have been treated like a rising star, and Max would have been mentoring her herself most likely.

"And then? What?" Danny prodded. "She treats them like crap?"

"No. They're just gone. Done. Like they never existed."

Had Helena called Max to come over? For help maybe? Given how upset Max looked in that clip the station kept replaying, Shane wondered, had she discovered the body?

He clenched his jaw and turned away. What the hell did he care? He'd stopped thinking about her years ago.

CHAPTER 4

A month later

IT'D BEEN A long week, and Max was really looking forward to her workout. She intended to heat up on the treadmill, work her glutes to the max on the elliptical, and then switch to some dreaded lunges. Today, which was a Tuesday, was all about legs. Her favorite playlist full of dance tunes and girl power pop music would get her through.

Her Friday spot was all about her upper body. Most days in between she did yoga or pilates in a different venue.

This gym, CRANK (forever written in all caps everywhere) was special—because it was *private*. Zeke trained models, actors and the like here. But any hours he wasn't teaching he rented out. A win-win. And the best part was, nobody overlapped. Everyone who signed up also signed a contract. You were on time—both coming and going, or you were out. Period. There was enough time between spots that you didn't even pass in the stairwell.

When you were known for your looks, you didn't always want to huff and puff and get blotchy, red-faced, or sweaty in public. Max sure didn't, and it wasn't like she was gracing the covers of any magazines. More importantly, the alone time was crucial for her well-being, even on a normal week.

Ever since Helena had been killed, people had been hugging her and asking her how she was doing and giving her concerned looks. They meant well, of course, but it was disconcerting. And she had the awful feeling that Detective Iocavelli was keeping close tabs on her. So, she didn't say much, and she tried hard to focus on her business and keep to a normal routine. But Max still thought about the young girl at the oddest times, and if she didn't distract herself quickly enough, she saw Helena's body all over again. Laying like a tortured rag doll on that cold floor.

Max shuddered, and paused on CRANK's stoop to double-check the automated text she'd received with today's code. She pressed it into the keypad, pushed through the vestibule, and jogged up the stairs. The building was nothing special, inside or out, until you got inside Zeke's gym. Then it was chrome and rubber and red squishy flooring and giant glass windows on two sides. Max smiled. It made working out sooooo much nicer. She opened her music app on her phone as she keyed in the code again, this time on the pad outside the studio door. Even from the hallway, the bluetooth would start to sync up. She didn't want to waste any time and bounced a little on her feet.

A click, and she was in. She hit play and let the door swing shut behind her. Immediately a peppy beat from the newest Demi Lovato song blasted from the hidden speakers. Max turned to set her bag on the table and peeled out of her outer layer. She dumped it on top of her bag along with her sunglasses, and immediately headed for the treadmill.

She hopped up, set a fifteen-minute hilly course, and watched the display as it picked up speed. In only a couple of minutes, she was running hard. Adrenaline and relief coursed through her. She lifted her chin and looked out the window at the street action below. As her gaze tracked to the right, she caught a reflection in the glass and gasped in shock.

Someone was *here.*

Max stumbled and nearly pitched off the treadmill. She righted herself, fighting a wave of embarrassment, then realized the prone person's reflection hadn't even budged. She jabbed the pause button and jumped off the machine even as her brain sped with possibilities. Had the client before her fallen asleep, or had some sort of medical emergency? Or…

Please *no…not again…*

Max crossed the room—torn between rushing to help and moving cautiously toward danger. The treadmill behind her finally slowed to a stop. So did Max. Her music still blared, but the loss of that whir made the place feel suddenly empty. More terrifying.

She forced herself forward. "Hello?" she tried.

As soon as she rounded the big weight machine, she *knew*. The worst *had* happened. Again.

Max froze.

A lean woman with a blond top bun lay on a bench, beaten to a pulp. Her legs were stretched out straight, and her arms hung off the bench. Squares of yellow gels were taped on the insides of both elbows. Max did not want to think about what that might mean.

Bile rose in her throat, and she had to turn away. She covered her mouth with her hand and took shallow breaths. She forced herself to move closer, to look. In case there was any chance—*please God*—this woman was breathing. She couldn't tell by the chest and suspected she'd have to check for a pulse—and then she saw the eye.

One eye, open and completely lifeless. The other was swollen shut and covered in blood. Her whole face was…just destroyed.

Max cried out and ran for her phone, her purse, the door.

She exploded into the hallway, sobbing and simultaneously attempting to enter her passcode on her phone. "Oh

God, oh God," she chanted. Her fingers refused to work—the code on her phone didn't take, and she had to start over.

She stumbled to the steps and sat, leaning against the wall. *Breathe,* she told herself, and tried again with the code. This time it worked. Next, she dialed 911.

"Someone's been killed. Murdered," she told the operator, her whole body shuddering. She gave the address and said, "I found her. I'm alone, please send someone fast." Her voice wasn't working right and it was all she could do to get the words out, but the dispatcher kept her talking, answering questions.

She could still hear the pounding beat of her playlist from inside CRANK. It seemed sacrilegious, and she felt like she should turn it off. But it was all she could do to focus on the dispatcher. Max scooted down a step, and then another and another as they talked. She didn't want to be anywhere near that body.

A barbell had been near the floor, with blood and hair caught on one end. The woman's face and head had been beaten badly—so violently that there was no recognizing her. Much of her hair was matted with blood. Max whimpered and pressed her knuckles hard into her lips to stop the noise. The woman's running shoes had been scattered throughout the room, along with her socks. Most of it made no sense.

Like her elbows, her feet had yellow color gels, black tape holding it down corner to corner…gaffer tape or maybe electrical.

Which could mean only one thing: The same person who killed Helena was responsible for this. She shut her eyes and shook her head, wanting desperately to deny that fact.

She heard sirens, which quickly got louder and louder, until they were screaming.

The dispatcher spoke again and asked her to go down and

open the door. Max wasn't sure her legs would hold her and told her today's code. Another minute and she heard a click. Thank God.

"Third floor," she whispered to the woman on the phone, even though she'd told her before.

Max clutched her purse to her chest and huddled close to the wall as numerous sets of feet pounded up the steps from below.

When the officers came up, their guns were out. Two stayed with her, the others pounded past. She shrank back, her hand clutching the phone tight to her ear.

"They're here," she told the dispatcher.

"3A?" she heard someone ask. Both she and the dispatcher answered. "Yes."

"Same code," Max said, and one of the cops yelled that to his counterparts.

She heard them enter, shut her eyes and let the phone drop to her lap.

"Ma'am, please stand up," one of them said.

She forced her eyes open, only to see their guns still pointed at her. Did they think she'd done this? That she was capable of such a thing?

She searched their faces, but they wore impenetrable expressions. One reached for her purse and slid it across the step before picking it up. The other gestured for her to hurry up. Habit had her picking up her cell phone from her lap—she thought it might even be still connected to the call. With one hand braced on the wall, she pushed up on shaky legs.

Yes, she thought, as their eyes swept over her and the other poked around in her bag, *they're making sure I'm not armed.* Was this standard operating procedure? Or was it because she was now linked with two murders? Scary, scary thought.

"Okay, come on." He motioned for her to precede him down the stairs.

In only a tank top and capri leggings, she shook with cold, goosebumps covering her arms as she wrapped them around herself. Once outside, the paramedics wrapped her in a blanket and began checking her vitals. Her zippered jacket must still be inside, she thought, feeling that if only she could have that she'd be warm again. The sirens had stopped and she heard the male paramedic murmur something about shock.

An officer stuck close, arms crossed. Another one stood a few yards away on the opposite side. Both watched her. Numerous police and first responder vehicles blocked two lanes of traffic. The street surrounding them was already snarled with cars, and pedestrians gathered at the barricades on the sidewalk to gawk.

She didn't care and barely registered the chaos. Her brain was worming around the most awful, terrible questions.

Was that body, that poor woman, another model? And if so, was she from another agency, or Max's own?

———

Once the paramedics deemed Max well enough, the taller officer took her elbow. Before she realized what was happening she was ensconced—imprisoned essentially—in the backseat of an official police vehicle.

"Hey!" she yelled and pounded on the window. Then she flipped him off in typical New York Italian fashion. How dare they treat her like a criminal!

No, she thought, a *suspect*.

And as soon as she thought of that mangled body upstairs,

she burst into tears. Because now that she was feeling slightly more like herself, she realized—between the hair, the build, the tennis shoes, and the eye color—who the woman was.

Win Michaels. One of Max's models. Twenty-two years old, Win had been with Ivory for three years. She was a quiet but determined tall blond, with skin as clear and smooth as porcelain. Rather androgynous-looking, which was extremely desirable in the field nowadays, she'd recently started getting real traction.

Although Win had also been a little unreliable of late. Max had assumed the model was getting too big for her britches, but the placement of those color gels made her wonder. And she could only think of one thing. Had Win begun using drugs? Heavily? And if so, how had Max missed it?

Max prayed it wasn't true and yet knew, somehow, it was. She felt the disappointment of that like a physical blow. Much the same way she'd felt when Detective Iocavelli had shown up at her office about a week and a half after Helena had been killed.

Without preamble, he'd asked, "Did you know that Helena Castle was pregnant?"

Max had reared back in her chair, but although Iocavelli watched her closely, she wasn't capable of making her face do anything. She was shocked. Horrified. Heartsick. So many thoughts had raced through her head. Why had Helena signed a contract if she was pregnant? Her poor parents—had they been told? Would they feel that news like another loss, or would they be furious at their daughter? The killer, that sick bastard, had he known? Had Helena even known?

Finally, she answered the detective. "I had no idea. How many weeks?"

"About eight, give or take," Iocavelli said.

He asked her a few more questions, none of which she remembered now, and excused himself to go re-question some other Ivory employees.

Now, Max had some of those answers. And so, surely did the police. Because the placement of the color gels was telling. The killer must have known Helena was pregnant, which meant Helena herself had known. As for Win, those gels weren't on her stomach, or her face, or anywhere random. They were very purposefully placed. Max had had her head in the sand. But the killer hadn't. Oh, Win…

Max out and out sobbed for Win and all over again for Helena, curling herself down over her knees so that no one could see her face. Vanity didn't much figure in right now, but this kind of falling apart deserved a bit of privacy.

Finally, she petered out. And that's when she realized the goddamn police had her purse. She had no tissues, no compact mirror, no lipstick, no phone. *Jerks.*

Max bent over again and used the inside of her tank top to mop her face and hopefully wipe the worst of the mascara from under her eyes. Her nose would just have to stay stuffed up.

Then she leaned her head back and shut her eyes.

———

After hours' worth of questioning at the police station—far less friendly than she'd enjoyed the first time—Max was finally reunited with her purse, phone and freedom. Max's best friend Miranda and her fiancé, Eddie, picked her up and escorted her home. She'd filled them in on the ride, and now she sat on the couch, totally spent. Her knees were pulled up under her chin, her hands shoved underneath her legs. Tissues littered the floor. She couldn't breathe from her nose and could barely see for crying so damn hard. Cucumber slices and expensive cold creams would be pointless on eyes this puffy.

But her friends refused to leave her, and despite living in a doorman building she was grateful not to be alone in her apartment. Miranda sat on the coffee table facing her and alternated between rubbing Max's legs and shoving fresh tissues at her. Eddie—the one straight male on earth Max didn't think twice about looking this bad for because she knew he only had eyes for her bestie—hovered nearby, sliding in and out of the kitchen. Occasionally he asked a gentle question or added a calming word. He looked concerned, though—and that alone worried Max.

"I just can't understand it," she whispered. "Why? Why them? Why my girls? And what if it happens again? This insanity is right out of a serial killer movie—but it's *really happening*. If there is another..."

At that Miranda glanced sharply at Eddie. He nodded.

"What?" Max asked as she snuffled.

"We think you need to hire protection for your models, and maybe for yourself," Miranda said gently.

"You mean bodyguards?"

"Yes."

Max squeezed her eyes shut, trying to process. She wasn't exactly on her game here. "How would that even work? How many people would that take? I've got models who work in every corner of the business, in every city, in—" Sheesh, she couldn't possibly calculate the complexity or expense of something like that right now.

"Whoa. Just start small," Eddie said. "You've got two models, both female, both based here in the city, both young..."

"You've described practically ninety-five percent of the models at every agency in New York."

"We're only talking about *your* models," Eddie said. "Right now I don't give a rat's ass about the other agencies."

Again, it begged the question Max had been asking herself all along. Why *her* agency? Was that just happenstance so far? Would a competitor's model end up butchered or bludgeoned next month? Or was there something—a grudge or an obsession—about her company specifically?

She hadn't even voiced those questions when Eddie said, "In both cases, the perp knew when those girls would be alone. That points to inside information."

"Maybe he knew their habits because he'd been stalking them?" Max shook her head almost as soon as she'd fielded the question. "No. Helena didn't have any habits. She was brand new here, and I was pretty much running her schedule."

"Exactly," Eddie said. "So as far as we know, this is about your agency, your models."

"This is so messed up," she murmured and dropped her head on her knees.

"You seriously need to consider protection," Miranda said.

Max turned her head but kept it resting on her knees. In her peripheral vision, she could see Eddie nod.

Miranda asked, "What's the name of that guy who used to work for you? The one who wasn't exactly happy to be let go?"

Max snorted. "You mean the one who let me know exactly what he thought of me in a drunken Irish rant? Yeah right."

"But he's been in the bodyguard business for years, right?"

"Yes, but Shane O'Rourke would *never* help—he'd probably love to see me and Ivory tank. Heck, he'd be the first one to stick pins in a Maxine Ricci voodoo doll." Max cringed. Shane's version would likely be a little ice sculpture kept in his freezer. He'd called her a soul-sucking ice queen, after all.

Shane O'Rourke...

He'd been great. She'd immediately spotted that magical

something. An inner fire that transferred to both print and screen. The raw confidence and swagger of a young man who believed himself invincible, the physical power that came across when he was virile and fit and had energy to burn. But male models didn't have much longevity in fashion. And there came a point when Shane wasn't booking the jobs like he once was. They'd put him out there as much as possible, but clients want what they want. She didn't believe in wasting anyone's time, plus there was a cost associated with holding on to models who weren't cutting it. Shane had aged out, pure and simple. Despite the gorgeous face, killer bod and previous successes, she'd had to tell him his career—at least with Ivory—was over.

He didn't take it so well. She found out just how not well when she bumped into him next.

Surely, he'd matured and moved on by now. But she'd bet anything his opinion of her was still lower than low and that he still laid the blame squarely on her shoulders. Rumor had it the Irish could nurse a grudge even longer than the Italians and the Jews—both of which she could vouch for as being a very, very long time. Like lifetimes.

"No," Max said. "There's just no way. I'll just google bodyguard companies and see who has the best ratings."

"Not sure trusting reviews on the internet is the way to go in a life and death situation," Eddie said.

Oy. She shut her eyes. "You two know any VIP's who could recommend somebody?"

"The only big name *I* know is in jail," Miranda said. She and Eddie shared a look. "With all the famous models and actresses you know, there must be plenty who've needed protection for travel or big events."

"I'm barely functioning at the moment," Max said. "Let me think about it."

"Do that," Miranda said. "I'll call Aggie a little later. She might know someone."

Max chuckled. "She probably does." Max's grandmother Aggie had run in a wealthy crowd as long as she could remember. Furthermore, she was full of surprises.

Miranda moved to sit next to Max, who tilted like an egg-shaped Weeble at Miranda's tug. Her friend wrapped her up with one arm and stroked her hair with another. She whispered quiet shhh's every now and then.

Max shuddered out a breath. And despite the sweatshirt Miranda had popped over her head earlier—she'd surely never get that jacket back from the crime scene, nor did she even want it—she was still cold. The warm press of her trusted friend felt good.

Eddie held up a bottle of Kentucky whiskey. "More? Or wine maybe?"

The shot they'd given her first had been welcome. She'd barely been coherent when she arrived from the police station, and it'd helped calm her a little.

She shook her head. More surely wouldn't do her any good. Besides, her stomach felt sour, and she wasn't sure round two would go down or stay down.

Not while she was wondering which of her models might be some madman's next target.

CHAPTER 5

SHANE KICKED AT the radiator and swore. Every year this crappy building O'Rourke Security occupied got crappier. Joe always said they'd find better space—but he never managed to make it happen. Either it was a bad year and they were hustling to get jobs and make ends meet, or it was a good year and they were just too busy.

This was a bad year. Not horrible, but ever since Joe had insisted he join him in the ownership—and all that came with it, like the financial matters—Shane had had a clearer understanding of where exactly they stood. They'd pay everyone on staff and take their own salaries, they'd pay rent and utilities, but the bonuses Shane was secretly hoping for wouldn't be possible. And unfortunately, he'd been counting on that.

Shane had blown through money back when he was modeling. It had seemed like it had grown on trees in those days—until his tree got razed. Once he'd realized he didn't have enough cash left to do what he'd promised for his sister, he'd reigned it in. Eventually, he'd begun investing and had done pretty well. But when his sister Janet's teenage twins Anna and Niall came to live with him, he'd purchased a three-bedroom apartment in a doorman building in a safe neighborhood. He'd been grateful he could, but there went the bulk of his nest egg.

Yeah. A bonus would have helped. He needed to keep the twins in their parochial school, per Janet's wishes. Not exactly a bargain, but their tuition was more manageable than most of the city's private schools. Anna was bright as could be and a hard worker to boot. She'd channeled grief into something positive, and would go far with the right opportunities. Niall, on the other hand, had too much energy—negative energy since the death of his mom—and a penchant for trouble. Much like Shane at the same age, Niall needed a watchful eye and a quality school, or they'd be courting disaster in no time.

Like history repeating itself, Shane often thought. Shane had been motherless as well and had crossed the pond the minute he'd turned eighteen. However the twins had been sent here, younger because he was the one his sister had listed on her will as their guardian. That, and he'd failed her. Hadn't pushed to bring her over like they'd planned. Hadn't realized just how badly she'd needed his protection and intervention. An exit route. If only he'd known...

Dammit, Janet, Shane thought, as he stalked around the office, I'm gonna need a little help from above here.

A sharp rap on the door sounded and Shane jumped. He talked to his sister often enough, but he sure didn't expect to be answered.

Joe swung open the door and walked right in—as he always did.

"Sorrelle just served us."

"He's suing?" Shane gaped. "Holy—"

Joe held up a hand. "It isn't the first time we've been sued, and it won't be the last."

Shane cursed vehemently and spun to face the window. He stretched his arms up and gripped his head like he could keep it from flying off.

"We'll fight it," Joe said. "Keep a lid on."

"We'll fight it?" Shane said and turned to stare at Joe. Had he lost his mind? "It's my fault. I let her get herself killed. How the hell do we fight that?"

"There's more to it than that." Joe dropped into his chair. "She was constantly pulling that cac, and you were on it nearly every time. Just the once, she had a second's head start, because she flipped the deadbolt to lock you out. It's *her* fault. It's the whole reason Sorrelle hired us in the first place—because he sure as shite couldn't control that girl."

Joe was more upset than he was letting on—the Irish slang was a sure sign. His normally largely Americanized accent had grown thicker, too. It was the same for Shane when he got worked up. No matter how many years away from home.

Shane fisted his hands. It was everything he could do not to put them through the wall or the window. He had to find a way to stop this train wreck. O'Rourke Security was well established and respected, and Joe was right. There was the busted door to prove it. But the truth hardly mattered when it came to litigation. A lawsuit—if nasty and long enough—could wipe them out.

And he'd been worried about a bonus. Hah. The thought that he could be the downfall of everything his uncle had worked for all these years…

No, it couldn't be. It wouldn't be. Shane would find a way to make it all right. No matter what it took.

———

The second Max gained consciousness from an uneasy sleep, grief flooded her. Win had been a crazy beautiful woman, inside and out. To have had her life cut short, so violently, was just…

There weren't words. Tears leaked from her eyes as she stared at the ceiling.

Her mind spun round and round the question: who would—*could*—do such a thing? The propensity toward the kind of violence both Helena and Win had endured was beyond her. She simply couldn't imagine anyone they knew… and yet, it was *someone* both women had come in contact with. Therefore, it was likely someone in the business or at least someone who followed it closely. Her hand fisted in her pillow. Maybe—even probably—Max knew this madman, too.

She heard a soft snore and looked to her left. Miranda was tucked into a ball under the covers next to her. Half the time they had movie nights or ended up talking into the wee hours, they'd wind up falling asleep where they were, head to foot and foot to head on the couch. Sharing Max's bed was hardly any different. Dear Miranda had insisted on staying through the night. Wonderful Eddie had slept on the couch. Despite the fact that there'd been no attacks or threats toward Max herself, he'd been unwilling to leave them alone or unprotected. Max was truly blessed to have friends like these.

She gave herself time to feel it all—good and bad—crying as softly as possible so as not to wake her friend, then reached for a tissue and dried her face.

Her greatest fear was that there would be another attack, another victim, before the police even had a handle on who was doing this. Eddie had implied that this perpetrator was someone who had insider information or someone close to both victims. Her mind skittered over Helena's first week in the city and Win's more established connections. She thought of her staff, her freelancers, all the various vendors they used. It was impossible, she just couldn't fathom. Not anyone she knew could possibly…

As far as Max could tell, the police also had no leads. Except maybe for her.

Max rolled her eyes, still somewhat pissed that they'd

suspected her. *Mannaggia*, they still did, but with not a spatter of blood or even a scratch on her in either case—they didn't have much choice but to let her go. Max prayed that all that evidence the techs had spent hours collecting would yield something meaningful. Something clear enough to lead to an arrest, so this could be over.

But she needed a contingency plan in the meantime. The most important thing was keeping her employees safe. Eddie and Miranda had the right of it: she needed to hire protection. A whole staff, however many it took.

No time like the present to get started, she thought, and slipped out of bed. She headed for coffee—already made by Eddie by the smell of things—and would attempt to vet the list of bodyguards that they'd cobbled together last night with Aggie's help. As it turned out, Gram did know a few people.

Two cups of coffee and some fancy scrambled eggs later—Miranda was right, her man knew his way around a kitchen—Max shut her laptop and slouched back in the kitchen chair.

"Crap, crap, crap," she muttered.

"No good?" Miranda asked. She'd slept in and therefore missed the volley of phone calls and internet searches.

Max blew out a long breath. "Nope, not even close to good."

Eddie explained to Miranda what he'd overheard from Max's phone calls and mutterings. "Basically they are all either too small—like one or two guys—or already booked."

Miranda poured a cup of coffee and inhaled deeply as she held it to her nose. "Any of them work with models?" She shook her head. "Nevermind. I can tell by your face."

Max sighed. "Supposedly they've worked with actors, politicians, and heads of companies. But no models."

Max had been thinking about it. She couldn't have just anyone. Her models went all over the world, all over the city, to photo shoots and go-see's, to fittings and consultations, to salons and gyms, and more. And that was just for work. She needed someone who understood that. Who knew the routine and wouldn't hamper it too much. Who knew the players and might recognize when something was amiss. Anybody else would be walking in cold. Every call, every appointment, would be a new situation.

There was only one. Shane O'Rourke. He knew exactly what it was like in her world. And he'd been good. He'd gotten it.

Besides, she'd seriously called every protective services outfit that looked halfway legit already. The only one left?

O'Rourke Security. And from what she could see his company was big enough and experienced enough to handle her needs.

Miranda said, "So...."

"So," Max grimaced. "I'm getting showered, putting on full war paint and dressing to kill. Then I'm going to see Shane."

Miranda clapped.

"This is not a clapping matter," Max said.

"It is, too," Miranda insisted. "You've never failed in your life. Shane will be on board in no time."

Max shook her head, nowhere near as confident given his feelings about her—which he'd told her in no uncertain terms. Harsh words—harsh enough that she believed she still remembered them all. Besides the ice-queen comment, he outright called her a bitch and a *kierney*. And whatever the heck that meant she'd known by his sneer of disgust that it was maybe the worst insult of all.

"The first step is getting in the door. I doubt he'd agree to see me, so you make the appointment under your name." Max slid a steno pad across the table to Miranda and tapped the bottom of the page where she'd written his number.

On the way out of the kitchen, she kissed Eddie on the cheek. "Thanks for the sustenance."

She was going to need it, and a healthy dose of chutzpah, too.

She'd looked up Shane's agency on the web. O'Rourke Security appeared to fit the bill. And believe it or not, they'd been one of Aggie's recommendations. One of her wealthy friends had used him. By all accounts—the personal recommendation and additional internet reviews—he was damn good at what he did and so was O'Rourke Security overall. But more than anything, he knew her business. The fashion industry, her agency, models, stylists, photo shoots, and on and on…

Shane *was* the one for the job. And she'd do whatever she had to to get him to take it.

First order of business: swallowing her pride. Even groveling, if necessary.

Second, making an offer even he couldn't refuse.

CHAPTER 6

THE RECEPTIONIST ALERTED Shane that Miranda Hill was there to see him. He stood and stretched, relieved to escape the paperwork he'd been slogging through. He crossed his small office and opened the door.

But any initial pleasantries died on his tongue the second he saw his visitor in person. Instead, he had to hold back a curse. This woman *wasn't* Miranda Hill.

It was Maxine Ricci.

The bane of his younger, wilder existence. He had the briefest fleeting thought that she was here to offer him modeling work—some silver fox shite, which he was nowhere near old enough to qualify for, or some seasoned thirty-something commercial—and then he caught himself.

He shouldn't have been surprised. He'd met Miranda Hill years ago through Max, and had remembered that they were friends when Miranda had gotten all that press attention after the E-Train Disaster. He'd seen yesterday's news about the model beaten to death at some elite gym, so he didn't even have to guess why Max was here now.

Or wonder why she'd used her friend's name. The last time he'd seen her in person, he'd acted like a drunken, bitter adolescent—despite that fact that every word he'd slung had been true.

Shane crossed his arms and leaned against the doorframe. "Max," he said.

Jaysus, he thought, but she looked as good as ever. Sinfully beautiful, perfectly poised and stylishly coordinated. She rarely showed much skin, and yet she exuded sex. Hot as hot got—on the surface. He was likely one of the few who knew the truth: she was stone cold when it mattered.

"Shane," she murmured.

"Uh..." Dawn, O'Rourke Security's receptionist, looked from one of them to another. Shane guessed she was more thrown by his unusually poor manners than the unexpected name.

"Change the name on the appointment to Maxine Ricci, Ivory Management," Shane said to Dawn.

He turned his back on Max and returned to his office. She could stay or go. He didn't really give a shite. It wouldn't matter what she said. Her business had once turned his head so far around that he'd nearly lost himself. He was not selling his soul to her a second time.

He rounded his desk and dropped into his chair, pushing it back so that he could prop his feet insolently on the desk. She wasn't getting VIP treatment from him. And damn, what was it about her that always made him act like an immature ass? It wasn't the five-year age difference, that was for sure.

Max walked in smooth like a cat on her heels, always the sexy heels—probably steep designer ones, and shut the door firmly behind her. Tight, printed cropped pants, that hinted at a luscious arse before disappearing under a fitted blazer. Her hair was black as night, thick and shiny, and loosely waved to just below her shoulders. She dropped her bag—another high-end whopper, he was sure—into the chair in front of his desk but she remained standing. She crossed her arms over her chest and leveled those luminous dark eyes at him.

"You know why I'm here," she said.

"The answer's no," he said.

She didn't react—she wouldn't. This one was as cool as they came. As the youngest agency owner when she'd opened Ivory at only twenty-three and subsequently one of the most successful now, she was no slouch when it came to holding her own. She was sharp and wily, motivated and hardworking. Also truly talented in her field. He doubted any of that had changed.

"Hear me out," Max said.

Shane rolled his eyes.

She acted as if she hadn't seen that. "I need executive protection for all my models," she said. "Starting immediately, for as long as it takes for the police to figure out who the hell is responsible for murdering Helena and Win." A shadow passed over her face, but she plowed on. "It could feasibly be months' worth of work for you and your team."

He crossed his arms behind his head. This might be kind of fun. How far would she go?

Max uncrossed her arms and gripped the back of the chair. "I'll guarantee a month's pay minimum—for every bodyguard on your staff—even if the police nail him tomorrow."

"Not even tempted," Shane said.

"I'll pay top dollar."

"No doubt."

"Twice your going rate," she said, and he could hear—just a hint—of frustration in her voice.

He lowered his arms and relaxed more comfortably in his reclined position. "I'm not interested in working with you, no matter what you're willing to pay."

"What are you interested in?" She narrowed her eyes, and he noted that the knuckles of her fingers turned white.

"Not a thing where you're concerned."

"You want to model again? I'll sign you right now and make sure you work."

He laughed. "Oh now I know you're hard up." Had she gone insane?

"What about your niece or nephew? You want them signed?"

How did she know about them? The surge of protectiveness he felt was almost scary in its intensity. He slid his feet to the floor and leaned forward. "Don't go near them," he said. "Ever."

She released the chair, stood up straight, and let go of a breath.

"Listen. I know you don't think highly of me," she began.

He raised an eyebrow.

She sighed. "All right. You despise me. I know it, you know it."

Then she raised her chin. She rounded the chair, tossed her expensive bag to the floor, and slid gracefully into the seat. She was a queen, and like magic, the crummy wooden chair became a throne.

She opened her mouth, then closed it again. Wow. Shane had never seen her at a loss for words. Maybe she'd do it again. Like a fish.

"Listen, besides the fact that this is a good thing for your agency." She slid a glance to a particularly large crack in the plaster wall to his left. "I know you care about the well-being of your business and your employees. I knew you once." Now she looked him in the eye. "You were a good guy. And I doubt you've changed that much."

She'd surprised him a little with that—which only made him more wary. He wouldn't put it past her to stroke his ego all the way to a contract.

"I can't imagine you don't care about women being murdered, and a madman on the loose." She swallowed, her eyes shifting to that crack again. "Win had just been booked for Milan. And Helena was…"

Her lip quivered and her eyes became wet. Shane's jaw almost hit the floor.

"She was a baby. Brand new to it all." Her voice was quiet. "She didn't even have her comp cards yet. You know what that means. How green, how young she was. How big her hopes and dreams were."

Shane felt something in him start to soften. Was it young Helena's story drawing him in, or Max's feelings about it?

"You've been there," Max said, leaning forward just a little. "You get these girls. You know who they are, what drives them and what they need to do. You know where they need to go, who they need to see, and what their crazy schedules are like. A lot of the players are the same. The requirements certainly are. I need someone who won't hamper all that, someone who can work *with* it."

Her words were heartfelt—somewhere in there she apparently did have one—and he felt himself slipping.

Max continued. "I've considered restricting the models. But that's too dangerous. They may not listen, or even if they started out cooperating, they'd get stir crazy. They want to work. They'll want to keep up their beauty and health regimens. They'll need to socialize and everything else. They'll be out and about regardless of what I say. And I can't have that. I can't lose another girl."

He frowned, and her chin snapped up.

"I know what you think," she said. "But it's not about what's best for business."

Shane remembered, all right. After an ill-chosen bar fight one night, Shane had crossed paths late at night with Max.

She'd been dressed to kill, obviously leaving a party with some conquest who'd stepped to the curb to hail a cab.

His foul mood had fallen right out of his mouth. "Well, if it isn't the soul-sucking Ice Queen."

"Shane." Max gave him the once over. "I almost didn't recognize you."

"No? This face you once said would melt women's hearts all over the world?" A harsh, sarcastic tone belied the words. Besides his overgrown hair and beard, he sported a split lip and a swollen eye. He waved a hand in front of himself with a flourish. "You're just as responsible for this mess as the melting."

She shook her head, the streetlight glinting on her black hair. "Your choices are your own."

She turned to go, and Shane grabbed her wrist.

"Hey—" Max's date said, taking a step toward them.

"It's all right," Max said looking down her nose at him. "He's harmless."

The bloke didn't look too sure, but returned to the curb. He kept one eye on Shane.

Shane was confident he could take that sucker and ignored him. But Max's comment stung. It made him feel even more like nothing. How did she always manage to keep twisting the knife?

"Don't you care? Don't you care that I'm the first in my family to make real money? I've made promises." He swayed a little and used his grip on her wrist to steady himself. "You're responsible for people's livelihoods."

"Let go," Max said, her eyes on fire, her expression furious.

He let go fast, suddenly realizing what he'd done. He'd grabbed her, and his grip was far too tight. He hadn't meant to touch her. Not like this. His boss. His *ex*-boss. He wasn't the kind of guy that would hurt a woman. How far gone was he that he'd lost sight of himself? He shook his head hard, mortification channeling itself into anger.

"*Jaysus*," Shane said. "How did I not see what you are? How did I not realize it? All that mentoring and support you offered? What an act! You don't care—about me, about any of us." He mimicked tossing a jacket over his shoulder like he'd been taught. "Not unless we're wearing designer suits made of dollar bills. You say it's *just good business*, but the truth is you are stone-cold to the core."

She turned toward her date.

"Watch out, mate," Shane called. "She comes on all hot, but you'll be kissing icy pavement in no time."

"You are so out of line." Max snapped. "Go home and sleep it off."

A cab slid to a halt then. Max strode to the curb and slid in as gracefully as if she'd spent time on the runway herself. She wore a long-sleeved body-hugging dress with a scooped neckline and strappy heels. The ensemble showed off curves made perfectly for a man's hands, collarbones a man itched to lick, legs a man would give nearly anything to have wrapped around his hips. Shane swallowed hard.

The date got in behind Max and slammed the door. He leaned forward to talk with the cabbie. The rear window was down, and Shane could see Max clearly. She raised her chin and looked straight ahead. Ignoring him, and all she left in her wake.

The cab took off, and Shane yelled. "An ice-cold bitch and still a fecking *Kierney*."

To this day, Shane regretted that last more than any of the other.

"This plan," Max said now in his dingy office, "is actually terrible for business. But I'd go farther. I'd shut my doors tomorrow if I thought that would work. It won't. The end result would be the same. They'd be out there," she flung out an arm, "exposed and at risk. So the only option is to protect them." She paused. "I cannot bear to have anyone else hurt. Especially when I have the power to keep it from happening—with your help. You are the right agency—the right man—for the job."

Shane had desperately wanted to shield himself from her. But it was no good. He related to her pain—the guilt and horror of not being able to protect those you cared for or even those you were hired to look after.

And as a hot-blooded male, he was drawn to her. Worse, his younger self—apparently still buried way deep down—ached to please her. *Jaysus*, but he was tempted to give her his every heart's desire.

But he just couldn't see this working. It was a bad, bad idea, no matter how well she spun it.

"Let me spell it out," she said. She stood, braced her hands on his desk. Her posture and her blouse, top two buttons undone under the blazer, drew his gaze—as it was meant to. Straight to her very generous cleavage. The smooth skin and hint of roundness he could see caused his pulse to quicken.

As did her words. "I. Need. You."

————

I. Need. You. Max had said. Her parting shot before she'd scooped up her bag and walked out, shutting his door behind her.

I need you. Words plucked from Shane's wildest fantasies. In that sultry, sexy voice. Formed with those generous, wide, red lips. And the killer? Beautiful dark brown eyes just *begging* him…

Shane groaned and shifted in his chair, horrified that he was physically reacting, too. He couldn't feckin' believe it. All this time, all that crap behind him, and he still—*still*—had the hots for his old boss.

Was she *that* good, or was he just doomed to be a bloomin' idiot forever?

Shane bent and thumped his head against the desk repeatedly. If he knocked himself out, surely he'd wake up sane and his stiffy would have taken a nap, too.

A tentative knock sounded on the door. "Shane?"

It was Dawn. She'd likely heard the thumping.

"Give me a minute," he called. Blast it all to hell. She'd think he was in here jerking off or something.

He jumped up, crossed the room and yanked open the door. Dawn had scuttled back to her desk and Joe had just come in. He looked a little awestruck.

"Was that who I think it was?" Joe grinned. "Your old boss?" He gave a low whistle. "Now I know why you were loath to leave that crazy business."

Shane shook his head. That was Max for you. Men of all ages, even happily married monogamous ones, literally panted after her. Like dogs in heat.

"That's Maxine Ricci," Dawn chirped. "The owner of Ivory Management—that modeling agency where those two models were just murdered!"

She must have been googling like mad, once she had a name, Shane thought.

"Then she definitely needs us," Joe said.

Shane scowled. "She may need us, but we don't need her."

Joe gaped at him. "The hell we don't."

"It's no good," Shane said.

Joe narrowed his eyes, then cocked his head indicating that Shane should follow him into his office.

"What's she want?" Joe asked.

Shane told him.

Joe's eyes practically bugged out. "What's the problem?"

"She's a shitty person. She doesn't hold to her word."

"Who cares? That's why we have 'em sign binding contracts." He shook his head, obviously incredulous that Shane would even dream of passing up this job. "I thought you were going to tell me she's broke or wants us to work for free."

"On the contrary," Shane admitted grudgingly, "her agency's successful. Very. I suspect she's got family money behind her, too." Shane shifted—doubly uncomfortable at this next. "She's offered to pay us top dollar for a guaranteed month minimum."

Joe threw his hands out in a *then-what-the-hell* gesture.

"It's impossible," Shane said. "We don't have enough of us to cover all her people."

"You talked numbers with her?"

"I don't need to. I know how they operate, and I know she's got even more people than she had back when I was there," Shane said. "We can't possibly protect them all. We'd be setting ourselves up for failure."

"Maybe we hire out," Joe said.

Shane didn't like that. There was a certain level of trust one built with a team—even a team as big as theirs. "You always told me that was a bad idea."

But even as he replied, he was thinking of angles. Probably, they didn't need to offer protection to the office staff or the male models. Only the female models. And Max had mentioned restricting them. She was right, that alone wouldn't work. But in conjunction with protection...restricting them just enough to decrease the manpower needed...

"We need this," Joe said. "Bad blood between you two or no. We simply can't turn it down. Not with the Sorrelle suit dangling in front of us like a noose."

"You always say this business is cyclical. Some years good

and some bad," Shane pushed. "But that it always comes back around."

"Yeah, " Joe said, "and Ms. Ricci's models are exactly the ticket we need to get us out of the slump and keep us out of the red for a good long time." Joe rolled his eyes. "Knuckle-head."

Shane rubbed his jaw, working a spot on the right that always ached when he was stressed, ever since it'd been bro-ken.

Hell. It looked like he'd have an aching jaw for the near future at least.

He'd have done well to remember that Maxine Ricci *always* got what she wanted. Men, models, contracts, placements. Why should he be any different?

CHAPTER 7

SHANE CAME UP out of Penn Station and walked toward Ivory Management. More accurately he barged along at an obnoxious clip, just wanting to get this over with. He'd known after Joe's dressing down that he had no choice but to take this job, and he'd largely come to grips with the idea overnight. But it still felt just a little like sidling up to the devil to be dealt another round.

No wonder. The last time he'd stepped foot in the place, Max had called him into her office and had point blank told Shane she was terminating his contract. He'd actually laughed. "Yeah, right."

"I'm serious," Max said and crossed her arms. "You aren't booking like you used to. You're oversaturated. And aged out."

"Aged out? I'm barely twenty-four years old," Shane scoffed.

"This isn't banking," she said, a hard glint coming into her eye. "Surely, you didn't expect this gravy train would continue forever."

He shook his head. "I'm *not* finished."

"You're finished with Ivory," Max said. She'd turned her back on him, striding to her desk. For once it wasn't the fine rear end shown off to perfection in a cream- colored pencil skirt—the one he'd been lusting after secretly—that had him gaping.

That day, when he'd walked into her office, he'd felt more sure of himself than ever, positive he'd booked something big. Instead, Maxine Ricci had sucker punched him. No warning, just *boom*.

Shane had sucked air in through his nostrils and drawn himself up to his full height. He'd show her. He didn't need Ivory to succeed. He had the looks, the body, and the charm. He'd already proven himself. He knew what this business demanded of a person, and he sure wasn't afraid to knock on some new doors. Any other agency would bust a nut to have him.

He spun and walked out, absolutely cock-sure that in no time at all he'd be looking down on Maxine Ricci from a brand-new billboard above Times Square.

But that was nothing really, compared to all that had happened later. Because things hadn't gone as he'd planned. Max, unfortunately, had been right. The other agencies didn't want him. He could have paid *them*, and they'd still have said no. Was he really washed up? Or were they all so used to trailing Max and Ivory Management that they couldn't think for themselves anymore? He'd never know.

Shane tried to go back to amateur boxing and took another hit. Surprise. The fighters had gotten younger while he'd been pansy-assing it in the fashion world. Camera fit was not fighting fit. Especially when you were the ripe old age of twenty-four.

He was filled with shame and nearly crippled with despondence. The only things he'd ever been good at had been lost to him. He felt powerless, like he had no control over his own destiny. Anger seemed to be always churning too close to the surface, constantly landing him in some dicey fights. He did some pounding. And got his arse handed to him plenty, too.

Uncle Joe caught on and called his dad, who told his older sister Janet, who pinned him to the mat for not telling them himself.

"I'd ne'er had quit my job if I'd known you lost yours, ye imbecile!" Janet had yelled over the phone.

He'd promised her he'd bring her to the States. That he'd buy her her very own bakery in New York.

"I still will," Shane said, although he didn't sound convincing even to his own ears. "Someday."

As awful as he'd felt then, it was nothing compared to how he felt later. Because little did he know, it'd be Janet, more than anyone else, who'd pay the price for his failures.

Shane shoved thoughts of his sister away, at the same time he pushed through the glass front doors to the street level lobby of the building Ivory Management was in. It hadn't changed a bit.

The security person at the desk called upstairs, and Shane was given a temporary pass to get through the turnstiles. Security wasn't bad, Shane thought as he waited at the elevator bank, although there were always improvements that could be made.

Ivory was on the fourth and fifth floors, and by the time he exited the elevator, he had to force his tight jaw to release. He pushed through another set of glass doors into the wide, decked out lobby area of Max's agency. Low, white leather couches, glass and chrome side tables, and a modern receptionist's desk. Open at the bottom, surely so you could see the legs and shoes of whomever sat there. Today it was a young woman (one he didn't know, thankfully) with strawberry blond hair. Pretty, and efficient. Not runway material, though. He wondered if she was doing commercials or maybe part work—legs or feet or something—then shook it off.

He was here only to talk to Max.

"Follow me, please," the young woman said.

He and the receptionist rounded a corner—

"*Oh. My. God.* Shane O'Rourke?"

Shane cringed and stopped short.

Cameron Bender had planted himself in their path, dead center of the corridor, wearing an over-the-top look of shock on his face. He was dressed in a plaid shirt and chinos, cut tight and rather short per the current trend. Once Max's lowly gopher, Cam had worked his way up to be her right-hand man. He practically ran things around here.

"How's it going, Cam?"

"Better now, I dare say." Cam put a hand dramatically over his heart. "*Whatever* are you doing here?"

Shane inclined his head toward Max's office, but didn't manage any words before Cam spoke again.

"Oh." A fluttery hand shot to his lips. "I know. Come then," he said to Shane. "I've got him, Sue-Sue," he told the receptionist.

Of all people to see, Cam wasn't the one Shane would have chosen. Not only had Cam once had the hots for him, the man was also one of the few who might know what a bad place Shane had ended up in after Max fired him.

Shane had spiraled out of control pretty fast. He'd always been a physical sort, who needed an outlet, and despite being boxed out of the organized amateur fights, his fists had still been his go-to. There were always fights somewhere, and Shane knew too well how to start 'em. A few drinks too many, and he didn't much care about the right or wrong of it. Soon enough a guy who'd seen him pick one too many and nearly get himself arrested led him to an underground fight club.

Even Uncle Joe and Aunt Tricia hadn't known about that time. Oh sure, Joe had known Shane was getting into some trouble—Shane couldn't hide every black eye and split lip—

but he hadn't known the extent of it. Cam, however, knew—or at least Shane suspected he did.

During that time Shane had once spotted Cam in the crowd of a fight club. He'd known those guys would tear somebody like Cam to shreds. So Shane had pushed his way through a bunch of sweaty, yelling, testosterone and alcohol-laden men, to warn him.

But when he grabbed his shirt with a "You have to leave, *now*," there'd been no recognition in Cam's eyes. Only belligerence and defiance.

Cam had shoved back. "What the fuck, man?"

Shane reared back arms held wide—because the voice wasn't Cam's. Deep and rough, and not a hint of femininity. And once he took a closer look, the hair was different—slicked back and darker. No glasses. And the clothes were all wrong.

The guy looked him up and down, puffed out his own chest and leaned in menacingly. "You want to fight? Huh?"

Shane took another step back, bumping into someone behind him. "Sorry, you look just like…" He shook his head.

"Oh. My little brother." The guy bounced on his heels, eyes now darting between the action in the ring and Shane. This one had come in hot. "He'd never come here."

"Yeah, I know. That's why I—" Shane shook his head.

The guy smiled—and for a split second, the guy looked so much like Cam, Shane was once again taken aback.

Cam's brother said, "Hey, I know you—"

But Shane didn't wait to hear the rest. Sometimes people did recognize him from modeling, despite the fact that he had been hiding under scruff, shaggy hair, and sweatshirt hoods. He turned, shoving through the crowd toward the makeshift bar—just wood planks on top of cinderblocks, with coolers stacked below. He raised an arm and signaled with two fingers. The bartender sailed a beer through the air over other people's heads and then followed that with another. Shane snagged both out of the air easily, chugged one and took the other with him out to the street, buttoning his shirt as he went. Luckily he'd already been in the ring once tonight, because he had no interest in fighting while there was an audience that knew him, or even knew *of* him.

He never knew for sure if Cam's brother had told Cam where he was spending his time or not. Two more unlikely brothers—identical in looks only—there never were, he thought. Jaysus, that was a long time ago, now.

And hopefully after all these firsts today, he'd stop thinking about the past and start thinking about this job.

"Max has been *beside* herself," Cam told him now. "You know her, she hides it well, but *still*."

When they reached Max's office, Cam gave a short series of raps, and then, his weight on the doorknob, he leaned into the room while he swung it open.

Shane braced himself. Maybe instead of a low-cut blouse, she'd be wearing a red body suit and sporting horns and a forked tail.

Cam wasted no time scolding Max. "How *could* you forget to tell me that Shane O'Rourke was coming to visit?"

Shane moved through the doorway, and nope—regular clothes, although on her, they were…

Cam was still prattling on. "You *know* nothing's been the same since he left."

Max crossed her arms, one hip pushed out. Her lips twisted in a wry smile, as she glanced at Cam. "Maybe for you, darling."

Ouch, Shane thought.

———

Max suspected that Cam had always had a thing for Shane O'Rourke. Her assistant had never let her forget his displeasure when she'd let Shane go. She, too, had hated to do it, but he'd gotten just old enough and just over-saturated enough. Male models simply didn't have the same careers that women did in this business. Even among the successful women models, only the few elite top models (think the Heidi Klum, Cindy Crawford, Christie Brinkley, Naomi Campbell-types) could keep working into their thirties, forties, and beyond. And even then, their income didn't come from modeling itself. They had sense enough to land advertising deals, start fashion lines or exercise programs, sponsor a line of body products or makeup, or write tell-all books. Heck, sometimes they simply married another famous person— singer, business mogul, movie star—thereby remaining in the limelight.

Max would bet her favorite vintage Chanel that Cam was positively salivating this time around. Boy Shane had been sexy, but Man Shane was...*wow*. She'd worked hard to ignore the wave of lust she'd felt when she saw him yesterday, thinking it'd been just the shock of seeing him so...matured. But no. Here it was again.

Which was inconvenient.

But it wouldn't matter—she had her rules. She didn't sleep with anyone she worked with. Period. Anybody else? Fair game. Rules were meant to be broken, of course. But Maxine Ricci never broke her own.

And she did hope that Shane being here today meant they'd be working together. Was he here to accept her offer? Why else would he have come?

"Cam, leave us, please," she said, as she narrowed her eyes at Shane. She'd hoped, and even actually prayed, that he'd been swayed by her argument and would see his way to accepting her offer. But she couldn't read his hard expression at all.

As he exited, Cam muttered something about missing out on all the good stuff, but she didn't pay him any mind. The door clicked shut.

Shane stared her down, holding her eyes. She thought she saw a muscle in his jaw tick, but couldn't be sure.

Neither of them moved a muscle.

She hardly wanted to be the first one to give in, but she was fairly certain they could easily stand here like this for hours.

Enough with the games. She dropped her arms and stood up straight to face him. "Should I take your arrival as a yes?"

"I'll agree to the terms you offered yesterday." Shane paused. "As long as you agree to my rules."

She pursed her lips, sensing she wasn't going to like all of *his* rules. And yet, they were talking about guarding her models, not laying out the groundwork and safety words for an S&M encounter. How bad could it be? "Which are?"

"First, you and I need to talk. I need a full disclosure: an account of both murders, background on the women, their careers as you saw them, everything you witnessed those two days, everything that's crossed your mind since."

Max hated to even think of the murders. "The detectives know all of that. I'm not hiring you to investigate. I'm hiring you to protect."

Shane spread his arms wide. "We can't protect adequately unless we have every bit of information. The best way to spot a threat is to see what's unusual, abnormal, out of character. I'm going to need information on *every* person your models will come in contact with."

She nodded. That made sense, she supposed, but sheesh it was going to take one helluva lot of time to prep him.

As if she'd spoken aloud, he said, "Until you can compile

that, go over it with me, and I can disseminate the information to my team, you'll have to have everyone lay low."

"How low?"

"As low as possible. If they aren't in an ambulance on the way to the ER, they shouldn't leave their homes or let anyone in. Ideally, they shouldn't be alone to start with. Or, hell, go with safety in big numbers—have a giant sleepover here and binge watch America's Next Top Model."

"This is insane." She threw out her hands in exasperation.

"So is your killer."

She inclined her head. That point definitely went to Shane. "Second—"

"Oh my God. We're only on number two?"

"*Second*," Shane said, and Max was now sure he'd developed a tick in his cheek. "I'll need a list. Every model you think could be at risk. Everything on their schedule as far as you know it. Get their input on any obligations you don't know about: social, work demands, beauty-related. Everything."

"Of course."

"Next, you and I sit down and cut out half of everything they are doing."

"What?" She shook her head emphatically. "No."

"Max…"

She could hear the warning in his voice but couldn't stop herself. In a voice much too loud, she said, "The whole point in hiring you is so that we can all still *work*!"

A disgusted expression crossed Shane's face before he threw out his hands and turned his back on her. Her office was big, obnoxiously so, and yet two strides of his long legs—ensconced in perfectly tailored gabardine—and he was yanking open her door.

"Wait!" she said.

But he slipped into the hall and headed for the elevator.

Madonna! What had she done? He couldn't leave, she couldn't let him.

Max had to run to catch up. She just prayed her Manolo's didn't catch on the carpet. He'd already pushed the button, and the doors slid open.

Max jumped in front of him and put out a hand to halt him. He kept coming, and at that moment, so did the elevator doors. She reacted on instinct, splaying out her arms and legs, her hands and feet stopping the elevator and her body blocking him.

His eyes and mouth went wide with shock and then he barked out a laugh so loud, she knew the whole office would hear it.

She scowled and stepped out of the elevator, toward him. Shane entered into a fit of hysteria. He actually howled. Like a hyena or a, a—well, whatever it was, it wasn't pleasant. And it certainly wasn't manly. Neither were the tears streaming down his face, the schmendrik.

"If you're going to carry on like that, at least do it in my office." She grabbed his sleeve and tugged, and the man was so weak with mirth that he actually complied.

Well fine, Max thought as she slammed the door shut behind him, at least she had him where she wanted him again.

"The almighty Maxine Ricci, like a flying squirrel," he managed.

She rolled her eyes and waved her hand. "Go ahead, get it all out." She could take a little ribbing. She was half Italian after all, and in that culture, insults and teasing from family and friends were a form of art. And as a New Yorker? Well, she could handle it even from somebody who didn't even like her.

"Mother, Mary, and Joseph, somethin' I ne'er thought to see."

Oy, she thought, she hadn't heard his accent so thick since he first walked through her door. Not that he'd ever tried to shake it—surely, he knew it was part of his charm. And she almost—*almost*—enjoyed seeing him so lighthearted.

Shane swiped his forearm along his eyes, and she cringed. That beautiful suit jacket would need to go straight to the cleaners.

Max crossed to one of the leather cubes that faced the window and sat with her back to Shane. Knees and toes pointed in, elbows braced on her knees as she waited, ignoring him until he pulled it together.

She could see Shane's reflection in the glass. He slid big thumbs under each eye and then bowed his head, wagging it from side to side. He'd always had really thick, really dark hair—almost as black as hers. His shoulders were exceedingly wide—man-o-shevitz had Shane O'Rourke filled out and matured. When he was modeling, he'd been pretty—in a rough, edgy way. Like he'd come from the wrong side of the tracks—and he had, essentially. The wrong side of the pond, anyway. He'd been raised by his dad. She had no idea whether his mom was dead or absent, but apparently he had been drinking and getting in trouble at a rather young age. He'd come to New York and a young model he had dated was savvy enough to see that the same qualities that made him so attractive to her—sexy charm, boyish energy, and rough good looks—would work for modeling. Max had signed him, and although he'd taken to it quickly and worked hard, there had remained a little wildness in him.

And now that edge had…hardened further. Both outside and, she sensed, underneath. Most men softened with age, both physically and in spirit. His transformation was the opposite.

He'd be an incredible turn-on in bed. That body, that face,

those eyes, that accent. Mmmm, she'd have to make him talk during. Tell her what he wanted.

Shane set his hands on his hips, and under his gaping jacket she could see the nice cut of his dress shirt taper into a trim waist. She also spotted a glimpse of the brown leather holster he wore.

Her shoulders slumped. A gun. That's what her world had come to, and she'd do well to remember it.

Eventually, she realized he'd straightened and was regarding her silently.

Finally, she sighed. "I'm sorry," she said. "For being…" Apologies were not her strong suit.

He crossed to the other stool, pushed it off to the right some—a safe distance, she thought—but sat down facing her, his legs wide and his elbows on his knees, mirroring her own posture.

"I'm not trying to make this harder than it is," he said. "There's solid reasoning behind my requirements. One, despite the fact that our agency is one of the bigger ones in the city, we don't have enough available agents right now to cover all your models all the time. Unless you've reduced your roster since I was here?"

"No. If anything, our numbers are larger."

"Then we've got to strategize to make the most of what we've got. The fact is, exposure is risky. The more the models are out and about, the greater the risk. Period."

He waited for her to nod before he continued. "Furthermore, perception is really important. You want this guy to know you are taking precautions. That anybody who *is* out and about is covered by an agent. That the office has extra security, their homes are covered, etc. The harder it looks for him to get access, the less likely he is to try."

"Okay. That makes sense." She grasped her hands together. "Anything else?"

"Yes. One more thing. The most important thing."

He looked hard into her eyes, gauging something, looking for what, she didn't know.

"I'm not going to like it, am I?" she said.

He half smiled. "Not even a wee bit."

She sucked in a deep breath, raising her shoulders and then letting them drop. "Lay it on me."

His dark eyes flashed—and she wondered if his head had gone slightly naughty at that. If she'd been at a bar, picking up a guy, anywhere but work, she'd have laden the words with husky intent. But not here. And not with him.

Shane's smile had disappeared. He held her gaze and planted his final stipulation on her. "My word goes. Above all, I need full and unequivocal cooperation."

Hmmmm, yes, she had the fleeting thought that he'd prefer to take charge in the bedroom. She stood and strode to the wall-to-wall windows and looked out over Broadway, just south of Times Square.

He spoke to her back. "You do not argue with me, or second guess my instructions. You do as I say, when I say."

Max heard Shane stand.

"Your people," he said, "especially the younger ones, hang on your every word. They emulate you, they take your advice. You have to make it clear to them—they must comply with whichever agent is guarding them. It starts with you."

She spun, mouth open, but stopped short. He'd come up right behind her—close enough to touch. She could smell his aftershave—spicy and sharp. A wall of heat hit her, and she didn't know if it emanated from him or was simply her reaction to him. Tall, broad, sexy, attractive—and just so... *commanding*.

"Especially you," he said, his voice a low rumble.

She blinked. "What?"

"You'll do as I say, when I say."

Apparently Max still had her head in the bedroom, because heat shot south at his words. There was something about this older, more seasoned Shane that had her positively *wanting*.

She had no choice but to agree.

CHAPTER 8

AT SHANE'S DIRECTIVE, Max had sent an email blast to all her models instructing them to cease all travel, appointments, shoots, etc., for the next two days. Which meant that she and Cam had spent the next few hours fielding frantic phone calls and people rushing her office. One model simply couldn't miss that shoot—she'd never get the opportunity again. Another couldn't bear the state of her roots and refused to cancel her salon appointment. One had plane tickets for her fiancé's surprise birthday vacation, another had a father in the hospital who was dying…

When possible, Cam worked his magic and calmed them to some degree.

At first she and Cam tried to handle each individually. They begged the magazine to move the shoot by 48 hours. They explained to the stylist that circumstances couldn't be helped, and that Maxine herself was asking the favor of slotting her in later in the week. And on and on.

At her wits end in no time, Max called Shane.

His voice sounded rough when he answered, as if he hadn't used it since he'd left her office this morning. She imagined he'd sound like that when he woke—and immediately pictured herself all but purring against his naked chest.

"A few things have come up that I need to ask you about," she said and began with Danielle—whose father was so near the end of his life. Shane knew Danielle from way back.

"We should be able to accommodate visits to the hospital," he said. "Once a day, for a couple of hours."

"Thank you," Max said. She was relieved. If it'd been her grandmother Aggie or her great-aunt Cora…well, she was glad she had something to offer Danielle.

She tapped her pen on her pad. "I've got a laundry list here of exceptions to ask you about, but I can see this really isn't going to work. I need to organize all the information you need, and I can't even get to it. Even with Cam helping. How do other companies handle this kind of chaos?"

"You're going to have to play hardball."

She groaned.

"Max," he said, "you're the queen of hardball."

"Damn," she said.

"It's just two days—and who knows, maybe we can improve that. Lay down the law." He paused. "Don't hesitate to scare the shit out of them."

Max shut her eyes. "I'll call a meeting. Can you get back up here?"

They agreed that he and Joe would join them late afternoon to answer any questions. Max hung up, slumped in the chair, and pressed the heels of her hands to her eyes—the masterpiece that was her eyeshadow be damned.

Shane had a point. And she *was* the queen of hardball. On the other hand, it was kind of nice to have somebody who had her back.

And wasn't that a surprise? She and Shane O'Rourke seemed to be finding a comfortable footing. Either that or he was a master at hiding his misgivings.

———

Max turned all her ringers off, gave strict instructions to

both Cam and Susan that she wasn't to be bothered and even locked her door.

She sat for an hour with a list of everyone that Ivory Management considered to be actual employees: all models; office staff such as receptionists, bookers, payroll, etc; and in-house specialists including photographers, makeup artists, trainers, and more. The bulk of the names were the models, of course. So far, the women who had been killed were models, one age eighteen, the other twenty-two. So it stood to reason—didn't it?—that the other groups were safe.

She scanned every line on the list as goosebumps rose on her arms. Was someone noted here the killer? Surely it wasn't a woman. Her eyes jumped from one man's name to another.

Uneasiness seemed to always lurk under the surface lately. She rubbed her arms and felt her chest tighten. Trying to picture her employees as deranged murderers was not helping anything. She never got anywhere with the wondering—except causing herself further distress.

There was a much greater chance the killer *wasn't* an Ivory employee. Right?

Right. She knew all these people, personally. She'd hired them. Traveled and lunched and brainstormed with them. No—just no. She couldn't believe there was some violent sicko on her payroll.

Max got up and stretched, then walked to the windows to survey the scene below. Like a reset button, sometimes you had to walk away in order to start again. She rolled her neck and then her shoulders, then deeply inhaled and slowly exhaled. She returned to her desk, willing herself to focus only on the task at hand.

Out of the list of models, she made a new list. Priority would go to anybody in that same age range, say to age twenty-four.

Tier Two was…all the remaining models. Because there was no other way to sort. Helena and Win were at different stages of their career. They also had different hair color, different body types, different attitudes…

Both groups were way too big. Shane was absolutely right. There was no way around it. They'd have to limit their whereabouts.

She sent the document to Shane via email so that he could see the numbers, then hit print and leaned back in her chair to stare at the ceiling. She'd been raised to pray. Lately, she found herself actually doing it. *Please, please, keep all these people safe.*

The printer hid in the credenza to her left, and Max got up to retrieve the printout. She put it facedown on the desk, in case she wanted to make notes later.

Next, Max pulled out a steno pad and sat, pen in hand, thinking. She had to prepare for the meeting they'd called. What would she say to her mutinous troops? What *could* she say? It wasn't going to be easy no matter how she framed it.

An hour later, she entered the viewing room, where they normally replayed training videos for new models. Everyone who'd been in the office was gathered together. About fifteen all told. Cam sat near the front and waited patiently. The head stylist Marc murmured something to Damien, their in-house photographer who practically reclined in his chair. His eyes shifted from his phone to Max, but his bored expression didn't change. He was definitely the type who didn't think rules applied to him. Although Max was sure he wouldn't be the only one.

Most everybody started yammering at once. Max held up a hand for silence, and they hushed.

A laptop screen had been projected onto the big viewing

screen, and Max knew that the rest of her employees had already logged in so that they could participate in the meeting remotely.

Cam had set up a video camera at an angle so that she could face both the people present and those who weren't. She looked to him, and he nodded. Then she looked to Shane and his uncle, Joe, who stood in the far back corner.

"Thanks for coming, everyone," she said. "I know this is unusual. I'm sorry to say, it's about to get more so. As you know, we've been targeted by a madman. Two amazing women, our friends, have had their lives cut short in the most violent, brutal ways." They'd all attended a service for Helena, and Win's would be held in a couple of days. Although it pained her not to say more about the women themselves, this meeting wasn't about them. "My sole goal now," she said, "is to keep the rest of you alive and well. Period."

She scanned the faces, making eye contact with everybody and then returning her attention to the camera.

"I've hired an executive protection agency. O'Rourke Security is the best in the city. The owners are Joe O'Rourke and his nephew Shane, who was for many years one of our own—a point that certainly works to our advantage."

A murmur went through the room, and those that knew him, either personally or through his print work, turned to look at him. Many nodded or smiled a greeting. The newer models turned to look for curiosity's sake.

Like Shane, Joe was tall, broad, and in good shape, but likely about twenty-five years older, with quite a bit of white in his beard. There hadn't been time to greet him before the meeting, but Max had felt his silent assessment of her since the minute she'd walked into the room. That made sense, she figured. Not only were they going to be working together, he and Shane were family and surely Joe knew that Shane had felt wronged by her all those years ago.

"Gentleman." Max beckoned them forward.

When they'd joined her at the front of the room, she introduced both men. But they'd already determined that this should be her show. The O'Rourke's would only jump in if necessary.

"Here's the situation," Max began. "O'Rourke's team is large, but not large enough to cover all of you, all the time. We need time, maybe 48 hours, to make the assignments and sort who needs coverage when. So for the next two days, you'll buddy up—with family or roommates or friends—and hunker down. Go home—don't commute alone—and stay there."

Voices erupted, and she heard the sounds of disbelief and horror.

"Enough," she said sharply, and the room quieted. "Hear me out. As soon as possible, we'll resume work on a restricted schedule. The most important bookings will happen *with* your assigned bodyguard."

"I've got dibs on that one," one of the newer models said loud enough for the whole room to hear as she ogled Shane. A few other women giggled. Max gave her a sharp look, and noted that Shane hadn't reacted in the slightest. Anyone who believed sexual harassment happened only to women had never been part of the modeling world. Now wasn't the time, though she'd be cataloging it for later.

"O'Rourke will cover as many of you as possible, wherever you need to go," Max said. What can be rescheduled to a later date, will be. I promise you, we will do our best to keep you working and to keep you as beautiful as always."

One woman raised her hand before she spoke. "This seems a little extreme," she said.

"It is," said Max, "but so are our circumstances. You'll note that I didn't take this measure after Helena died. But now there's been another murder." She looked out over those gorgeous faces she knew so well. "*Two* female models from *our* agency. That increases the odds substantially against us."

"What about us?" asked Marc, her resident head stylist. He gestured to himself and a couple of male models.

She nodded. "I'll be frank. Right now, we plan to focus largely on the women, especially those in the same age range as Helena & Win." She hated this part, but it was what it was. "By necessity, we'll allocate less support to those of you that are male. Likewise for those of you who are staff. But," she hastened to add, "we'll be constantly assessing things. If we receive new information from the police or discover that anyone else is a target, we'll adjust."

In fact, she'd spoken with Officer Iocavelli this morning, and he'd sounded frustrated. They had no leads, no motivation, and the only commonalities were the ones she already knew about. He was still waiting for the crime scene and forensic analysis from the second murder. She prayed they'd come up with something soon and had made him promise that he'd share any information that might help her to keep her team safe.

Max rolled with the impromptu question and answer session. She'd been more amenable to Shane's rules and restrictions, once he'd explained the *why's* behind them. Hopefully the same candidness would ease some of the misgivings for her models and staff.

A model named Chrystina asked, "How do we know it won't be some other agency next? Or that this psycho isn't already done? Or that Helena and Win didn't bring this on themselves somehow?"

Max crossed her arms as she thought of the gels taped with

an X on each body. There was something specific, some message the killer was trying to impart, or some reason he chose them...but no one could possibly bring *that* on themselves.

"We don't," she said. "For all we know he'll choose someone from another agency next week, or someone from a club or a bar. For all we know, he *is* done. As much as I wish that were true, the police don't think so."

She glanced at Shane, thinking of what he'd said on the phone. He nodded, his face still that same expressionless mask—what she was already coming to think of as his on-duty face, except for the eyes. They held a certain grimness.

She continued, "What I can tell you is that no one on earth asks for what happened to Helena or Win. I saw them. It was violent, angry, destructive..." She swallowed hard.

The room was dead silent now, and everybody leaned forward. Even Cam—and she realized she had never really told him about those days—what she'd really seen, what it'd really been like.

"...truly disturbing." She took a shaky breath, needing to make them understand. Not to cause them pain, but to take this seriously enough to stay safe. "Helena was stabbed, dozens of times. Her front and her face all cut up. Blood was everywhere." She almost whispered now and still her voice felt loud to her, so loud with words she hated to speak, hated to even think. "Win was beaten—blood and bones—mangled to a pulp. At first I couldn't even tell it was her."

Tears had filled her eyes now.

"You and I, we appreciate more than most the human form, physical beauty. Our friends didn't die beautiful." She swallowed hard. "They died wrecked and ugly."

Cam's hands rose to cover his face. Max could see tears glistening in a few others' eyes. She took a minute to gather herself.

She looked first to the model who asked the questions that had led her here, and then to the rest. "So, I'm not taking *any* chances. I'm stacking the deck in our favor, and I'm playing for keeps—keeping each of you alive."

She breathed deep and moved her hands to her hips. "Here's the deal. First the short lockdown, then the restricted schedules for as long as it takes. If you don't comply with any part of that, your contract is terminated. The minute you break a rule, you're gone."

There were some surprised intakes of breath, but a few people nodded assent as well.

"Cam," Max said.

He rose and began to pass out the agreements and pens.

"After you bring Cam up to speed with every appointment you have for the next two weeks—business, social, gym time, everything—we'll spreadsheet it. Then we'll sort and let you know your modified schedules and who will be assigned to you when."

Just one more thing, she thought.

"Don't forget—while I'd hate for any of you to walk, you *are* expendable." She made sure her voice sounded matter-of-fact and unapologetic. "There are people knocking on our doors right now, ready to fill your designer shoes and take your spot in next month's Vogue. Right now, I don't care what spots we lose. What I can't abide is seeing another of you dead."

There, she thought, as she turned and walked out. *I've done all I could.*

CHAPTER 9

MAX AND SHANE retreated to her office after the meeting. Let Joe answer any further questions. Let Cam collect papers and report in later on who was the most amenable and who was the most disgruntled. She'd done her part.

"Nice job in there," Shane said after he shut the door.

"Scary enough to keep everyone, you think?"

"Your employees usually take what you say to heart," Shane said. "At least they used to."

She grimaced. Being influential was sometimes a blessing and sometimes a curse. Either wonderfully rewarding, or a really tough road.

"If they walk," Shane said, "they're stupid and short-sighted."

"Thanks," Max said, and slid him a glance. Yeah, she was paying him, but he didn't have to say that. She didn't normally look outside herself for validation, but in these horrid circumstances, it meant something to have his support and to know she wasn't in this totally alone.

A knock sounded on her door. Someone must have been right on their heels when they left the meeting.

"Perhaps the exodus begins," she muttered. Then she called, "Come in."

It was Damien Closse, her in-house photographer. He sauntered in and raised his chin by way of greeting Shane. She introduced them briefly, then Max moved around behind her desk but remained standing.

"What's up?" she asked. Out of the corner of her eye, she could see Shane assessing him. Closse had dark hair cut in an edgy style and tats that snaked up his arms and neck and even invaded his ears. He wore black skinny jeans, black boots, and a short-sleeved black T-shirt. Adam Levine-like, except far rougher.

She'd described Shane just yesterday as rough—but although there was an underlying current of something just slightly untamed in him, she knew instinctively that Shane was of good character. Damien?

Let's just say she wasn't a fan of Damien personally, but so far, she hadn't found anyone better behind the camera. He was a master at lighting, had surprising vision, and a knack for drawing out the models' personalities despite his abrasive nature.

Damien threw himself in a chair in front of her desk. "You people are way off base with all these precautions."

She raised her eyebrows.

"You're wasting our time and your money," Damien said.

"That so?" she asked.

"I told that dick all he needed to do was follow the needles."

Max knew he meant Detective Iocavelli. The detective had questioned nearly every person at Ivory that Helena had met and went at it again after Win was found. Damien was abrasive and uncouth, but at least he cut straight to his point.

"Win was in deep," Damien said. "And that innocent-looking farm girl, what's-her-name, wasn't what she seemed. Very first time I met her, she asked me where to find a good time." He smirked and looked at Shane. "I told her I was the best time around."

Max grit her teeth. Someday he was going to get them sued. She'd spoken with him before about steering clear of the models. He'd blatantly laughed in her face and said, "They chase me, boss lady."

After this was all over, she'd focus on finding a photographer who was supremely talented *and* tolerable.

"Thanks for the tip." She sat and pulled up to her computer in way of dismissal.

Damien shrugged. "Just telling you." He pushed out of the chair, gave that man-to-man chin thing to Shane again and sauntered out.

"Good guy, eh?" Shane said.

"Obviously, I didn't hire him for his personality." Max blew out a breath. "Would you lock the door?"

Not only did she prefer to block out Damien from her thoughts, she really didn't want to handle any resignations herself. She wasn't, at the moment, inclined to persuade or coddle. What she wanted was to make tracks, so that business could continue sooner rather than later to whatever extent possible.

"We'd better get to work," Max said to Shane. But even as she rose and handed him the list she'd printed out, she wondered: *had* anybody walked out? Just up and left her and Ivory?

She hadn't lied, this business was harsh. The models *were* replaceable. Her bottom line might dip through this, but it would recover. Still, she'd chosen each and every one of her models because they were unique and talented, and each one of her staff because they were amazing at what they did. She would hate to lose them to another agency. But she'd hate far more to see any harm come to them.

It would be what it was. No sense worrying when you could take action. Or as Grandma Aggie often said: wasting time worrying was about as useful as trying to pick poppy seeds off a bagel one by one.

Max gestured to the big table on which sat a cup of pencils and pens, another with fat markers, and a stack of lined notepads. Often she needed to spread out print ads or head shots and really see it all together. The oversized surface was great work space, and the privacy of her office allowed her to mark things up, take notes, and sort without comment or curious eyes.

She rounded the table and chose a spot where she could look across the office to the bank of windows with its cityscape. Shane sat beside her.

They went over her list versus how many agents he expected to have on day one. More would become available, he said, as their current assignments wrapped up.

Shane frowned. "You don't have yourself on this list."

"For obvious reasons."

"Which are?"

"I'm not a model, and I'm not even close to the right age range." *Duh*, she thought.

"But you are the link."

"My company is the link—maybe," Max said. "There's nothing that points to me, specifically, being the common denominator."

"You don't know that. You're splitting hairs."

"I don't feel I'm at risk. More importantly, I really want the manpower on my people."

Shane gestured to the pages with an angry flip of his hand. "You meet the criteria for a target. You're female and you are an employee of Ivory. Put your name down on Tier Two."

"Fine," she bristled, but did as he asked. She'd promised she would, didn't she, in order to get him to stay?

They discussed more employees and each corresponding tier, and then Shane shared the numbers he'd sorted on his end. They would have to do some juggling for sure. Yet it was still impossible to finalize anything at this point. They didn't know if anyone had chosen to leave the agency. Nor did they have schedules yet. Likely they wouldn't have everything ready to compile until tomorrow morning.

Although she was focused, Max was incredibly aware of Shane. She could smell his scent—the spicy aftershave that had grown more faint this late in the day. Different from when she had visited his office yesterday morning and when he'd visited hers early today. Little by little she'd begun attuning herself to the nuances of his voice and accent, his gestures and how he held his body. She subtly catalogued the length of his strong hands, the way his hair waved just so, the line of his jaw.

She was, and always had been, an extremely sexual being. She didn't apologize for it, she embraced it. Why not? You were what you were.

But usually, she could surf a different channel when she was working. Turn it off or tune it down. Not, it seemed, when she was working with Shane. Not yesterday, not this morning, and not now. Was she just off because of these extenuating circumstances? Maybe subconsciously focusing on his maleness and her attraction to him as a distraction? Or was it simply... *him*?

"Max?"

Her eyes snapped up. Sheesh—she'd been staring at his hands, imagining what they could do to her. "Sorry," she waved a hand, "I was lost in thought."

"Do you want to talk about it now?" he asked, those black brows slashing downward. "We need to anyway."

If they spoke aloud about what she'd really been thinking, she'd combust. But she knew what he meant. He needed to hear about the murders. "There won't be a good time," she murmured.

"No," he agreed.

She uncrossed her legs and pulled her chair into the table. As if a wooden barrier would protect her from the memories that had been haunting her dreams. She propped her elbows and forearms on the table and interlaced her fingers.

Max took a breath and started at the beginning. Because how did you start at the end—the end of someone's life? She told Shane why she'd gone to meet Helena, going up to the apartment with her key when there was no answer.

He asked a few questions now and then. The words came faster and faster, and she ended up telling him things she hadn't intended to. About why she'd chosen Helena, about how young and naive the girl was, about how she prayed her parents never saw crime scene photos so that they could remember her always as so fresh-faced and beautiful.

"What I wouldn't give," Max said, swiping under an eye when a tear escaped, "to go back in time and to have let her be. To have my Ivory representative just pass her by in that mall, choose someone else. To send her back to that farm, alive and well, never knowing the awful fate that would destroy her."

Shane reached over and squeezed her hand. The comfort was both welcome and unexpected—so much so that she slammed her eyes shut to keep Niagara Falls from escaping.

His hand disappeared, and she sucked in a deep breath. She heard him move away, probably running from the room. Most men did not do well with tears. *She* did not do well with tears. Her eyes popped open to check and she sniffed. No— he was rooting around, pulling open the slim drawers of her desk. How dare he—

"Tissues?" he asked, head bent to his task.

The desk was a sleek thing, not conducive for stashing

a box of tissues. "Behind you, on the shelves, in the basket." Hidden because, according to Cam who'd arranged the space, who needed pedestrian items like tissues amongst the display of famous photos and awards? Especially when you never cried and rarely even got a stuffy nose.

After Shane had handed her a wad and deposited the box on the table, she took a deep breath and told him about Win. It was no easier. She—mostly—held it together.

By the time she'd finished talking, the light outside had begun to wane. In fact, she felt as if she'd packed a week into this one day.

"I think we've done as much as we can for tonight," she said.

"I'll escort you home."

"I meant, you could go. I usually work late." It was already late. Really, she just needed some breathing room.

"Can you work from home? Because you just gave all your employees a hard-line about the buddy system."

"So I did," she said. "All right, give me a couple of minutes." She didn't have the energy left to fight him. Besides, he had a point. She transferred a few documents to their cloud-based service, stuffed a few paper files in her oversized bag, and tidied up the table.

She flipped off the lights behind her, and they stepped into the empty hallway and headed for the elevators. Everyone else had been sent home after filling out their paperwork. Max had wanted them to have daylight for travel and enough time to sort sleepovers, etc.

"You should alert the cleaning staff," Shane said. "The assailant could look for someone alone and working late."

"That's a good thought. I'll be sure to have Cam call them in the morning." As they hit the street, she asked, "Do you mind if we walk it?"

"It should be okay, since you're with me." He looked everywhere but at her. Not avoiding her though, she realized. He was already assessing every person, vehicle and doorway he saw for potential threats. This new situation was going to take some serious getting used to.

"Choose a route different than you'd normally go," Shane said. "Habits are dangerous."

Max thought about that, and more as they walked. The pavement still held the heat from the early October sunshine, and after a few blocks, she paused to remove her lightweight trench coat.

"I'm still hoping that this guy is already done," she said, "but if not…if there'll be another, do you think we have some time? Since there were almost four weeks between Helena and Win?"

"Yeah, I think we probably do," Shane said. "With luck the cops will solve it before anything else happens."

"That's what I'm hoping. I'd dearly love to see the bastard fried."

They walked on and Max considered asking if he wanted to grab dinner. She'd heard his stomach rumble hours ago. It wasn't unusual for her to skip lunch or just nibble for dinner. But a man his size probably needed three squares a day, and then some. But she kept her mouth shut. They'd do best to keep this as professional as possible—although already today, they'd crossed some sort of invisible line. That do-not-ever-let-anyone in your chosen field see you cry line. *Ugh.*

No, she thought, no dinner.

Despite the pedestrian dodging and stopping and starting at every corner, the walk had felt good. Always helpful in terms of sloughing off a little of the work day.

When they arrived outside her building, she said, "Thanks for the escort."

"You're not alone tonight, are you?" Shane asked.

"No, a friend…" she trailed off. She had planned to get dressed up, enjoy a drink, some music, and multiple orgasms with her friend Scott, at his place. For about two years now, they had enjoyed each other off and on. It was an ideal scenario when she didn't feel like dealing with finding someone new. Scott offered a good time, no strings, and no discussion of their respective businesses. She'd already cancelled, however. She simply didn't feel like it with all this going on.

"Is he already here?"

"No." He could assume whatever he wanted. He didn't need to know that she'd decided to remain alone, unless she got squirrelly, at which point she planned on calling Miranda and Eddie.

"Let me come up then," he said.

"That's awfully forward," she teased.

He didn't even crack a smile. "I want to do a site check—make sure your place is secure."

"Oh," Max said and grimaced. Why did she suspect she'd have been more comfortable if he'd been actually coming on to her? And why did she feel so *un*comfortable about having him poke through her personal space? She was weirding herself out.

He took her elbow—*again* with the elbow thing, had they gone back in time a whole century?—and steered her into the building. She nodded to the doorman, who didn't blink an eye.

He was accustomed to her bringing men home, although they didn't usually steer her like a toy car for God's sake.

———

In the elevator, Shane mused over the irony of heading to Max's apartment—for business. Years ago, he'd entertained numerous fantasies of getting together with her. Then, there had been years he'd have rather seen her burned at the stake.

Even last night, Shane had been torn between making sure he was the one assigned to Max and dreading spending that much time with her. Not only because he still—blast it—thought she was a knock-out, but because she'd surely run rough shod over most of the other guys on his team. They were good—they wouldn't have jobs with O'Rourke if they weren't—but there were few men who couldn't be influenced by Max's particular brand of sexy. Add in headstrong, determined, and smart, and you had a recipe for trouble.

No, it had to be him. And chances were this job was going to be more stressful than the average.

Now? Today? He didn't know what he felt. He was here in a professional capacity, and yet, the professional distance he usually maintained with clients was already…blurry.

He suspected he'd always find her attractive—as in insanely hot. He just did. Period. Maybe that was just a physical thing. Pheromones that matched up or some animalistic mating instinct that just existed, defying will or logic.

But seeing her cry earlier? Well, his shell had cracked a bit. He'd never have suspected that Maxine Ricci had any *softness* about her.

As the doors slid open, Shane reminded himself that he was here to work. He scanned the hallway and then motioned for her to come out. Four apartments to a floor meant she must have a large place. No surprise really, as she was quite successful.

She led him a short distance down the hall and opened the door with a key. That lock was okay, but he would recommend better. He entered first into a good-sized foyer styled like a fancy mudroom. He checked the closet first.

"Stay near the door," he said.

"Oh, come on," she said. "It's a doorman building."

He ignored her, and she crossed her arms.

He'd been right, her place occupied a whole corner of the building. Oversized windows on two sides would provide loads of light in the daytime and a great view of Central Park. The open kitchen and living area took advantage of this with a large, cushy L-shaped seating area and an additional spot for conversation, or maybe reading. Somehow he couldn't picture always-busy Max sitting around with a book and a cup of tea. Some work and a Red Bull seemed more her speed.

Shane could hear Max tapping her foot in the foyer. She'd been in those heels all afternoon and walked—what, over thirty blocks? Did she slip them off under her desk when she was alone? He'd overheard a model once telling a friend that she'd always walked on her toes as a child and that therefore heels were more comfortable for her than anything flat... maybe Max was the same.

A cozy office and two bedrooms sat on the exterior of the building as well, still windowed, but less exposed. One with a full-sized day bed and trundle mattress underneath, the other with a king-sized bed.

The walk-in closet had a three-way mirror, a padded bench, and was full of designer duds perfectly organized by color. He'd been in plenty of models' closets (and bedrooms) and would have expected no less. As he crossed the master bedroom, he couldn't help but note the elegance and intimacy of the room. Low lights, subtle accents, built-in speakers, candles—battery operated, he noted—everywhere. The furniture was classy, but he couldn't help but wonder what was hidden in the bedside drawer. A warehouse-sized box of condoms, surely. He doubted this particular woman needed jelly—except maybe for some extra fun. Probably some toys. What exactly was oh-so-sexual Max into?

A stab of desire shot through him when he entered the bathroom. The shower was glass-encased and big enough for two—or three. And nearly the whole room was mirrors. Did she often shower with her conquests, getting off on seeing the action?

There was also a bidet, of course.

A linen closet held towels and beauty products galore, but not enough space for a man to hide.

From the back of the door hung a silk robe in a rich purple, and he had a flash of Max in it, the robe open in front to showcase her...

Hell and damnation, he thought.

He stalked back to the foyer. Although he thought he'd dragged his mind fully back to the job, his voice was gruff when he said, "All clear."

She'd set her purse on a bench and hung her coat on a hook. She looked tired, but her hair and clothing still looked impeccable. Maxine Ricci was not the type to rumple.

"Then you're officially off duty for the night..." she said.

"Officially, not until I actually leave you, but yeah," he returned.

"Long day," she said, and he wondered if she was stalling. Did she not want to be alone?

"Indeed," he said. "Do you want me to stay until your man arrives?" They hadn't officially begun the executive protection portion of their agreement yet, but he had slight misgivings about leaving her alone. Not professionally—she was Tier Two, it was too early, there was a doorman, he'd cleared her space, and she wouldn't be alone—but...lust was making things murky already, he thought grimly.

"No," she said quickly. Her gaze skittered past him and back before she said, "Would you like to stay for one?"

His heart seized, even though he was sure she wasn't asking

for a romp in the bedroom. He raised an eyebrow, although he was careful not to show anything but a serious expression.

"Naughty man," she said.

And wow—that particular sexy smile had the power to bring a red-blooded guy to his knees—especially one who'd never been graced by it directly before. And of course he hadn't. She'd likely thought of him as practically a child way back when. Come to think of it he'd also never seen her flirt at work before. At other events, yes. But never with an employee or coworker.

"I meant a drink," she amended.

"I know. I think I'd better leave you to it," he said. "It'll be another long day for you tomorrow."

For him, too, he thought. Because, like today, the bulk of it would be spent alone with Max.

CHAPTER 10

MAX FOUND Gia Serra waiting for her bright and early Friday morning. Gia's almond-shaped golden-brown eyes looked serious and her normally wide smile only reached half-wattage.

She held two paper cups from the nearest coffee joint. "Coffee or tea, your choice," Gia said.

A peace offering or a delay tactic. Max knew what was coming.

"Thanks," she said, and reached for the coffee. Gia, she knew, preferred tea. Except the model wouldn't drink it until later, when it was cool enough to put a straw in. No reason to stain perfectly bleached teeth. "Follow me."

Max didn't want to have this conversation in the lobby. She didn't really want to have it at all, but she appreciated that Gia felt speaking to Max was the right thing to do. Max lead the way to her office.

Gia was an accomplished model and a good soul. With a slightly olive complexion, brown hair, and luminous eyes, she was also incredibly moldable. One day she could look like a wealthy siren, the next like she'd never been anything but a surfer chick. Often snatched up by clothing, perfume or jewelry designers, she'd had years of success in print, mostly magazines. She'd never become a difficult diva-type however, nor had she ever taken the work for granted. At thirty-one years old, she *was* starting to book a little less frequently, however.

Max held in a sigh when Gia shut the door behind her. She was right then. Gia was here to resign.

Max gestured to the chairs in front of her desk as she set her bag and the coffee cup down. She hit the button to wake the computer. The model gripped her cup with white knuckled fingers, and Max hoped she didn't squeeze so hard it'd burst.

Max straightened and crossed her arms, having decided to make this as painless as possible for both their sakes. "So," she said. "You're leaving."

Gia nodded. "I'm sorry. I took the night to think it over, but yes."

Max sighed in earnest this time. "You're not done yet. You know that right?"

Gia shut her eyes for a moment. "I'm glad to hear you say that. I'm not ready to call it quits, but I do think it's time to reassess."

"You could just as easily reassess while you work," Max said. That would be as close as she came to asking Gia to stay. In this crazy situation, she didn't feel she should push one way or another.

Gia smiled, looking slightly more at ease now that the conversation was well underway. "I know, but it would be tough with the current circumstances. I was thinking of getting some true perspective. Maybe at the Bodhi."

"Oooh-la-la," Max said. The Bodhi was an up-and-coming premier spiritual and wellness center, popular among models and actors. It was well known that supermodel Molly Sims credited her detox and fasting experiences at the Ashram and We Care retreats for landing her that famed Sports Illustrated spot—the very one that had launched her career into the stratosphere.

"I know," Gia said, shaking her head. She stood and looked

Max in the eye. "Thank you, Max, for everything. I know how much I owe to your guidance and I don't want you to think I don't appreciate—"

Max interrupted. "I understand. I really do. Call me when you figure things out." She reached across the desk and squeezed Gia's hand.

"I will," Gia said.

Max's heart felt tight as Gia took her leave. She'd always liked Gia and had always believed in her future as a model. Today was no different, and Max sent out a silent plea to the universe that Gia would quickly find the answers she was looking for and continue to succeed.

Once Cam had taken care of Gia's resignation details, Max and Cam spent the bulk of the morning compiling a complex spreadsheet of everyone's schedules.

At one point, she'd growled in frustration and thrown her pen.

Cam had scolded her. "Patience, patience."

She came close to wringing his neck. When he suggested color-coding, however, things finally came together. Tier One people were highlighted red, Tier Two orange. Any appointments that weren't high priority were coded the same, but tinted fifty percent of the color.

"Okay," she said slumping back in her chair, "we've gone as far as we can." Thank goodness for Cam, or she'd have torn all her hair out.

"I'm still not sure this is all necessary," Cam said, pursing his lips.

"Neither am I," she said, "but it's what we've got to do. Call Shane for me and tell him we're ready for him?"

"Ooooh, silver lining," he quipped and exited her office for his own desk just across the hall.

An hour later, Shane strode in looking exactly as Cam had implied. Silver lining, indeed. Handsome and sleek in a perfectly cut gray suit, he wore a clear earpiece this time, with a squiggly wire that looked like it must be clipped to his collar in the back. She wondered who exactly he was connected with.

"How's it going?" he asked.

"It's not quite business as usual, but it's going," she said.

"How many quit?" he asked.

"A few—all models, no staff." She named them for him. Max shrugged for Shane's benefit, but in truth, she felt the loss of each one keenly. She'd given them her all over the years. She could certainly understand the urge to distance oneself from a threat—and this was a life or death whopper.

But she wished that they could see that she was doing everything in her power to keep them safe. Would they be safe out there alone? Surely another agency wouldn't offer protection. And sadly, her models likely wouldn't thrive with any old agency like they would have with Ivory. That wasn't conceit, it was just that she had a knack and vision and experience. She was good at what she did. Damn good.

"I'm sorry," he said, and he looked like he meant it. How odd—that he'd gone from considering her an evil witch just a couple of days ago to…to what? Was he actually concerned about her, or her company? Did he care what those models had meant to her personally? Likely he was just being polite.

"It is what it is," she said. God forbid she should get all maudlin and weepy again today—especially in front of Shane.

She waved him over toward the desk. She clicked a few times with her mouse to bring up the spreadsheet on her monitor.

He came to stand just over her shoulder, and she noted that the enticing aftershave smell was back in force.

"Let me show you the list so we can start making the assignments." She pursed her lips. "I don't know how your team is going to manage all this."

She learned, however. The first thing Shane did was chop. Chop, chop, and more chop. There'd been some obvious non-important purely social lunch dates, shopping excursions, etcetera, that she'd known would go, but he was positively ruthless.

At one point, her mouth dropped open. Shane chuckled and pushed it closed with a finger.

Cam came by about that time and poked his head in, "Need anything?"

She'd heard Shane's stomach rumble some time ago. "Would you mind running down and getting us a bite from Dominic's? Sandwich for this guy and a salad for me?" She looked to Shane, who nodded, and then to Cam.

"Thanks, man," Shane said.

"Don't forget something for yourself," she called as Cam left. "It's on me."

Cam was back in what felt like no time at all, and they switched to the more comfortable seating in front of the windows.

"Mmmm, this used to be my favorite," Shane said. "Just as good as I remember."

"The menu never changes, and Cam's got a memory for these things," she said. "He'll make a good wife and mother someday. Far better than me." She couldn't even see herself in those roles, honestly.

"He hasn't found the right guy yet?"

"Nope. He dates sometimes, but they never seem to last long."

They made general conversation while they ate, and then when they'd put their plates and wrappers on the coffee table, Max decided it was time to tell him the rest. She gestured to his earpiece and the black piece clipped to his lapel.

"Is someone listening to us?"

He shook his head. "It works more like a walkie-talkie."

Okay, then. She tucked her legs under her and shifted to face him. "Detective Iocavelli—"

"Danny's my cousin," Shane interrupted.

"Oh," she said, then smiled. "Surely from his Irish side of the family."

"Aye," he said, and the mood was light for just a few seconds longer.

"He said not to share the details with anyone, that they can make or break a case," she began. "I intended to stick to that. But it's occurred to me that if my agency's models are this psycho's target, that it could be someone who works closely with us or…"

Shane said the words she didn't want to, didn't even really want to think on. "Someone on the inside."

She nodded. "You're going to be *way* involved. Assessing everyone. So I think you should know all of it, the detective's directive be damned."

"You have my word not to share it with anyone," Shane said, "except maybe Joe on a need to know basis."

Even though she knew Joe would be doing more of the behind the scenes work, that seemed reasonable. She nodded.

Then she took a deep breath. "Both girls were…." God, she hated to even picture it. And there wasn't a word for it. "They both had color gels taped onto their bodies with black tape in the shape of big X's. A yellow one over Helena's belly, and her face." Max moved her finger from her own hairline to her chin, and again, in demonstration. "Win's were smaller yellow gels taped here, on both arms." She turned an arm and traced the X over the inside of one elbow. "And on her feet, on the tops, near the toes."

Shane looked as grim as she felt. "So," he said, "there's yet another link. And one very sick bastard out there trying to tell someone something."

Max grasped her hands tightly together between her knees.

"Your cousin isn't exactly chatty," she said.

"I'm sure he's got all kinds of laws and procedures to follow," he said.

She nodded. "He did share that Helena was pregnant. Too early to show."

Shane cocked his head sharply, then froze.

Max continued. "He said there are no reports back yet on Win, but I believe she was using."

Shane shook his head. "Like Closse said. Follow the needles." He pushed up from the low couch and walked to the windows. "The gels likely highlighted or showcased flaws then," Shane said. "Personality flaws or physical flaws?"

"Maybe both," Max said. "Both women had marred their bodies by their choices—one with pregnancy, the other with addiction—and the killer was surely calling that out. But to what purpose? For whose benefit?"

"This changes everything." Shane spun and looked at her, his expression incredulous. "This almost makes it seem he was working *for* your agency, not *against* it. Purging the ranks, eliminating those who weren't...what? Worthy? Perfect? Weren't what they seemed?"

She frowned.

Shane continued. "It's clear that the killer *knew* things.

Private, intimate things. Things he wouldn't know if he wasn't close with them. Particularly Helena."

"Right. I should have known Win was using." Max swallowed a fat serving of guilt. "Nearly anybody might have, but there's no way I could have known Helena was pregnant."

"She obviously confided in someone. But she'd have been terrified to tell you."

She winced. "I'm not that intimidating."

He raised an eyebrow, but didn't smile.

"Besides, she *should* have been worried," Max said. "I'd just signed her. She must have already been pregnant when I did. At what point she found out herself however, who knows."

Shane nodded. "You'd have terminated her contract."

"Or not signed her in the first place," Max said. "And she'd still be alive, having a beautiful baby out in the Midwest."

"It's not your fault," Shane said. "You didn't pick up that knife, nor did you hand somebody a barbell."

She sighed. "I keep telling myself that."

Shane paced the length of the windows, then stopped dead and leveled his gaze at her. "It had to be someone here." He gestured to indicate the building.

"Or someone outside, who'd be close to them. A stylist or photographer or nail tech? Maybe somebody they'd both partied with."

"Max, think this through," Shane said. "That might make sense if it was only Win. But Helena would have to *trust* somebody to tell them about the pregnancy."

"She could have been fishing for information. For termination maybe? For the name of a clinic in the city, since she was totally new here."

"There's google for that." Shane crossed his arms.

"Helena could have gotten drunk and spilled the beans to anyone who seemed like a sympathetic ear," Max said.

Shane raised an eyebrow. "Most women know better than to drink while they are pregnant."

Max sighed. "If she was set on an abortion, she wouldn't have cared." Then she shook her head. They both knew she was just playing devil's advocate.

"Danny," Shane said, and she realized he meant his cousin, Detective Iocavelli, "will be thinking the same thing. But just in case, you should tell him all of this."

She nodded. Max hugged herself.

"Do it now," he said.

She looked up at the sharp order—really looked at him. His face looked like a thundercloud. Ominous and angry.

"Then," he said, "you and I have a score to settle."

She narrowed her eyes but crossed to the desk to retrieve her cell phone and slid into her chair. He wanted a fight? Fine. She much preferred feeling angry to being upset and scared. Those feelings were so unlike her.

While she conversed with Detective Iocavelli, Shane faced the street, with his back to her. Arms crossed, legs slightly apart, the back of his suit jacket stretched tight across his broad shoulders. She watched him the whole time, and he didn't move an inch. He used to be so full of energy, constantly in motion, his fingers tapping when he could have been still or dancing across the room instead of walking.

When Max told Iocavelli that she'd hired O'Rourke Security, he said, "Good choice. I'll call Shane later to make sure we're on the same page."

After she'd hung up, she leaned back in her desk chair, crossed her legs so that her pencil skirt rode up—just a bit. She wouldn't try to seduce Shane, of course, but he was ticked off about something. Distracting him a little might be smart.

"So you want to tell me about the bug up your ass?" she asked, not one to beat around the bush.

He shook his head, then turned. She saw his gaze flick to her bare knees and then back to her face. No reaction. So much for distraction then.

"You want to play around right now?" he asked. "Make light?"

"No." Instantly, she felt contrite. "Just say your peace."

"You *aren't* Tier Two." He said, his voice tightly controlled. "You let me drop you off at home last night, without protection, and you aren't Tier Two."

"Shane," she began, in the most reasonable tone she could manage. But he didn't let her reason this away.

"You knew everything you just told me, you had to have thought through the implications, and yet, you chose… you *chose* to be stupid."

"Come on," she said, launching herself out of her chair. "That's hardly—"

But he plowed on, getting louder. "Even if you hadn't determined yet whether to go against police orders and tell me everything, you should have accepted my offer to stay until whoever you had coming over could get there."

It had seemed smarter, she thought at the time given her attraction to him, to make him go. But she wasn't about to say that. "I *really* don't think I qualify as a target for this guy."

He completely ignored that. "From what you've just told me, the killer knew intimate details about these women. He didn't pick randomly. This is either an inside job or awfully close to it. And you are a big link. Hell, you *are* Ivory," Shane said. He rubbed his jaw but barely paused for breath. "I can't do my job if you're hiding things from me. I can't protect you if you aren't being reasonable."

"I have now told you *everything*, and I'm hardly being unreasonable." Her hands fisted. "I seriously don't think we can make *any* assumptions. Short of calling attention to these women's flaws, we can't infer anything. Plus, I don't have anything to hide. I don't hide who I am—I'm exactly who I appear to be." She threw out her hands, frustrated that he didn't see what she did. "I'm not sure we can apply logic to a psychotic killer anyway."

"Are you being purposely obtuse?" he asked with a scowl.

"I could ask the same of you," Max said and stared daggers at him.

Somehow during this conversation, they'd squared off face to face. Another step and she'd be able to feel the heat pouring off him. His anger seemed unwarranted to her, but maybe he knew something she didn't. Maybe he hadn't been totally forthcoming with her. Maybe like some caveman, he just wasn't voicing his thoughts very well.

"Let's agree to disagree for now," she said.

He made a sound of disgust. "Fine. What's your situation tonight?"

She narrowed her eyes. What did her Friday night plans have to do with anything?

He shook his head at her, then he moved in even closer. So close that she had to look up at him.

"Here it is then," he said. "You'll either cancel whatever *friend* you've got coming over tonight, or you give both me and Danny his full contact information so we can both run background checks. If we clear him, I'll stay at your place until he arrives, pat him down, interrogate him, and then let you have your fun."

Horror must have shown on her face, because he asked, "You don't like that idea?"

There was nothing comforting about his smile now.

Shane said, "You'll like this one even less. You get *me* for a sleepover—which means no action for you."

"What I really don't like," she snapped, "is you constantly referencing my sex life."

"It's common knowledge that you keep awfully busy playing the field. What was it you just said?" Shane cocked his head as if he were thinking. "Oh yeah, that's right. You don't hide who you are." His eyes were hard. "I'm just being realistic. All the cards on the table, remember? So I can do my job?"

This was exactly the reason she held fast to her rules, the most important one being no flirting or sex with anyone she worked with. Some rules were meant for safety, this one was all about drawing a hard line between her private life and professional life. Max did not appreciate Shane mixing the two.

She scowled. "I *don't* hide who I am. You're the one making it sound dirty."

He snorted. "I don't care how it sounds or how you do it. All I care about is clearing *who* you do it with."

The *stugats* on this one! Max jammed her hands on her hips and glared.

He rolled his shoulders once and then waited, his eyes narrowed on her, seemingly having vented the worst of his anger.

"Any other options?" she finally managed to ask in clipped tones.

He shrugged. "You got any girlfriends you sleep with?"

Short of shouting *va fancul*—choice Italian for go F yourself, which she refused to yell here at the office, she was stumped for words. The *shmendrik*! And mind, that Jewish slight was nowhere near strong enough.

Her default took over. She raised her chin and lowered her lashes. "You'd like that wouldn't you?"

"Not really," he said with a bored tone. "Male or female, I still have to do that background check and escort you there."

She seethed but refused to let him see it. She spun and sashayed toward her desk to gather her things. Muttering, she said, "This whole thing is going to be a joyride from start to finish, isn't it?"

CHAPTER 11

HIS FATHER HAD always yelled. The morning after was nothing new. But at least in later years, it was confined to the mornings.

After a woman left their house, usually hollering right back, his dad would go on and on. About his mother, he'd say, "She was never the same after she had kids. Her breasts ended up swinging like a mutt's balls. She got fat, in all the wrong places. And she started pissing herself when she so much as coughed. I couldn't stand to look at her anymore, and I certainly wasn't going to bury my prick in that. See that? It's all your fault you have no mother. You boys ruined her."

It wasn't true, though, he *had* slept with her again, over and over. Because he was also fond of the phrase *A man's gotta do what a man's gotta do*. But the railing got worse and worse, and when she showed signs of being pregnant a third time, Dad made her take something and locked her in the bathroom. Nailed in two boards to keep her in there.

He'd been young, he didn't know how young at the time. He'd lain under the bed on the rough planks of the floor, trying to watch, trying to understand what she was meant to *take care of*. He'd have heard everything from anywhere in the house anyway—it was small. With only the one bathroom, the rest of them now had to use the great outdoors for their business. The room he shared with his brother had mattresses on the floor. But there, under his parent's bed, all dusty and musty, he didn't have to see his father's face. And he could see his mother's feet.

Nothing's happening, it's meant to be, she'd screamed.

His father said it was all her fault. That she'd let her body go to rot. That she'd never make any money now. That she'd never hit it big. That nothing on earth was meant to be. Everything was what we made it.

Two days. Two whole days of screaming and pounding—*You bastard! I hate you! I'll never forgive you for this!*—and nothing had changed.

Except her screams. *I need food*, she'd begged. *The baby will never live through this anyway, just let me out.*

And then, finally, he'd understood. All the things his father constantly berated her for were going to get worse. The yelling would never end.

How long did it take for a baby to be born? Would she just walk out with one in her arms? Would she be changed already when she came out, her stomach bigger, her breasts longer? Or was it the feedings that had made his father hate her so much—*sucked the life outta your tits*—as he'd heard him say so many times…Could the baby suck the life out of the rest of her? Could the baby die from all the noise?

Whenever his father would go out, she would call for him. So many, many times.

"Open the door, honey, please. You can do it. Find the crow bar. We'll run away. He'll never find us."

His brother had disappeared. Gone to a friend's or slept in the woods or somewhere. So it was just him.

He'd looked, but he hadn't found a tool that would work. He'd tried the door, but couldn't reach the wood pieces at the top, and couldn't budge the one at the bottom. He didn't try very hard. He was scared.

He'd pleaded with her to just make it go away. *Make Daddy happy, Mommy, please.*

He'd been so torn. He'd loved his mother. And hated her for her weakness. Sometimes, when she looked beautiful and happy, he wanted to be her. To climb up on her lap and melt inside her. He wanted to be able to move like her and to dress like her, especially when she danced.

He loved his father. And hated him for his meanness. He *never* wanted to be him.

He watched his mother's bare feet through the crack in the door. Always, her feet remained beautiful, he thought, with brightly painted toenails. So pretty. She walked around and stomped and sometimes her feet would disappear, but then they'd come back.

Eventually his father told her *you're not getting out until it's done* and slid a wire hanger under the door. He didn't know what that meant. But his mother went crazy. There was more name calling. *Bastard, Bastard, Psycho Bastard.* She'd long since become hoarse with it. And the sobbing went on and on. She hit things, she ran a lot of water.

After what seemed an eternity, it became quiet. And then it was quiet for what felt like forever.

She never did come out.

CHAPTER 12

MAX HAD HAD no choice but to phone Miranda and ask if she could impose on her and Eddie. They didn't mind, of course, but Max felt like a grounded child—both resentful at being restricted and shamed despite having done nothing wrong.

She truly didn't feel she herself was at risk, but it also wasn't kosher to impose all these stipulations on her models and staff, without being willing to follow them herself. She'd just been so focused on taking care of everyone else, that she hadn't thought this far ahead.

She'd gathered her things, then she and Shane took a cab to her apartment. She packed a bag, while he poked around checking window locks, playing with the intercom system and who knew what else. On the way out, he spoke with the doorman and gave him his card. He took a pen from the desk and scribbled something on it. Once outside, she asked what he'd given him.

"Danny's number," he said, and that was the end of it.

The cab ride to Miranda's place was spent in silence, and that was just fine with Max. She had nothing to say to him anyway.

Although she was calmer now, she still thought he'd been unnecessarily harsh. And offensive. And crude.

And it's not like they were friends, or lovers, or even really colleagues. At the moment, they were working together because she'd hired him, because she was paying him. The minute the killer was caught, or at least the minute the police considered him no longer a threat to her employees, they'd part ways, and she'd likely never see him again.

In the meantime, she'd have to follow his orders, put up with his angry outbursts, and try very, very hard not to notice how good-looking he was, all while spending one helluva lot of time together.

So much for that fleeting feeling of support and common ground she'd enjoyed yesterday. She must have been delusional. Max stared out the window as the cabbie weaved and jerked through the traffic and lights. This was going to be a long, long few weeks.

When they buzzed in to Miranda's first floor brownstone apartment where she both lived and ran her business, the dog was technically the first to greet them.

"Hellooooo, sweetheart," Max said and bent to rub his ears. Eddie's dog was a gorgeous, well-trained Shepherd mix. "This is Stripes, and you remember Miranda," Max said to Shane.

"Nice to see you again," Miranda said warmly. Eddie had joined them, and Miranda introduced him to Shane. The two men shook hands and, Max thought with a roll of her eyes, sized each other up.

"Where should I put this?" Shane said, raising Max's overnight bag.

"I'll take it," Eddie said. "Come on in."

"Thanks for taking care of my girl," Miranda said.

"He's being paid, you know," Max said, still a little angry.

"You'll have to excuse her," Miranda said sweetly, "sometimes she can be a real jerk." She shot that last word to Max.

Max decided she'd had enough. She harrumphed—*sheesh*, she sounded like her grandmother Aggie—and took herself off to the kitchen.

"Seriously," Max heard Miranda say as she rummaged around in the drawer that usually held the wine opener, "she's just really out of sorts with all this."

Shane replied just low enough that Max couldn't hear it, and she told herself she didn't care.

Eddie was nearer the kitchen, so she heard his invitation. "I'm sure you want to make sure Max'll be secure so come take a look around. I installed some surveillance cameras not too long ago."

They moved down the hall.

Miranda came into the kitchen and crossed her arms just as Max was pouring her first—probably not her last—glass of Pinot Noir.

"Want one?"

"What has gotten into you?" Miranda asked.

"You have no idea how awful he was to me this afternoon. And anyway, you're supposed to be on my side." She knew she was practically pouting but couldn't help herself. She was tired and worried, and yes, the words Miranda had used, *out of sorts*, were apt.

"I'm always on your side," Miranda soothed. "Pour me a glass."

When she had it in hand, her expression turned mischievous. "Can you tell me now, or do I have to wait?"

"Ugh, I'm not sure I want to tell it."

"We tell each other *everything*, remember?" An oath they swore way back in college one drunken night. Miranda had been a film major, and Max had taken a photography course as part of her fashion degree. It was love at first sight. Well, okay—it was a meeting of the minds and a fair amount of hilarity during a partnered field assignment, but still.

Max didn't want to relay what Shane had said in front

of Eddie—even though Miranda told him practically everything, too—so she filled Miranda in as quickly as she could.

Miranda narrowed her eyes. "Hmmm."

"Hmmm? What kind of response is that?" Max said, "How about you poor thing, or what an a-hole, or —"

"Ladies," came Shane's deep voice behind her, and Max jumped, sloshing her wine all over her silk blouse and new skirt. "Goddammit!" She spun on him. "Don't sneak up on me like that."

"Sorry." Shane smirked. "Just letting you know I'm taking off. I'll call you later when I get through the scheduling."

He and Eddie both headed for the door, Stripes trotting along beside them.

Miranda whispered, "You've got trouble. He walks as silently as Eddie. Like jungle cats, the both of them."

Max sighed. She'd have to remember that fact.

CHAPTER 13

NEARLY A WEEK passed and nothing had happened. Shane knew Max felt the pressure of having a near-constant guard, but so far she was cooperating. She continued to be forthcoming with him and had been accepting of his presence, and that of the other agents he'd assigned to her, without fuss.

Every time he was scheduled as her guard, he prepped himself. But nothing worked. A wave of lust hit him like a blowtorch each and every time. The scent of her perfume lingered with him, even after she'd left a room. He'd listen for her throaty laugh from down the hall. He'd begun dreaming— flashes of bare skin, dark, silky hair, and full red lips—nearly every night.

It was insane. He felt like a teenage boy, obsessing over someone out of reach, stirring himself into a frenzy—even though *logically* he really didn't want anything to do with Maxine Ricci.

His body had other ideas though. When he leaned down next to her to point out something on the master spreadsheet, he ached to touch her. And that happened a lot. Because there was constant re-jiggering who got to go where and who was assigned to them. Daily, even hourly sometimes.

No real surprise there. Modeling was an on-the-move kind of business. You hopped to any opportunity that crossed your path, you crisscrossed the city, or even the country or the ocean, if need be to score a gig. Shoots ran late constantly and go-see's were cancelled regularly. And none of these people were the personality types that could abide sitting at a desk, or even staying in one building for long.

What did surprise Shane was the constant bickering. Had it always been like this? Or did Max happen to have a bunch of immature jerks on her roster right now? Chrystina didn't want to work with Armand again, Samara wanted only Brian, somebody else insisted her hair appointment was more important than so and so's nails, and on and on.

Maybe he was being too harsh. Everybody was on edge, frustrated by having their movements scrutinized and curtailed. And the longer nothing happened—a blessing, though they seemed to be losing sight of that fact—the more the restrictions grated.

"You've got to remember," Max said to Shane at one point, "to them, the gel nails *are* important." And on more than one occasion, she'd said, "Spare no expense. Cover as much as you and your team can manage, and make it work however you need to."

Max had promised to keep her people working and beautiful. So as long as there were enough bodyguards, she wanted to honor as many of the models' engagements as possible.

Which meant an awful lot of car services, and in one case, a private plane. Shane wondered about what all this was going to do to Ivory's bottom line—but refrained from asking Max about it. It shouldn't matter to him. In the end, he and Joe would make a pretty penny—both ensuring bonuses for all O'Rourke employees and covering their quickly mounting attorney fees for Daddy Sorrelle's lawsuit.

Not only was this job's volume enormous—not one asset to protect, but dozens—but there was no way to do site advance work. Other than Ivory's two floors, there was simply no way to preview every location involved, and there certainly wasn't time to make any of those sites more secure. The fact that they had no idea who the killer's next target was meant they were spread awfully thin.

He and Joe had discussed it at length, and this was simply going to be one of the more unusual protection jobs they'd ever taken. Joe had seen nearly everything in his thirty-plus years in the business, so that was saying something.

"We'll just have to be on our toes, and then some," Joe had said.

That made Shane uncomfortable. He'd followed procedure to the letter with Carrie Sorrelle, and it'd still gone south. Her fault, really, but if he'd only been one step ahead of her, had thought through just one more scenario...

No, don't go there, he thought, just as their car service pulled up to Capelli, a high-end hair salon. Shane remembered it well—in fact, the lead stylist had given him his first haircut in the States—after he'd been here going on two years. Which was ironic, considering that Keith Tomlin was one of the most well-known stylists in fashion *and* Hollywood.

Shane had sent his agent Armand ahead. He radioed, and heard the confirmation in his ear radio: site secure. Shane hustled Samara Tim inside, and then Armand slipped outside to escort Cam in. Max had opted to send Cam in her place. A high sign of trust, because Shane knew from experience that Max generally preferred to oversee these things herself. He was pretty sure she believed firmly in the *if you want it done right, do it yourself* philosophy. Well good for Cam—it couldn't have been easy taking orders from a hard-ass like Max for a decade plus.

Keith's face lit up when he saw Shane, and the tall, reedy man wrapped his arms around Shane and squeezed. Mostly Shane didn't mind. Some men were huggers, some back slappers, some hand shakers—the fashion industry just happened to have a few more huggers. The trouble was, the agent in him was freaked at having both arms hampered, even for a few seconds.

"Look who the cat dragged in," Keith said leaning back, his hands still on Shane's upper arms so he could look him over. "You need a cut, and a shave, but you look good. Better than ever."

Keith himself looked much the same—a tall, wiry black man, who had light brown eyes and long eyelashes but offset that slightly feminine asset by channeling an edge. The flat top hair cut with lightning bolts edged into the shaved sides and ear gauges were new. But the tight t-shirt and black jeans were standard fare.

"You too, man," Shane said. "Good to see you." And Shane meant it. Keith was a good guy and a true professional with loads of talent. Shane had always liked him. There were lots of relationships like these that Shane had walked away from when he left, so angry and bitter, cutting himself off entirely from this world.

Keith and Cam greeted each other warmly as well, but Shane sensed an undercurrent of tension, which immediately put him on high alert. Shane assigned Armand to watch the front entrance and sought out the salon owner himself. He'd prefer to lock the rear exit while they were there, and he also made a request that the volume of the music be turned way down. When he returned, Cam and Keith were deep into discussions about Samara's color and highlights.

Finally, Keith went off to mix color. Cam came to stand next to Shane. "He's so good but, uh-yi-yi, talk about stubborn," Cam complained.

He kept up the chatter through the first row of Samara's

foils, talking about how impressed he was with all of Shane's agents, how amazing Max was for her commitment to keeping everyone safe.

Cam leaned in close, putting a hand on one of Shane's crossed forearms. "She's a Madonna, don't you think? I'm in awe."

Interesting word choice *Madonna*, Shane thought. Idealized and revered, by men and young women alike, but certainly not virtuous—not in the traditional sense anyway. Not if you went by her reputation—a woman who loved men, loved the hunt, loved the conquest.

Maybe that was why Shane's particular case of lust was so bad. He'd been a player, too—before he suddenly became a dad, anyway. He and Max together should be a no brainer. And yet for him, she was off limits. And vice versa, he suspected. Though he *had* caught her eyeing him up once or twice.

Shane forced his mind back to the present. Interestingly enough Keith's eyes kept darting to Cam, and he seemed to be growing annoyed.

Cam saw him noticing. "Oh, don't worry about him." He turned his back to Keith and faced Shane more directly. "We had a *thing*. For a while."

Shane couldn't picture it. Cam was a good-looking guy: average height, fit enough, stylish in a preppy way, highlighted brown hair perfectly arranged, and trendy eyeglasses. Maybe it was an opposites attract kind of thing.

Cam shrugged a shoulder. "It's over now. That was part of the problem." He leaned in. "His jealously issues."

He glanced over his shoulder, then cocked his head and eyed Shane. "Maybe he should be worried in this case. If I thought you were even just a little bit…"

It wouldn't be the first or last time that Shane had been hit on by a man. "Cam," Shane said, "I need to concentrate."

Cam made a face, but his tone was reasonable. "Absolutely. You're right." He mimed dusting off his hands. "We both have jobs to do here." And he went off to keep an eagle eye on the highlighting process.

A short while later, Shane's radio crackled in his ear. Armand, who stood outside the salon, spoke loud and clear. "Suspicious incoming. Female, medium complexion, knit cap pulled low, big sunglasses, long winter coat."

This was the first thing an agent looked for: any person acting inappropriately. You weren't going to get a blinking neon clue, like a semiautomatic carried in on a silver platter. It was the little tells that pointed to something off. Neither sunglasses or a big winter coat were appropriate to the warm, overcast day.

"Intercept," Shane said. Another common agent tactic. Be visible, be a deterrent. What better tactic to scare off an assailant than actual contact?

Shane had positioned himself purposefully, with a good view of Samara in Keith's chair and Cam hovering over her, as well as the entryway and Armand outside it. He watched as Armand slid in front of the entrance. He spoke to the woman, and Shane knew that at least initially, Armand's tone would be friendly and helpful.

Shane kept one eye on his assets, in case the woman was meant as a distraction and a threat came from behind.

In no time, Armand had taken the woman's arm and steered her in the door, even as he shook his head at Shane. Negative—no threat. His expression confirmed that he felt no alarm, only displeasure and annoyance.

The female stomped a booted foot angrily and they were

obviously having words. Shane couldn't hear them through the various blow-dryers, running water, and music (the volume of which had somehow creeped back up), until the woman nearly yelled, "But my roots are showing!"

Chrystina. No wonder she had made a fuss about working with Armand. There had been no personality conflict, she was just angling for her freedom.

And sealing her fate as one of the newly unemployed—at least if Max stuck to her guns.

———

Liang "Lillian" Willken's photo shoot brought Shane right back to the old days. He'd never worked with Max's new in-house photographer Damien Closse, but everything else was so familiar. Max and Cam were in attendance, as were the head makeup artist, Kimberly, and head stylist, Marc, both of whom Shane knew. Plus, the steady beat of dance music, the shine of the lights turned this way and that, the rapid-fire clicking of the camera. Then there was the constant stream of directives and encouragement and the stop and start of the action when powder or water or a clothing adjustment was needed. Shane felt a rush—habitual he was sure—because he truly didn't have any desire to be back there.

Lillian was rocking it. Blue-black sleek hair in a trendy chin-length cut. Dangling earrings with loads of move-ment. Sky-high gold heels and a gold-lame type shift. The short dress was loose and boxy, but the allure was that it was nearly—but not quite—see through. Shane could imagine the finished product, a reader squinting at the spread, trying to decide if that was the curve of the breast they saw or a catch of the light.

Cam looked entranced, eyes on Lillian, his hand flying

over a notepad. Likely he was taking notes on suggestions, critiques, ideas for later. Photo shoots were organic and sometimes the best results were borne on the spot.

Max strode back and forth in platform heels. She'd shed her fitted jacket to show a loose gray sleeveless top with a long statement necklace and sleek leather pencil pants. As always, she looked fantastic, perfectly nailing the balance between trendy and classy and sexy. She gave the shoot her full attention, with no hint of her inner turmoil.

Shane was impressed. It hadn't been ten minutes since he and Armand had marched Chrystina into the boss's office and the young woman had attempted to apologize. Max had cut her off, sharply.

"No exceptions," was all she'd said to the girl, before she'd asked Armand to see her out. On the way back he was to instruct both the security guard downstairs and Susan the receptionist on the receiving floor that she was not to be let back in under any circumstances.

As soon as the door closed behind them she'd let loose. "What was she thinking? I told her she only had to wait a few days, *a few days,* before she'd have her turn." She looked at Shane. "Did she think we wouldn't notice? That word wouldn't get back to me? The *stunad!*"

Shane worked to keep a straight face. He always got a kick out of her propensity for dishing out colorful slights—both Jewish and Italian—or for gesturing wildly at times. Sure enough, she'd thrown out her hands and spun to pace the other direction.

"And the worst part is, nothing's happened. I might be losing my models for nothing." She uttered a noise of pure frustration. "I just don't know—I don't know anything anymore."

"Neither do I, but to my mind, it's a calculated risk worth taking," Shane said.

"Hah!" Max said. "I don't know, you don't know, the police don't know. This is crazy!"

The phone had rung then: Cam, letting her know that they were ready for her downstairs. She put her hands on her hips and blew out a long breath. Then she nodded firmly, and they were off to watch Lillian do her thing.

Now, Shane stood a ways back from the action of the shoot, watching the doorway, surveying all the players. The building's security was good, but the office was also high risk. So many of the models in one place—the one place that the two models who'd been so brutally murdered had in common. Given more time, Shane figured, Helena would have frequented the same salons and gyms and social hot spots, but she'd been so new to the city, those overlaps hadn't had time to occur.

Closse didn't have to call out. As soon as he lowered his camera and took a step forward, all the other action ceased. As per his usual, he wore all black. T-shirt, jeans, boots. Body art on full display. Max had told him that she'd hired Damien Closse because he was "The *best*. An asshole, but the best."

Shane would agree with the asshole part. There wasn't a lot about the guy to like.

Closse directed the stylist to add the wig. "Quickly now," Closse said, and motioned the makeup artist to add some shimmer to her lips. The whole time, he circled Lillian, assessing.

Then he moved in close to her and pulled the shift to expose more of one shoulder. She already had her eyes glued to his face, but he grasped her chin to tilt it up and caressed her lightly.

He said, "Just for me now."

She nodded, he stepped away, and immediately the wind

and music resumed. More clicking, maybe another five minutes, and then he called out, "Stop."

He strode forward, took Lillian by the arm and spun her around to face the screen. Then he came in close behind her, his front to her back, and put his mouth directly to her ear. He said a couple of sentences, tops, though Shane couldn't hear it from his post and he doubted anyone nearer could either.

When the action started again, Lillian exuded sensuality, like she was making love to the camera.

Or to Closse, Shane thought and slid a glance toward the photographer.

Closse had ceased clicking away. He'd actually lowered the camera a couple of inches—to just watch.

CHAPTER 14

THE PHOTO SHOOTS always brought him back. The lights, the pounding music, the audience. All that skin showing through the skimpy clothes, painted lips pouting just so, bedroom eyes that beckoned. Long beautiful hair tossed this way and that, the sinuous graceful movements, everything sparkly, catching on the light and reflecting it back.

So far back, to when he'd first come to appreciate the female form. No—to fall in love with it. The smooth expanses of soft skin—no coarse hair ruining it. The deep curves that drew the eye. The shadows that fell in the most enticing places.

Women were stunning creatures.

Growing up, they'd spent countless evenings in strip clubs, his dad ordering beer after beer. Dad wasn't the hooting, hollering type. But the girls liked his tips and seemed to think he was attractive. Attractive enough to bed. At least until the morning after.

For him, it was different. He could have—and did—spend hours upon hours just watching. With no real endgame. Each woman had different coloring, different hair texture, different lengths and proportions, different peaks and valleys. He longed to see them *take it all off*—as so many of the men would chant, including his brother in years to come. But he himself kept quiet, like his dad.

Later in the evening, he knew, he might get to see them in

all their naked splendor. And once he understood the pattern, he wished always, that morning would never come.

Watching Lillian today? What a rush. She was something to behold—simply spectacular. So gorgeous and fluid. Thin enough to show the underlying muscle and bone, but still curvy enough to nearly make him weep with longing. What he wouldn't give…

He liked her real hair best, not that the wig wasn't sexy… Her eyes, her lips, when she really got into it, she was just… There were hardly words.

He knew without a doubt that she would be a big star. She'd scored some decent spots already, and she had a shot, a good one, at the cover of Harper's Bazaar. Someday, he could even see her in the Sports Illustrated swimsuit edition— maybe even gracing the cover. Lillian had *it*—that intangible something that Max was so good at spotting and nurturing.

And between Max and him? She would go far.

He'd been disappointed in the past. But Lillian wouldn't be like that. He'd been watching for a long time, he'd seen her come into her own. And she was just as pure now as when she'd begun…

The times he'd been able to touch her had been simply amazing. Her skin had been even softer than it looked. Up close, her skin really was flawless, her lashes so thick, her hair so sleek and straight.

He looked forward to spending more time with her. Getting to know her even better.

Lillian, he could tell, would live in his night for a long, long time.

CHAPTER 15

ON FRIDAY AFTERNOON, Shane asked Brian to cover for him. Specifically, to stay with Max at Ivory until she called it quits, and then deposit her with her friends Eddie and Miranda. Max had looked relieved. Probably she needed the space as much as he did.

He'd been shorting the twins since he'd started working for Max, so he'd promised to take them boxing. They were old enough to use the city's public transportation and would join him right after school. Shane had gone home to change and then jogged the nearly forty blocks to Dub's gym in Upper Manhattan to warm up. He should have time to get in a good workout before they arrived. He figured they'd have dinner together afterward, maybe hit their favorite local pizza place.

It'd be a good break for Mrs. Costa, his neighbor and housekeeper as well. She loved to cook and loved to be needed, hugging up the kids every chance she got, but never hesitated to shake her wooden spoon and deliver a heavily-accented scolding when it was called for. Even when he wasn't paying her, she was always next door if they needed her—and often he did. Executive protection hours weren't always regular, and sometimes it was necessary to be gone days at a time. He could never justify this work if it wasn't for Mrs. Costa and Uncle Joe and Aunt Tricia. He couldn't ask for more protective, more loving caregivers for his kids, and considered himself and the twins blessed.

Dub's was basically a hole in the wall. Nondescript door outside with a rather small sign, and a rather bare-bones boxing club on the inside. Shane raised a hand to the guys he knew as he entered. He avoided any conversations, choosing to head straight for the locker room to wrap his hands. The regulars were used to that. When he came here, it was because he needed to let off steam, not waste time talking. Sometimes he'd indicate to the manager with a nod of his head that he hoped to pick up a match. Not today, though. Today, he'd be satisfied working up a sweat himself, because he wanted to be available to the kids when they arrived.

Shane shed his hooded sweatshirt and stashed it in his locker. He quickly wrapped his hands and donned his gloves. Then he headed for the bags.

The first punch felt so good, the second even better. He was full of so much tension, gathered up like a storm cloud between his shoulder blades. He needed to let it rain.

All the time with the Ivory Management job, constantly assessing and reassessing. Had he thought of every contingency? Was there anything else that could be done to make them safer? Would that schedule change or this addition affect anyone's safety?

And then there was working with Max—an entirely different level of stress. Somewhere in the last week or so the bitter taste of bad blood between them had subsided. He could admit now that she wasn't the stone-cold bitch he'd built up in his younger mind. She cared about her models, and she was willing to make the hard decisions for the overall good. Nor was she immune to the pain that came with those hard decisions. He supposed that it'd been the same when she'd let him go. He'd just been too immature and full of himself then to see it, not to mention scared for his future prospects. Max had only been doing her job, running her company as she saw fit.

He'd created his own bad place as a result. It wasn't remotely her fault that he hadn't had sense enough to step out of his own self-destructive way.

Shane bobbed and weaved as he danced around the bag, and all the while his arms moved like a machine. The physical relief was so welcome, he felt like he could keep it up forever.

As his old bitterness—which he'd clearly held on to for far too long—about being fired by Max subsided, somehow the other stuff—like respect—had creeped in. She was tough and determined, hardworking and savvy, funny and animated. She could be nurturing, but in a no-nonsense tell-it-like-it-is way, and like him, apparently had a protective streak as well.

She also happened to be the most comfortable flirt he'd ever met. A sex kitten wrapped in some classy fur. He'd entertained plenty of fantasies about her way back when. Hell what young, hot-blooded straight male didn't?

Sweat dripped into his eyes and his breath came harder. Shane kept up his rhythm.

His old fantasies had resurrected themselves, hotter than ever. All grown up. But the worst part was they felt...nearly real. Like they were just out of reach and might even arrive with tomorrow. He felt the sexual tension between them as if it were a tangible thing. And he was sure that that feeling wasn't one-sided.

He couldn't deny it any longer. His desire for Maxine Ricci had swelled to epic proportions.

Bedding the woman might solve everything. Or make it that much worse.

He faltered, his punch sliding right off the bag. He gave it a rest and let his head rest against the bag as he held it.

Just as he straightened a towel hit him square in the face.

Yanking it off, he found his cousin, Danny Iocavelli, grinning at him.

"Nice," Shane said.

Danny chuckled. "Couldn't resist."

They came together for a quick hug and backslap. Shane tugged off his gloves as they moved away from the bags. "How'd you know I'd be here?"

"I was nearby, so I called ahead to check." He inclined his head at Dub's manager.

Shane retrieved the towel, mopped his face and neck, and chugged some water from the bottle he'd brought. They chose a bench against the wall.

"How's the investigation going?" Shane asked.

Danny grimaced, a few of his freckles disappearing into the lines around his mouth. "It's not. We don't have much."

Shane grunted, none too pleased to hear that.

"How's the protective detail going?" Danny asked.

Shane could feel Danny's eyes on him. "Fine." He busied his fingers unwinding his tape. "I would've called you if I'd discovered anything."

"I know that," Danny said.

"Then what are you asking?"

"That woman, Max. She's really something." Danny raised his eyebrows.

Shane narrowed his eyes. "Yeah, she is."

"You got your best guys on her?" Danny asked.

"Yeah. *I'm* on her."

"Well then, watch her closely. It'd be easy to get sucked in with that one, if you know what I mean."

Shane's fists clenched. "Spell it right out so we're clear."

"She's a gorgeous woman," Danny said.

"And?"

Danny shook his head. "She's still a suspect, man. You know that, right?"

"There's no way," Shane said. "No way."

"Come on," Danny chided. "She's got more access, more connection, more motive than anyone."

Shane scoffed. "You told me yourself that wielding a barbell as a killing tool likely ruled out a woman. And how the hell do you figure motive? What's the point in killing off your own models?"

Danny shrugged. "Maybe she was furious when she found out Helena was pregnant. Maybe killing them off gains Ivory publicity. Even bad publicity sells, right? Maybe they had something on her. Maybe—"

"Jaysus. You don't know shite," Shane said. "Max cares about her people. She's torn up about the murders. She—"

"Whoa," Danny said. "Now I gotta worry that you're already blinded? That you're falling for her? You're the one that used the word *ruthless*, remember?"

Shane made a noise of disgust and rolled his eyes. Then he saw Anna and Niall burst through the door. Time to end this ridiculousness.

"They shouldna passed ye from playschool, Danny," Shane said, "no matter yer ma insisted ye were smart."

Danny laughed, the Irish making all well between them. Danny had actually grown up here, with heavy Italian influence, but he'd spent summers in Ireland visiting his mother's family, perfecting his brogue. The art and joy of insults was prevalent in both cultures. Shane had known Danny would laugh and let up.

As soon as the twins dropped their school and gym bags, Danny gave them playful punches and then big bear hugs. He asked some questions about school, told them to mind their Uncle Shane—except in boxing because if they really wanted to learn they'd do better to talk to Danny, himself—and invited them to visit his precinct anytime. Both kids basked in the attention.

"I'll leave you to your lesson," Danny said. "Mind what I said."

But he wasn't telling the twins. He was warning Shane with a hard look.

CHAPTER 16

BEFORE LEAVING for the night, he was on his way down the hall to deliver some newly developed photographs of Lillian's photo shoot so that they could be addressed first thing in the morning, when he heard the unmistakable sounds of someone throwing up in the bathroom. He frowned. Nearly everyone was gone except Lillian. He knew, because he always knew where she was.

She was impossible not to notice, not to track. She shone with beauty and grace. He couldn't help but be aware of her. An ever-present temptation—what he desired most in the world.

He listened as he approached—definitely the woman's bathroom—and then pushed the door open halfway. "Lillian? Is that you?"

"Go away!" she said.

"It's me," he said.

He entered and eyed the stalls, bending to check under.

Lillian was in the far one, standing facing the toilet.

He went over and knocked. "Are you okay?"

"Yes, I just didn't feel well." She sniffed. "I'm better now."

He heard her take some toilet paper and blow her nose.

He turned to the sink to wait and spotted her big bag open on the vanity. Half the contents had been strewn over the counter, and there were wrappers in the sink. With crumbs.

He leaned closer to investigate. He heard the toilet flush. A six pack of peanut butter crackers, two protein bars, an individual package of vanilla cookies. Vending machine fare. All gone.

No, no… he thought. It can't be.

"Don't—" she started, and shoved hard enough to push him out of the way of the sink. Frantically, she scooped the wrappers and shoved them in the trash can, then turned on the water. She scooped with her hands to swish and spit, then drink. Hurriedly, she cupped more water and flushed the crumbs down the drain. She grabbed a paper towel and wiped at the counter, her movements jerky.

He watched her hands make quick work of the mess, disbelief making him feel queasy.

"Don't judge," she said.

He looked up and met her eyes in the mirror and realized tears were streaming down her face.

"How could you?" he asked.

"I can't help it!" she said on a sob. "I've tried!"

He shook his head. Stunned. How could she treat her gorgeous body like that? The *damage* that bulimia could cause…

And just like that with the help of the harsh fluorescent lights of the bathroom and the smell of acidic bile creeping into his nose—he saw her with eyes that were wide open. Her nose was red and her lips had no color. Her eyes were glassy. She was too skinny. Her hair wasn't lush—it was thinning and brittle. All from throwing up. From treating her body like a garbage truck. Shove in the crap, crush it, and shove it back out, more disgusting than before.

He put a hand over his mouth, as his own stomach threatened to erupt.

"Does Max know?" he managed.

"No! Don't say anything! To anyone!" She grabbed his arm, her eyes pleading. Her waterproof mascara held, but the foundation and concealer under her eyes looked like drab, wet cement. Such a shame, because her brown eyes were still luminous, especially with the sheen of tears.

He twisted his arm out of her grasp and stepped back. "You need to get help." His breath was coming too heavy now. He couldn't stand her touch. She was a fake, an imposter. She wasn't beautiful. She was ugly. "If you don't, I'll tell her."

And he would. Because it wasn't fair. If he had that body…

He'd honor it, treat it like a temple, make it last forever, night after night. And it would be just as glorious in the morning.

"Where's your guard?" he asked.

Brian, he knew, should be downstairs any minute to take her home, after delivering one of the other women across town. Shane had taken extra measures for security at Ivory, like installing additional cameras up here, locking any unused space and more. The building was safe enough, but the models still required protection when coming or going.

"That's just it! I don't have any time alone." She looked almost panicked. "It's driving me crazy! I can't wait until all this is over."

He shut his eyes, dread filling him.

He suspected she wouldn't have to wait long.

CHAPTER 17

MAX HAD ARRANGED for Shane to escort her to the office Saturday morning. As soon as she opened her door and saw him, her breath caught. She should be used to the sight by now—but no. Just wow.

"Ready?" Shane asked.

He looked serious, as he usually did at first. Did he give himself a talking to on the way over? Thou shall not smile at Max today? Or was he always just focused on the safety aspect of moving a target—usually her—from place to place? It was kinda cute. Max hid her smile by reaching for her bag and then locked the door behind her.

She didn't want to think too hard on it, but she'd taken extra care with her outfit. More casual than usual given that it was Saturday, and yet she'd wanted to look great. A printed tank top with movement, a cardigan that had a habit of falling off one shoulder, skinny jeans that accented her legs, and heeled suede booties.

She'd felt Shane watching her over the last two weeks—likely the same way she sometimes watched him. Serious attraction existed between them, and she fantasized about what might happen when all this ended. Because when it did, they'd no longer be working together. Her most important rule—no flirting or sleeping with anyone she worked with—would no longer apply. And by then, they'd have *serious* stores of pent up lust. The sex would be explosive.

She couldn't help wanting to fan that flame a bit.

Once they reached the office, Shane checked in with the security guards, getting the reports from the night, and then they went up to Ivory, stopping first on the fourth floor. He did a quick sweep, locking doors behind him, and then continued up another floor to the office suites. It was quiet, and she could see the vacuum marks on the lush carpet in the reception area. The cleaning staff always came Tuesday and Friday evenings.

She waited there, as was their routine whenever they arrived before any other staff, while he swept the area.

"All right," Shane said, and motioned for her to join him.

She sighed. This was such a drag. They continued on to her office, and she immediately crossed to her desk and booted up her computer.

"I'll just stay until Brian arrives," Shane said.

"Make yourself comfortable."

"Want some coffee?" Shane asked.

"Sure. Thanks."

He already knew how she took it and headed off to the kitchenette. He apparently rarely drank the stuff, so she expected he offered in order to give her a few minutes of privacy.

Max typed in her password, then froze when a warning message came up. "Incorrect password. Allowable number of attempts exceeded. Contact your administrator."

Goosebumps erupted on her arms. She pushed back from the desk.

Shane said, "It'll take a while for the machine to—What's wrong?"

"Someone tried to access my computer," she said, but he was already at her side reading the alert for himself.

"Don't touch anything," he said. "Does anything else look disturbed? Different from how you left it?"

She stood and thought back. "No." She kept a clean desk, finding it easier to concentrate if it was clutter free. "Do you want me to check the drawers?"

"No." He handed her her purse from the floor. "Call Danny, while I talk to the guard downstairs."

Detective Iocavelli answered on the first ring. Her voice was slightly shaky when she said, "Detective, it's Maxine Ricci. Someone's been in my office, trying to get on my computer."

Shane squeezed her arm and moved to the hallway as security answered his call.

Iocavelli asked her all kinds of questions: *Are you sure, when did this happen, have you checked who was in the building, are there security tapes?*

"Shane is checking now."

"Okay," he said. "I'll be over shortly, and I'll send someone to dust for prints."

Her brain was past the initial shock and processing again. She told the detective, "That'll only make sense if whoever was here arrived *after* the cleaning staff."

"Cleaners don't often clean keyboards well enough to remove fingerprint oil. On the other hand since you tried to log on, there're probably no liftable prints anyway—at least not on those keys. Let's see what Shane can find out."

"You know," she said, "it's possible it's nothing."

"Yeah. Have Shane call me." Iocavelli clicked off.

Max crossed her arms and tucked her hands and even the phone under her armpit. She went out into the hallway and leaned against the wall near Shane. He eyed her up, and she saw concern—for her?—written all over his face.

She could hear most of the conversation and gleaned that there'd been numerous people in the building last evening. Of the staff: Cam, Damien, and Damien's assistant Rory. Two models: Lillian and one of the male models named Leo.

Plus Shane's guard, Brian, who'd come to escort Lillian home. They'd all trickled out as the cleaning staff had arrived.

When Shane hung up, he said, "It's not nothing. This is exactly why I asked you to change your password."

"You think someone is trying to access information only I have."

He nodded, and looked grim. "Yes. You still have the USB drive?"

"Yes." He'd asked her to make sure she didn't have the models' schedules and guard assignments anywhere cloud-based or anywhere that could be hacked. Instead, it existed only on the flash drive, which she carried with her. He had a version of the same, and they verbally contended with any changes. A little archaic, but infinitely safer.

She'd felt bad not sharing it with Cam, and knew he felt hurt about that. She trusted him, but Shane didn't trust anyone.

"Show me," he said.

She dug in her bag, feeling for the little zip pouch, praying it was there, and that nobody had touched her things. It was just a purse, but still…it was personal. She held it up and unzipped it.

"Voila," she said pulling out the little red flash drive, her shoulders dropping a fraction with relief.

Shane's phone rang then. He listened, and then swore.

He told Max, "The camera in this hallway was tampered with. A hood, a dark cloth or bag of some sort, was used to cover the lens for just a few minutes."

There went her hopes of this being nothing. Someone had tried to access the schedule. "That means…"

"That means something's up. Likely our guy is getting itchy. Wants to know who will be where when."

"I don't like this at all."

"Neither do I," Shane said. "And it'd sure be a helluva lot easier to counter an attack if we knew who was next."

"I'm..." Max felt unsure, such an unaccustomed feeling. She rubbed her arms. "I'm scared," she whispered. Then more vehemently, "*Damn* him."

"You should be," Shane said, and much to her surprise he stepped forward to give her a hug. She hesitated only a second, then eased into him. He rubbed her back. "This guy might attack *you*, to get his hands on that schedule."

She shivered and he increased the pressure of his arms, tucking her in even closer. Max breathed him in, and found his scent slightly spicy, earthy, and all male. She almost felt that if she could just stay here, right here in his arms, she'd be safe, for good.

"Scared is good. Scared is smart," Shane said. Then, he stiffened and stepped back, his hands on her upper arms maintaining a safer distance. As if he'd just realized that he'd crossed a professional line.

And he had. Max shut her eyes and gathered her strength. She'd always relied on herself. She wasn't the type to lean on others. Especially men. She turned away from him and moved into her office.

"There've been no attacks on other models from other agencies, and now he's proven he can just waltz into your office, as easy as you please, because he belongs here." Shane scowled. "No doubt now. The adversary is definitely an insider."

"I wish you'd stop calling him that," Max said, sharply. "That sounds so reasonable. He's a psycho, a killer. *Adversary* is just sugarcoating."

Shane inclined his head. "We'll step up security right away."

"How are we going to do that?" She knew frustration

sounded loud and clear in her voice. "Your guys are maxed out, and my people are already at half their usual level of activity."

"We restrict them further," Shane suggested.

"No." Max rubbed her forehead. "They're out of their minds already. And we'll scare them needlessly—they'll know something's happened."

"Actually," Shane said, "we should tell them there's been an incident."

She shook her head. "That's a terrible idea. They'll think the worst."

"On the contrary, if they are scared, they'll be more careful and more alert," Shane said. "Even if we don't change the schedule, just *pretending* we are is a good deterrent. Everybody will think it's someone else who's had their appointments curtailed."

Max nodded. That might be okay, although she hated to worry everyone. Still, if it kept them safe... "Like what you told me before," she said. "If this a-hole believes we're taking extra precautionary measures, he'll be less inclined to strike."

"Exactly," Shane said.

"But," she said immediately keying in on the down side, "that means this could go on indefinitely."

He gestured toward her computer. "We're already seeing some of his frustration. I'm betting he'll act rashly soon enough, because he desperately needs whatever it is he gets out of killing."

Max shut her eyes. There was that, too.

CHAPTER 18

ONCE THEY'D STEPPED into the private elevator of the Upper West Side building, Max turned to her ever-present shadow Shane and opened her mouth to explain Aggie, who was one half of the Wise Ones, as she and Miranda called her grandmother and her Great Aunt Cora. Tonight was their standing Monday girls-night-in dinner, and the sisters were…

Shane narrowed his eyes at her. Those gorgeous, dark brown eyes, always trying to read her.

Max shook her head. There was no prepping him on this.

Shane stepped in front of her in preparation. She could have told him he'd be blocking her from an attack of a different sort, but she rather liked ogling his back half. Tall and broad, his jacket pulled tight over wide shoulders. His hair was cut shorter than when he'd worked for her, exposing his strong neck. From what she could see, he was as in-shape as ever.

The door slid open and two old ladies rushed them before stopping short. Max peered around Shane's shoulder. "Aggie and Cora, meet Shane. Shane, these are the Wise Ones. Aggie's the one in all the jewelry." Always overdoing a trend, Max thought. "And Cora's in the pink."

The elevator buzzed. "Oh, Miranda's arrived, too," Cora said and waved them forward. "Come out, come out."

Max had told Shane who'd be in attendance tonight, so he

already knew that Miranda would be here. In fact, originally, Miranda was her buddy-escort home. But given the attempt on her computer, Shane had decided it was best if he remained to see her home himself.

As the door slid shut behind them, Shane said, "We'll wait for the elevator. Then, I need to check the apartment."

Max sighed. He was so staid in this role. She'd begun to long for the days when he wore a cocky grin and thought nothing of running around the studios half-dressed and dancing to a funky photo shoot soundtrack.

Aggie gave one of her best harrumphs and crossed her arms.

Cora, always the peacemaker, said, "Max told us you'd need to. That's fine." Out of the side of her mouth she whispered to her sister. "Such bad manners."

Aggie snorted. "I'm not ill-mannered. I'm simply too old not to call it like I see it."

Max saw Shane's mouth twitch. "Nice to meet you, ladies." He shook both their hands.

"This is the one who hates you?" Aggie asked Max.

Sheesh, Max thought. Had Miranda told them *everything*?

Aggie waved her hand up and down as if encompassing Max. "What's not to like? Men have been falling at her feet since she hit puberty." She eyed Shane with suspicion. "What's wrong with *you*?"

Max groaned. She absolutely could not look at Shane. This was why she *never* introduced men to The Wise Ones. Not that she kept any of them around long enough. Long-term was not in her repertoire.

Still, she'd have to make it a rule. *Never* bring a man she wanted to jump to meet Aggie and Cora. He'd be good for nothing after they emasculated him.

Thankfully, just then the elevator dinged softly behind

them, and Miranda stepped out. She took one look at Max's face and said, "Darn! I missed it. I *so* wanted to see the welcoming committee at work."

"You missed a doozy," Max muttered and slid a glance at Shane. He looked like he was about to bust out laughing even as his eyes scanned the elevator for ride-alongs and who knew what else he was trained to search for.

"I'll give you the play by play later," Cora whispered to Miranda as they hugged.

Shane greeted Miranda, then set off to do his sweep.

"He's as good looking as that bodyguard in that Whitney Houston movie," Aggie whispered. But since she didn't hear that well, it was about at a regular speaking voice level.

Miranda grinned.

Cora said, "Kevin Costner doesn't hold a candle to this guy."

Max just shook her head.

"How are you doing, sweetie?" Cora asked Max.

"Been better."

Miranda squeezed her hand and held on. They watched Shane duck into the hallway off the living room. When he returned, he swept out a hand with a half bow. "Ladies, enjoy your evening together."

"You're not joining us?" Cora asked.

"No, ma'am, I'll just be nearby."

"I told you I shouldn't have had an extra place set," Aggie said to her sister.

"We'll bring you a plate." Cora said to Shane and moved away. She turned back to him, however. "We're counting on you to watch over our girl."

"Yes, ma'am," he replied.

————

True to his word, Shane had only hovered in the background. He seemed to always be on guard, listening. He'd cock his head and then slide through Aggie's big penthouse rooms like a specter or maybe that jungle cat Miranda had likened him to. Other times he stood sentry at the elevator or the door to the stairs—despite the fact that it remained bolted. What Max couldn't tell was if he was also tuned in to their conversation. She sure didn't feel she could speak freely, not that she was feeling especially chatty. Aggie, unfortunately, hadn't had the same inhibition.

Regardless, Max had survived and Shane had held his own, which was a relief. She'd even seen some of his old charm come out—with Aggie and Cora, at least. Which made it glaringly obvious that he'd been holding back when it came to interacting with her. Sure, he'd been supportive when she'd broken down that first day, and he'd comforted her when they discovered someone had tried to access her computer.

But overall? He'd definitely been careful not to engage too much.

Then again, maybe she was reading too much into tonight. Maybe he just had a thing for sassy old ladies. And why in the world did it matter to her what he thought of them, or vice versa? Or even what he thought of her?

She wasn't dating him. He didn't even *like* her much, she thought, for all that they'd come to occupy some common ground lately. This was only a job for him, one he'd taken on reluctantly.

In fact maybe, she decided, she was only weirded out because she'd never once brought someone home and introduced him to The Wise Ones. It felt oddly intimate to do so tonight, even though she and Shane were only working together.

After they'd seen Miranda off in a cab toward her apartment on the Upper East Side, Max and Shane headed to her place on foot. She slid a glance toward him as they walked. He wore a little smile on his face.

"What?" she asked.

He said, "That was a whale of a time."

So he *did* get a kick out of meddling Jewish grandmother types? Max asked, "Meaning you had fun?"

"Yeah. I've never seen you actually uncomfortable before. It was refreshing."

She scowled. "What the heck does that mean?"

"It means, Black Widow, that I enjoyed seeing another side of you."

What was she to make of that? And…

"Black Widow?"

"Oh, come on," Shane said. "You tear through men. All that's left is a pile of shredded clothing in your wake."

Max *enjoyed* men. She loved to flirt with them and make them want her. She loved to explore their bodies and make them react. And on the flip side, she loved how they made her feel. Desired, sexy, hot. She loved heating up, and she loved good sex. Nothing wrong with that. She was careful who she chose to spend nights with—no one dangerous, no one psychotic, no one needy. That was another of her rules—meant to keep her safe. The minute she got even a hint on her uh-uh meter, she cut her losses and made a gracious—or forceful—exit, but that didn't mean—

Dammit. By calling her that, Shane made her lifestyle seem both sordid and cold.

"That's what you think of me?"

A look of discomfort passed over Shane's face, and then his jaw set in a stubborn line. "It's common knowledge."

She thought back to the long-ago altercation they'd had after she'd fired him. He'd called her all kinds of names. The

English of course she'd understood loud and clear. But like her use of Italian when she really needed a whopper, he'd switched and lambasted her for being such a *kierney*. Maybe like tonight, he'd been implying that she was a cold-hearted slut. Obviously, it was pretty derogatory.

Back then she'd figured that his anger at her was partly a reaction to the blow she'd dealt him and partly truth. After all, most people tended to be *more* honest when they were three sheets to the wind. But she'd hoped the last couple of weeks of working together had erased some of his intrinsic dislike of her. Had maybe helped him see her as she really was. Not an ice bitch at all. Apparently not.

"Wow, you sure know how to make a woman feel special," Max said. "No wonder you're single despite that face."

She picked up her pace. She refused to walk beside him. If she thought she could shake him, she would, but she knew full well he wasn't going anywhere until he'd seen her home and sniffed through the corners of her apartment with his nose to the ground like the rat he was.

A rat who most definitely wanted her.

Too damn bad. He'd lost his chance. Not now. Not when the job ended. Not *ever*.

This Black Widow didn't even need to chew him up and spit him out. He'd managed that all on his own.

————

"Wow. Grumpy much today?" Anna asked, and screwed up her face at Shane.

Shane grimaced. Apparently his regret over that comment to Max last night was manifesting itself in shortness with the twins this morning as they all scrambled to get out for school and work.

"Sorry," he said and gave her a kiss on the forehead. "It's nothing to do with you two."

"What is it to do with?" Still holding her toast, she crossed her arms and regarded him steadily. So much like his sister that he actually answered.

"I wasn't very nice to the woman I'm working for last night. Said something I shouldn't have." He'd thought of apologizing to Max, but honestly it was better this way. If she was angry, she'd steer clear of him. Less temptation. Less distraction.

"What did you say to her?" Niall asked, though he barely paused from shoveling cereal in his gob.

"Nothing I care to repeat. Suffice it to say, I was teasing, but she didn't take it that way." He'd really blown it, letting his guard down, teasing her as if she were a friend or a girlfriend. He should know better. They were colleagues, *temporary* colleagues at that.

Anna raised an eyebrow. "You've known her a long time though, right? You used to work with her. Aren't you friends?"

"It's important to maintain a professional relationship when you're working with someone," he explained.

A gleam appeared in Anna's eye. *Uh-oh.* "Ooooooh you li-i-ke her..." Anna sang.

"No, he doesn't." Niall said, looking up from his bowl and rolling his eyes. "He only took the job 'cause he had to."

"All right," Shane said, wondering how Niall had come up with that juicy bit of intel. "Time to pack up." And thank God for it. Enough was enough with the teenage interrogation.

But his mind stayed squarely on Max during his commute to her office. Did he 'like her' as Anna had charged?

There was nothing *not* to like about her. He could honestly say he respected her. He'd let go entirely of his old bitterness about the past, and he was man enough to admit that he should never have nursed that grudge in the first place.

He should have been grateful for the experience and the plump bank account, right along with her faith in him early on and her subsequent frankness about his dismal future in modeling.

As for the Black Widow thing, some men would be jealous or intimidated. Her sexual prowess and active sex life didn't bother him, except for wanting her himself. Not a good idea in a working environment—especially in his line of work. Too distracting.

What really worried him is how he'd felt when she'd cried. It'd been all he could do not to pull her in and whisper sweet words into her hair and stroke her back until she'd calmed.

And when he *had* comforted her—instinctively reached for her and pulled her to him—after they'd realized someone had been in her office trying to access her computer? It had felt so right, he'd wanted never to let go. Such a powerful urge to safeguard her forever had overcome him.

He'd worked hard after both incidents to keep his distance. Not to let himself get wrapped up in her emotionally. For God's sakes, never to touch her...

Down the line—well, astute Anna seemed to have the right of it. He'd be open to getting to know Max better. Much better. Thoroughly. Intimately.

But right now there was only the job. It was on him and the team to keep Max and her people safe. Nothing mattered beyond that.

CHAPTER 19

MAX WAS SLEEPING over at Miranda and Eddie's—again. On the couch. They were wonderful and she felt at home, but she longed for her own space, her own bed, her glorious closet instead of a pre-packed bag. Not to mention, less wasted time crisscrossing back and forth between apartments.

No sooner had she cracked open one eye, then she heard her phone vibrate where it was plugged in on the kitchen counter. Or maybe it'd been the vibrating that had woken her. Who would be calling this early? Other than the streetlamp, it appeared to still be dark outside.

Max groaned and shoved the covers off, then padded to the phone.

Shane.

Instantly, she was alert—and worried. They hadn't spoken more than necessary since the Black Widow comment, so she knew he wouldn't have called unless it was something important.

She yanked the phone off its charger. "What happened?" she asked.

"Another murder," he said, his voice heavy. "It's Gia Serra."

"Oh, no. *No.* Oh, God…" Max sank to the floor, her back against the refrigerator, knees tucked up and head bowed.

Gia had tendered her resignation when they'd instituted the restrictions. So she hadn't had protection. Max sobbed, but quickly covered her mouth, trying to hold it together.

Max had hinted that she'd like her to stay, but was reluctant to push. Oh God, she should have *pushed*.

"Max?" Shane asked.

Max took a shaky breath. "Tell me."

He took a deep breath. "She was found by her boyfriend, who came home around four a.m."

"He's in a band," she murmured.

"Yes. She was in bed, sleeping. Probably on painkillers. She'd recently had plastic surgery."

"Goddammit," Max murmured. Gia had been so worried about getting older and not being able to compete. She said she might go to the Bodhi, but she must have thought leaving Ivory was the perfect opportunity to have some work done. "What kind of surgery?" She didn't know why she wanted to know, but she did.

"Eye and neck lifts," Shane said. "The bandages were ripped off, and…the attack was concentrated there." He cleared his throat. "The weapon was a knife."

She whispered, "Like Helena."

"No." Shane's voice was gruff. "Her throat was slit and her face was…"

Max felt her shirt getting wet and realized she was crying. "Just say it, I have to know."

Shane sounded as if he was crying, too. "Her eyes were violated and pieces of her face were… sliced off."

"Dear God," Max said and sobbed. She couldn't be quiet any longer.

Miranda appeared next to her and rubbed her legs and arms. She took the phone and spoke with Shane. After a minute, she asked, "Is there anything Max needs to do?" She nodded at his response, and said, "Okay." And then, "Of course."

"Wait," Max said and she snatched the phone back. "Were there gels and tape?"

"I don't know," Shane said. "I'm not supposed to know, so I couldn't ask Danny. I told him I'd let you know. He said he'll have questions for you. When you're up to it, reach out, unless he calls you first."

"Okay," she said. "What do we do now?"

"We double down. And it wouldn't hurt to pray."

———

Other than returning home to sleep, Shane expected to be at Max's side going forward. Shane had sorted Anna and Niall's schedules. He'd handed Mrs. Costa a wad of cash so that she could go to the grocery as many times as needed or handle anything else that might come up. He'd given the twins some extra money, too.

He and Joe gathered all of his agents—who weren't on duty this morning—at the office for a debriefing.

"Nearly all assumptions we've made to date," Joe said, "are off the table. Every model on Ivory's roster is now high risk. This Gia was thirty-one years old."

"Are we covering the other two models who walked?" Brian asked.

"No." Shane grimaced. "They've signed with other agencies already. We recommended that they secure protection themselves or ask their new employers to do so."

Joe said, "We'll call you with schedule changes—only the most important going forward."

The agents left with heavy hearts and a renewed sense of the importance of each assignment.

"You have any bright ideas?" Shane asked Joe once they were alone.

"No," the older man sighed. "Just keep doing what we're doing. The adversary seems to be escalating. He picked an easy target this time, but at some point, he'll get bold—or desperate—and go after somebody we're guarding. God willing, we take him down."

Shane had been thinking the same thing. "Is it wrong to hope it's on my watch?"

———

Shane arrived at Miranda's apartment just before noon. Max had already talked to Detective Iocavelli, and there was a color gel. Yellow again. One piece that covered from Gia's eyes to her neck, secured by two long strips of black tape in a large X.

"It's him," Shane said. "Not a copycat." Given that Gia had no longer been working for Max and her agency, that had been a remote possibility. However, according to Danny, no one in the press had gotten wind of the color gels.

Shane explained that they could no longer sort priority by age, or by anything really, and therefore the need to reduce activity even further.

Max's eyes and nose were red, and she hadn't yet put on any makeup. "I don't care," she said flatly. "If they can't understand that we've got to take extra precautions, that it's even worse than before…."

Stripes, Eddie's dog, rested her head on top of Max's feet, as if he knew she was the one who most needed comfort and warmth right now.

"Gia hadn't hired anyone to protect her. And her boyfriend's show schedule would have been easy to find with a simple internet search," Shane said. "I keep thinking about the timing though. There was a month between the first two attacks. It's only been about two weeks this time. He could be escalating. Did Danny say anything about that?"

"No," Max said and cringed. "But he doesn't share much,

at least with me. I was surprised he told me about the X's. He's far more interested in my alibi."

Eddie gestured to Miranda and explained. "He asked both of us a fair number of questions, establishing a timeline, making sure we could vouch that Max was really here all night."

Shane shook his head. How Danny could still suspect Max was beyond him. She talked big and she was tough, but she simply wasn't capable of such a thing.

"I've cleared my schedule," Shane said and looked at Max. "I don't want you alone, even in the office, going forward. Certainly not at home."

She blanched.

Eddie said, "I need to go home to the Poconos for a few days. I was originally thinking that I'd rather have Max here at our place than Miranda staying at Max's, but maybe they should both come with me. Just take a break from all this."

Max shook her head. "Thank you, but no. I can't leave. If my models and staff are here, then I have to be here."

"I'd like to eliminate Miranda from the scenario anyway. There's no reason to put another woman in harm's way," Shane said. "I'll stay overnight with Max. Every night until this is over."

Shane expected incredulity or an argument at the very least. He knew he was probably the last person Max wanted underfoot since that dumb Black Widow comment he'd made. But Max only looked at him and nodded.

CHAPTER 20

HE'D KNOWN WHAT Gia was up to, and it had disgusted him. He'd wanted to scream when she told him. Why? Why would you do such a thing?

He didn't though. Instead, he'd told her that she didn't need surgery, that she was as beautiful as ever, that she'd never be old in his eyes. But she could not be convinced. She'd kissed him on the cheek, told him she loved him, and said, "You'll see, it'll make all the difference."

And it had.

Her choice had killed her. Laid out in her bed, he understood, too drugged to have heard what was coming. He didn't know what was worse. Did he wish she had passed with only a second's alertness? Or was it better if they suffered—all these women who no longer deserved their beautiful bodies?

The thought of Gia stretched out in bed reminded him of the women always present in his youth. Always so much noise at first. Moaning and urging and demanding. They always said, *come on, baby, and yes, yes, yes.* His father always sweet-talked them. *Baby, you're amazing. Wrap your lips around me, baby. Look up at me with those beautiful eyes. My God how those tits would look on screen.*

Or ass or legs or whatever had caught his eye that night...

His father thought they were all stars, or would be soon.

He always saw what his father had. The women were

beautiful, each with some asset or another that was really spectacular.

Once they'd gone quiet, sleeping next to his father, always naked, he would creep in. Sometimes the sheet would cover them, sometimes not. His father was normally a deep sleeper, always having had one too many drinks at the club. The women were harder to gauge. He would listen to their breathing, try to determine how deeply asleep they were. If he was sure, he'd chance it, pulling the sheet ever so slowly off so he could see.

Some had dark hair and skin, others light. Some were redheads or blonds. Some were shaved nearly bald, others trimmed but more natural. Narrow hips, and lush, round ones. Flat tummies and ones that curved outward a bit.

And the breasts—what variety. Between the fullness, the placement, the nipples, the coloring… He'd been in awe, every time. Even the shoulders, the neck, the ribs, the knees, the hands and feet, all the way down to their toes.

Each woman was unique, each glorious in her own right.

He longed, positively ached, to touch and to feel. He never ever tired of looking, often staying up all night, sneaking back to his own room just before dawn.

He didn't like when his father woke, when he ruined it. If he didn't ruin it, the ladies sometimes got to come back, and he might get to view them again, maybe even in a different position, maybe see the expanse of their back the next time, or the slope of their other hip.

But if his father yelled, they never returned. He was too cruel, too good at exposing their flaws. And in the light of day, there were usually flaws.

CHAPTER 21

SHANE AND MAX had returned to her apartment. Max had been subdued the entire afternoon. She'd taken a long shower and spent a lot of time in her room.

He'd commandeered the TV in the living room—although he didn't let it distract him, keeping the volume low and often walking around to stay alert. He texted with the twins, spoke with Mrs. Costa, and slogged through some emails on his phone. He was used to killing time. Max, he figured, probably never took time out and didn't know what to do with it.

Finally, when his stomach had insisted, he'd knocked on her door. She'd opened it wearing leggings and a roomy off the shoulder sweatshirt. Her feet were bare and her hair a little mussed. He wondered if she'd been sleeping.

"Shall we order take out?"

"Sure," she said.

No, he thought as he really looked at her eyes, she hadn't slept. She looked tired under the light makeup she'd applied earlier today.

"What sounds good?" Max asked.

"Pretty much anything," he said.

She smiled. "I'm not really hungry, so you choose." She slipped past him and crossed the living room.

He followed and couldn't help but watch her walk. She was graceful and sure, her toes curling on the plush white carpet. Her legs looked long and fit in those leggings.

She opened a drawer in the kitchen and pulled out a slim folder. "Here are the best places nearby." She glanced out the windows. "Can we pick up or...?"

"Better to get delivery," he said, coming up beside her. Any departure or arrival Max undertook put her at greater risk.

She nodded and pulled out a few menus she spread on the counter in front of him. "These are your best choices then."

He chose a Thai restaurant, and after they'd placed their order, she offered him a drink.

"No, thanks," he said.

"On duty?" she asked.

"Right," he said. "Want to sit out here? Watch something or...?"

Why was he trying to engage her, rather than let her hide in her room? Normally, on a job he wouldn't. He'd be blending into the background, letting the principal do his or her own thing as much as possible. Why the urge to distract this particular woman from her worries?

"Okay," she said, a little hesitantly, "what were you watching?" She moved toward the couch and then stopped. "*Rocky?* Really?"

"It's a classic," he smiled. "They've got a marathon going."

She tucked into a corner of the couch, knees and feet under her.

"Did you go back to boxing? After?" she asked.

It'd been in his contract, when he'd signed with her—no fighting of any sort. Couldn't risk the pretty face, i.e. the money maker. Much like pro athletes weren't allowed to ski or race a car or whatever. Staying out of the ring had really been the only thing Shane had found challenging—it was the best way he knew to blow off steam.

Before he'd answered, a frown marred her face, and she'd said, "Oh, I forgot—"

"Sort of," he interrupted. He knew what she was thinking. He'd been sporting a black eye, a swollen lip, and dried blood in his overgrown facial hair that night he'd bumped into her and said so many alcohol-induced idiotic things he wished he hadn't. He did not want to talk about that night. He said, "I boxed. Unofficially for a while."

"Why unofficially?"

"Because I was too old," he said.

She grimaced, "Oh."

She wouldn't say she was sorry, of course. Maybe she was. Maybe she wasn't. It was a long time ago, and it really wasn't her fault.

"How do you box unofficially?"

By picking fights? By entering the basement shit holes in this city? The ones that teemed with sweat and stink and rage-filled testosterone? That time wasn't something he talked about, certainly not to her.

"You just do," he said.

The phone buzzed just then, signaling a call from the lobby. Shane was relieved. A change of subject *and* sustenance. Just what he needed.

He dealt with the delivery, and when he'd returned, she'd gotten plates, napkins and silverware. He'd have pegged her as a formal sort, but she'd set them up on the coffee table in front of the movie.

They ate in silence some, then she narrowed her eyes at the screen after a particularly violent scene. "Is that allowed? In real life?"

Shane explained some of the rules of boxing, what was legal and what wasn't. "I'm teaching my niece and nephew," he said. Then added, "And I do still box pretty regularly myself."

"Do they like it? Or is this more of a family requirement?"

Shane smiled. "They love it. Beg me to take them all the time."

"How old are they?"

"Fourteen. Twins. Anna and Niall."

"You'd be a good teacher," she said.

"I'd rather be a good father and role model, since I have custody of them."

She sat up straight. "You said you have it covered, but are you *sure* you shouldn't be home with them? You could assign someone else—somebody without kids—to me."

"It's all right. They're used to my strange hours."

She scowled. "If you want to be a good father, then you should…change careers or, I don't know, something."

"Immediately jumping to conclusions about me, eh?" Shane chuckled. "I do my best to make it up to them when duty doesn't call." He smiled. "Besides, when I'm home too much, they claim they're right tired of my crooked nose in their business."

She leaned closer to him. "Your nose isn't crooked."

"This week. Because it was broken back toward straight."

She smiled and shook her head at that, and he felt a strange lightening. It pleased him to make her smile. But she'd asked about the twins and that there was a serious subject. "I do worry, that it's not enough, that just me is not enough. But I've also got to support them." He explained about Mrs. Costa, and reminded her that kids in the city were more independent than most. Joe and his wife also spent a lot of time with the kids. "There's no changing careers, much as I wish there was sometimes."

"You see a lot of bad, I imagine," she said, pulling a pillow onto her lap.

"I do at that." Shane got up to clear the food and dishes. She sat for a moment and then followed with the remaining items. "How did you come to do this work? Was it only Joe?"

"It was largely Joe," he said, sticking her leftovers in the fridge. His were gone. "And sitting at a desk or making it through a college degree wasn't going to work for me."

He explained that his skills in the ring translated easily to martial arts and self defense. "Those courses were easy enough—no desks involved. And there are loads of executive protection courses out there. Some of them rip offs, but Joe had recommendations. Beyond that, I learned from him and his senior agents on the job."

Shane didn't know why, but he said, "There was another reason."

She waited patiently while he tried to gather the right words. Finally, he shook his head and just blurted it out. "The reason I have the twins. My sister was killed by her boyfriend."

Max sucked in a breath.

"Janet was older than me, had had the kids out of wedlock, and never married. We were close. After I'd been in the States a couple of years, she'd started saying she wanted to come over, making plans for her and the kids." The words were just spilling out of him now. "I didn't realize it was an escape plan. I didn't know what she'd been going through. The physical abuse. We'd planned for her to come over when the time was right, but that got delayed." He didn't want to guilt Max, to let her know that his sudden loss of income had mattered. "I'd only been killing time working for Joe until then." He cleared his throat. "It'll never make up for it, but I thought if I could help just one woman, then two, and… well, here I am. All in."

Max reached out and squeezed his hand. "I hope you can count pretty high," Max said and smiled. "Because you're good at it," she said. "From what I've seen."

"So says Joe, but you always feel you can do better," he said, thinking of Carrie Sorrelle. Just good wasn't enough.

She smiled.

He narrowed his eyes. "What?"

"That's so you. You always wanted reshoots, remember? You used to tell the photographers, 'Just a mite longer,'" she mimicked. "'I'm no tired a'tall.'"

He laughed and rolled his eyes. "I never spoke like that here."

"You did, too. When you got excited."

He'd prefer she think of him like the man he was now, instead of the eager lad he'd been then, but she was smiling again, so he didn't push it.

They returned to the couch, but the TV showed commercials. He asked, "What about you, did you always plan to be in fashion?"

"Mmmm," she said tilting her head side to side. "Maybe not always, but about the time I realized that clothes matter— that they have an effect on how you are treated, yes."

"So about the time you learned to turn men's heads?"

She swatted him, but didn't seem to really take offense. "It wasn't about me. When Aggie was dressed like a slouch, people treated her like a kooky old lady. But when she was dressed to the nines, they did her bidding without hesitation. If the kid in the bodega dressed like a hoodlum—even though I knew he lived in the same high-rent apartment building as I did—the owner watched him like a hawk. Like that."

"I bet you gave makeovers to girls at school," he said.

"Of course. Kara Hirschberg *needed* me."

"Why not makeup then or a personal shopper, or I don't know, anything else?"

"That's such a dumb question coming from you," she shook her head in mock disappointment.

He, in turn, acted wounded.

"You've seen my closet. I *love* clothes," she said. "And you've worked with me. I have a knack for spotting talent."

"You also have a knack for bossing people around," he said.

She went to swat him again, laughing, but this time he snagged her arm. She was just off balance enough, leaning forward as she was, that she fell into him. Close enough to kiss—so incredibly tempting—but he was caught in her eyes. Big, dark brown eyes, sparkling with laughter, that held his own.

She looked down almost shyly, and he released her immediately. She tucked her hair behind an ear and curled back into her corner.

"Another movie?" she asked, grabbing the remote.

It was folly—insanity, even. But what he'd like was to know if she'd thought at *all* about kissing *him*.

Later, when she'd dozed off watching Rocky III, he went and ran a quick check through her bedroom, enormous closet, and bathroom. When he returned, he nudged her awake and ordered her to bed.

"You're pretty bossy yourself, you know," she murmured, but padded off to the bedroom.

She'd offered him the guest room earlier, but he'd declined. For tonight at least he'd prefer to sleep out here, where he'd be more central. Able to hear and see more, faster, if need be.

Shane gave her time to get settled, then time to fall asleep, before he prowled through the apartment once more. He wouldn't be able to rest unless he'd covered the remainder of his mental checklist.

Max's bedroom door was open, lights off. He slid past—then stopped cold. There was just enough light to see that the bed was flat as an Irish soda bread farl. And still perfectly made up as well.

Max was not in it.

His heart beat fast, and he moved into the room quickly. He had a small but powerful flashlight in his jeans pocket and got it out, turning it on. Feeling the pressure to find her, and fast, he moved into the room quickly, sweeping the floor left and right with the light. He also called her name, softly. If she'd gotten up to use the bathroom, he didn't want to terrify her.

The bathroom door was half open, and he knocked softly and called again, "Max."

No answer and he pushed it open, immediately shining light into the corners of the room.

He swore and nearly ran to the closet. Not there either. He swept the windows but they hadn't been breached. What the—

He snapped off his light, switching to stealth. If someone were here, he'd prefer the element of surprise. The hall was empty. But the next room was the guest room and the door was shut. Shane braced himself—his mind racing with all kinds of possibilities—and slowly turned the handle with his left, while his right flipped the flashlight around and gripped it like a weapon.

He pushed open the door slowly, and nearly sagged with relief.

Max was curled up on the twin day bed. Under the covers, obviously under her own free will. What in God's name was she doing in here?

And how the hell was he going to get any sleep at all after that scare?

CHAPTER 22

SHANE COULD UNDERSTAND why Max was getting squirrelly. House arrest and curtailed activity had that effect on nearly everyone. He felt it, too, but he also knew there would invariably be an end to it. For as much as it seemed the job would go on forever, boom, something would happen, and it'd be over in a snap. He guessed what it came down to was that he'd learned patience.

Wouldn't his father be proud? Shane remembered bouncing on his toes outside the ring. He must have been maybe ten at the most. His dad had shaken his head and pursed his lips. But it wasn't until after that particularly disappointing fight that he'd gotten the lecture. "Ye've got to learn some patience lad, and it starts outside of the ring."

Shane smiled. He'd been the aggressor the whole fight, while the other boy had bided his time, waiting for Shane to tire, watching for Shane to leave him an opening as wide as the cliffs of Moher.

Shane had wanted to ask about Max's parents last night. She only ever spoke about her Grandmother Aggie, her Grandfather Giovanni who'd passed (and that marriage was apparently responsible for her Jewish/Italian heritage) and her Great Aunt Cora. No one at that dinner at Aggie's house had mentioned Max's parents either. He supposed it was none of his business.

He was here to keep her safe, and if necessary, keep her sane.

Which meant he had to get her some exercise. Yesterday, they'd gone to the office for a few hours, but that'd been it. She'd cancelled previously made appointments and even a scouting visit.

"I can't bring anyone new on during all this," she'd said.

She'd been pacing the apartment for the better part of an hour. She'd picked up magazines and discarded them. Stood in front of the TV and then moved on. Opened the refrigerator and closed it.

Eventually, she disappeared into her closet for a while. He heard her talking. Yet, her phone was on the kitchen counter…

He went to investigate.

Max tucked a pair of casual wedge heels back into a cubby. "Maybe tomorrow," she said.

Shane eyed the corners. Nobody was there but Max. She put her hands on her hips. He could see her expression in the full-length mirror, and she looked sad and lost.

"Max?" he said.

She turned then.

"Who are you talking to?"

"Oh, I…" She looked at the wall of clothing racks and drawers, then waved her hand in dismissal and brushed past him.

The woman talked to her shoes. Somehow, he didn't think she was crazy. Somehow, he thought it was cute.

He followed her back to the living room. Shane had never bothered to entertain or distract clients before, but everything about Max threw him.

"You don't want to go to CRANK?" he asked. She hadn't had a workout in at least a week as far as he knew.

She shuddered. "No. Probably not ever again."

"Maybe Zeke could come here?"

"You trust him?" she asked, one eyebrow raised.

"Danny checked him out after Win was found," Shane said. "But I'd have to run a background check and do some digging. I don't trust anyone blindly with an asset. Plus, I'd be here."

"Not worth all that trouble," she said.

"Yoga?" Like everyone else, Max had had to turn over her schedule so that he could allocate guards and weigh importance, so he knew her usual regimen.

"I don't care for the instructor that handles Fridays."

He slid her a sideways glance.

She crossed her arms and snapped at him. "I'm not that picky, but last time I did her class I couldn't feel my fingers for a week."

Yeah, he had to get her out of here so she could burn off some steam.

"How about I take you to my club? It's somewhere you've never been before—therefore unexpected—and we can take a circuitous route to get there."

"That seems like a lot of trouble, too."

"Come on," he cajoled. "I could use it as much as you could."

"You don't look like it." She wore a sour expression. "You look like you could sit around here, shoving in food and letting your ass spread, watching mindless TV and doing nothing for days."

He laughed. She really was grumpy. He tried to peer at his own backside. "Such a shame. Once upon a time, I was known for my fine arse." Then he tried to look at hers. "Want me to check yours?"

She swung around, effectively hiding hers from his view. "No!" she said.

Little did she know, he'd been checking out her tail for days. The woman slept in short shorts and a tank. She'd add a loose t-shirt and fuzzy socks when she was walking around, maybe only because he was in residence, but that hardly hid her rear.

"Go put on some leggings and a sweatshirt," he ordered. Please God, let her not wear a tank top or short shorts or anything else that meant he'd have to punch out teeth and wipe up drool at his boxing club.

———

When they arrived at the Dub'iaba (a very unofficial Dublin Irish Athletic Boxing Association), otherwise known simply as Dub's, Max looked around, and then stared at Shane. "There are no women," she said.

"There are some female regulars, but they must not be here right now," he said and shrugged. Shane watched a few male heads swivel their way. They didn't bother to hide their interest, looking Max up and down.

"And not one single elliptical machine. When you said club," she said, "I imagined cucumber water and mountains of rolled towels. You know, maybe a sauna afterward."

He laughed. "Yeah right. Welcome to the other side of the tracks."

She put her hands to her hips and looked around.

"You're out of the house, and you're safe," Shane said narrowing his eyes, "so what's the problem?"

She turned and glared at him. "There is no problem, I'm not nearly as snooty as you seem to think. I'm just sorting a new routine in my head, figuring out where to start."

Shane handed her a small towel from his bag. "There's a treadmill in the back corner. Will that do?"

Shane showed her where the bathroom was, introduced her to the manager, and left her at the treadmill.

He'd had workout clothes in his overnight bag and had changed at Max's, so he headed straight for the jump ropes. When he was warm, he went to get his wraps and gloves, then headed for the bags. Max was running on an incline, her phone grasped in one hand. Her cheeks were flushed, her ponytail swung jauntily, and she was happily mouthing words to whatever she was listening to through her earphones.

Shane threw a few punches and immediately felt some of the tension he'd been hauling start to release. When Joe showed up to help him keep an eye on Max, Shane would be able to really let go. He truly did think she was safe here, but he wasn't one to take unnecessary chances. So, for now, he'd positioned himself to see the whole place.

He picked up speed, arms flying, legs moving, dancing as fast as he could. He could feel Max's eyes on him, and he also noticed the other guys shooting her glances now and then. Luckily, they behaved. Surely, they assumed he and Max were an item, and certainly they knew he would joyfully beat them to a pulp.

Joe walked in, waved hello to Shane and Max both and started his own warm up. He and Joe had already discussed how they'd handle this. Granted, tuning her out entirely was like trying to stop breathing by force of will. It just wasn't possible. But he'd trust Joe with his life, and any of his principals' lives, too.

Shane nodded at the manager and headed off for some water. The next time a fight broke up, Shane was waved into the ring with a guy named Rex. They'd fought before, and they were fairly matched—though Shane had him two to zero.

Rex looked like he was coming in hot today. He and Shane circled each other. Shane threw the first punch, having no interest in doing a child's dance. He always loved a fight, and fight he would. It worked. Rex reacted by moving in, and Shane dodged. They were on.

In his peripheral vision, he saw Max jump off the treadmill. She crossed over to Joe and began a conversation. Shane could feel her eyes on him. Probably she was asking questions. He tried to ignore her.

He took a hit to the side of the head—just didn't move fast enough—and he swore. He needed to block out Max's presence entirely.

He and Rex got up close and personal, and Shane knew if he didn't get his head in the game, he'd be handing Rex this round. But then Rex slid his eyes to the right and hesitated just a bit too long. Shane struck and the point went to him. He turned to see what had distracted Rex and nearly spit out his mouthguard.

Max had ditched her sweatshirt—and was jumping rope. Her tight tank top and sports bra did more to accentuate what bounced than not.

She was grinning from ear to ear. She mouthed, "*You're welcome.*"

He snorted, shook his head and turned back to Rex. The minx.

———

Much to her surprise, Max found boxing fascinating. The only trouble was that her attraction to Shane had somehow been uncorked. With a big old popping noise, like when you opened a bottle of champagne. Seeing him box, spar, fight—whatever—was so hot. Okay, she'd ogled his muscles and admired his moves when he hit that bag, but once he got in the ring?

It was so deliciously *male* that she'd almost had to cross her legs.

On the flip side, she'd cringed and felt her heart seize a little when he'd taken that hit. She emphatically did *not* want to see him take another one. So she'd done what she could to help out.

She tired of jumping rope fast, however. *Way* harder than running. She retrieved her water bottle and swiped her forehead with her sweatshirt.

Just then a girl and a boy both in school uniforms entered the gym, crossed directly to the ring and commenced hooting and hollering. Shane's twin charges, no doubt.

Good-looking kids, both. Anna with blond hair, Niall's closer to brown.

Shane finished off Rex. Anna whistled with her fingers in her mouth, while Niall whooped.

The twins seemed to know Rex, as well, as they gave him some ribbing on the way out. He responded good-naturedly, "Dudes, you're supposed to wear the old man out and make it easier on me."

The twins went to greet Joe, and Shane approached Max. "You good if we stay a little longer?"

"As long as I don't have to jump rope. I can't take any more."

"I'm sure you're not the only one," he said, and winked.

He waved the twins over. "Anna, Niall, this is Maxine Ricci. Ms. Ricci to you," he said. "Max, these are the rug rats I was telling you about."

"Nice to meet you," they both said, but they were eyeing her up speculatively. Did that mean that Shane brought a lot of women home, and she was being rated in comparison? Or maybe he'd never introduced them to a woman before, and they were worried this was serious?

"Nice to meet you as well," she said, and then added, "I'm sorry to be the cause of your uncle being gone so much lately."

Anna's eyes popped wide. "*You're* the one that has all the models?"

"Well, I don't carry them around in my bag, but yes," she smiled.

The girl crossed her arms and turned to Shane. "She doesn't look *anything* like I imagined from what you said to Uncle Joe. She's *much* prettier."

Max tried hard not to laugh. She thought that maybe he didn't despise her anymore, maybe even liked her a little bit. But two weeks ago or so? Max could only imagine. The girl was probably expecting an old witch with leathery green skin, daggers for nails and an evil cackle.

"She looks a lot like she did on the news to me," Niall announced. "Just sweatier." The kid grinned.

This time Max did laugh. It was like contending with Aggie and Cora, just decades younger. To Shane, she said, "Couple of straight shooters you've got here."

"They'll be enrolling in manners classes tomorrow," he said, giving them a warning look. "Go change," he ordered. "We don't have all day."

"They're charming," Max said.

"They're a work in progress," Shane said, yet it was clear he adored them.

Joe joined them. "Has the Gia investigation led to any breakthroughs?"

"Not yet. Far as we know," Shane said. Neither had the follow-up from Max's computer. Dusting her office for prints had yielded nothing.

"I saw you're assigned to Samara tomorrow," Max said.

He nodded. Although Joe didn't usually do the personal

protection end of things anymore, they'd needed all hands on deck.

"Just remember," Max warned, "she's all bark. She's a softie deep down."

Joe laughed. "Thanks for the tip."

The twins returned raring to go.

"Feel free to watch or work out," Shane told Max. "Whatever suits you."

Mmmm. More Shane-watching would be quite enjoyable. But there were children present. Could she keep the desire from showing on her face?

CHAPTER 23

TWO MORE DAYS of laying low had Max increasingly on edge. Shane hoped the event tonight would be a good change of pace, despite the fact that it would be emotionally loaded. A big tribute to Gia pulled together by a number of Italian designers in a ballroom venue meant lots of beautiful people, very expensive evening wear and probably a fair amount of tears.

As for him, O'Rourke Security team was certainly earning their fees. They'd done pre-site work at the hotel, had a full team in place for those at Ivory who'd been closest to Gia and remained on high alert through the evening.

All had gone smoothly—until suddenly, Shane couldn't spot Max.

He spoke into his headset. "Where's my principal?"

Brian scanned, then looked at him from across the room. He shook his head.

Armand said, "She was at the bar a few seconds ago."

"That was the last I saw her, too," Shane said, and his anxiety level ratcheted up. "Everyone else accounted for?"

"Yes. We got it. Go," Brian said.

There was a door very near the temporary bar that led to the kitchens—the same door waiters had been streaming in and out of with appetizers. There was nowhere else she could have gone so fast.

Shane nearly ran into Cam. "Where's—"

"Hold your horses, cowboy," Cam said. "She needed some air. She went through that door."

"And you let her go?" Shane growled.

"I—"

But Shane didn't wait for the guy's excuses. He pushed into the kitchens and moved quickly through to the door at the far end that led into a hallway. The other door, he knew, accessed only refrigeration and storage. Serving staff glanced up but went straight back to their plating.

Max didn't know the layout like he did, and he'd wager she'd head for the exit sign which led to an alley. Shane ran, turned the corner and ran again, shoving through the door to a delivery area.

There she was not fifteen feet ahead of him—hustling along in her tight dress and heels toward the busy street. He swore she felt in heels like other people felt in sneakers. She startled at the bang of the door and turned, but he'd already closed the distance between them.

"What the hell do you think you're doing?" he said, then immediately hit his mike to let the team know. "I've got her."

"I need to be alone," she said, turning toward the street again.

"Too bad." He grabbed her hard and spun her around. "In you go."

"No, I don't want to be back in there. I can't stand being *watched* anymore. I just need some breathing room."

"Come inside. We can take a proper leave anytime."

"That won't do it." Supreme frustration sounded in her voice.

"Why the hell not?"

"Because I'll still be with *you*."

"There's plenty of space at your place," he said. "I'm not on top of you."

"You're always just *there,* and it's making me *crazy*," she said, her hands fisting with frustration. "This is so not me. Being a hermit—a hermit who can't even be alone! It's making me insane. I need to see people, to be out in the world."

"Public places are dangerous, transitions are dangerous."

"I *know,*" she snapped at him. "You keep telling me."

Shane didn't like it, but if it reigned her back in… "If you're that desperate, I'll take you out." It'd also be out of routine, unexpected, and therefore probably all right.

"I can't go out with you hovering over me," she said, those fists pumped in emphasis.

Ah, Shane thought. This woman who wore her sensuality front and center, who didn't make excuses for who she was, who lived life on her own terms, needed a release.

Fat chance. There was no way she'd be ending this little celibacy streak on his watch. But he could give her a little taste. Let her get a little attention, flirt some, blow off a bit of steam.

Of course, Shane would be grinding his teeth so loud they'd hear it across the Hudson, but okay. Okay fine. He'd deal.

"Where do you want to go? Huh? A bar?" He'd quickly sorted options. They were close to her own neighborhood. He'd seen her at this one place, years ago, working it. "You're favorite pick up spot? Let's do it."

————

Max scowled, angry at being caught, beyond frustrated at this whole situation. She felt like a misbehaving child and yet her desperate desire to escape stemmed more from her insane attraction to Shane than anything else. They were together 24/7 and it was too much. She was a sexual person by nature, and spending that much time with someone she wanted to jump—more than she'd wanted anyone, maybe ever—was killing her.

Shane had grabbed her arm—and basically steered her around the corner and into the very place she'd been aiming for. Twenty was a bar/restaurant that happened to get a fair amount of traffic, yet still felt intimate. The bartender, Samuel, knew her well. Sometimes he'd give her a wink—meaning he'd thought she'd made a good choice, other times a slight shake of the head indicating he knew something she didn't and she should steer clear. If he stayed neutral, he knew nothing, and it was her call.

Shane guided her all the way to the rear of the place, poked his head in the restroom, and then tugged her to the kitchen.

A chef, two other kitchen staff dressed in white, and a waitress all stared. Shane stepped forward. He had a quiet word with the chef, who nodded and pointed to the back corner.

"Stay," Shane told her and he disappeared into the stock room and then out the back door.

The staff looked her over. She wasn't a dog for God's sakes. She raised her chin, then turned to leave.

She hadn't even gotten past the restroom when that warm clamp returned to her elbow.

"You don't listen very well, do you?" Shane's breath hit the spot on her neck just under her ear, and the timber of his voice rumbling with that slight Irish lilt made her tingle. "What about in bed?"

She gasped, partly at his audacity, partly because that's exactly where she wanted him.

"Will you take orders there?" Shane asked, his voice still low and close. "Or do you still need to be in charge?"

The bite in his voice told her he was angry. The words told her he also still had some wild in him. Max felt heat pool between her legs. Oh God, now she was really in trouble.

When they reached the bar, he released her elbow and swept his arm out in front of him. He went to stand a few feet to the right of the front door. He could see the whole of the restaurant, the bar area, the main door and probably a good chunk of the street outside through the glass, she thought.

Normally, she'd have sat where she could see the bar, but tonight she chose a spot that put her back squarely to Shane. Samuel raised his eyebrows.

"Don't ask," she said.

"I'm guessing you don't want wine tonight," he said, even as he started making her an old-fashioned.

"You guessed right."

How in the hell was this going to work? She'd really, really, really needed to let loose tonight. To forget about everything, to exist only in the physical for a little while. But now that Shane was here and on her like fabric paint, there was no way on earth she could go home with someone. No guy in their right mind—and a right mind was key as she'd gotten tired of fetishes and kink a long time ago and she'd always had a healthy aversion to crazy—would take her home and bed her with virile Shane looming and scowling over them.

Just like he was now. Max could feel his presence, could feel his eyes on her. She wiggled back further on the stool and crossed her legs.

She took a generous sip of her drink. "Mmmm, thank you, Samuel. That hits the spot."

"How about for your shadow?"

She pursed her lips. "He'll decline. He's on duty. Needs to keep his wits about him."

She sighed. She hadn't thought escaping through. And she hadn't really meant to go out and go nuts, she'd only been acting on instinct, desperate for a little breathing room, a little normalcy. She should have known he'd be on her in seconds flat. He *was* her shadow now. There'd be no shaking him.

If she wanted a sexual release tonight, it'd have to be the do-it-yourself option later. But that really wasn't what she wanted or needed.

Max spun her glass, then centered it on the napkin. Although her plans had been foiled, she'd go ahead and enjoy the noise, the company and the drink. Let Shane wait. Let him stand there and brood. He'd be wasting his time. No one was after her. She was sure of it. There'd been plenty of opportunities for someone to harm her before she'd hired Shane and team. She wasn't a model, she didn't fit a model's physical mold either. Despite someone maybe wanting the schedule to pinpoint a model's whereabouts, she just didn't believe this was about her.

Just then, a blast of cold air hit her back. She didn't turn, but her ears perked up at the male voices.

A trio of men approached the bar.

"This seat taken?" asked a good-looking man in, oh, she'd guess his mid-forties, wearing a very well-cut suit and Burberry overcoat.

Oh, goody, she thought. Let the fun begin.

————

It was no surprise that the three men had zeroed in on Max and were so captivated that they hung on her every word, every gesture. Jaysus, it was like a choreographed dance the way they all stood when she got up to use the jacks, then swiveled to watch her strut down the aisle like a runway model.

What Shane couldn't believe was that this is where he'd ended up. Watching her—and watching everyone else watch her.

This was a particular kind of torture. He'd stolen some candy when he was young, booze when he was a little older and lifted a bill from old lady McKinnie's purse at church once. He'd started fights and broken men's bones more times than he could count just for the fun of it. Oh yes, Shane O'Rourke was headed to hell and he knew it—but apparently his hand basket had arrived a wee bit early.

And Max in particular was going to make sure his ride was every bit as uncomfortable as heading to the fiery pits of the afterworld should be. She'd accepted the trio's invitation to dinner, which included a round of appetizers, meals and already two bottles of wine.

Shane was roasting under his jacket and he positively ached with the need to pummel someone. Preferably the arse in the tan overcoat, the one who Max had *chosen*. While Shane had to force himself to stay in place, Inspector Gadget had definitely gotten comfortable, constantly leaning into Max, his arm stretched out behind her chair. Worse was when his hands kept snaking onto her thigh, her knee.

This situation was wreaking havoc on his concentration, and Shane had to force himself over and over to focus on all the patrons, the door, the street…

The bartender came over, wiping his hand on a bright white towel.

"Can I bring you a meal—on the house?"

"No, but thanks," Shane said.

"She must be a handful to watch over," the bartender said. "Everything all right? She's okay?"

Shane looked the guy in the eye. He didn't seem to be panting after Max. He seemed concerned about a friend. "Yeah, I'll make sure of it."

The bartender nodded, and Shane found himself thinking it was true. Yeah, it was his job, and he knew what he was doing, but also he'd do whatever he had to, simply because it was Max. The most beautiful, vibrant, sexy woman he'd ever met—no matter that she'd cut him loose way back when, no matter that he'd probably never have her.

"You sure about the food?" The bartender glanced at the foursome. "It's bound to be a while yet."

"Some water would be welcome."

"You got it."

When they finally had had their fill—*thank you, Mother Mary*—Shane breathed a sigh of relief.

They slipped into their coats and moved into the bar area.

Inspector Gadget put his hand on Max's hip like she was already his. He said, "Let's get together. Privately." She smiled, and Gadget said, "Give me your number."

Shane found himself cracking his knuckles. He forced himself to flex his fingers and drop his arms to his side.

"I'd like that," she purred. "But I'll call you."

She pushed a few buttons and then handed the tool her phone. He entered his number and handed it back. Then, he leaned in close, mouth at her ear and murmured something. She smiled, full wattage, and slid her hand from his shoulder and down his back to squeeze his rear.

She actually feckin' groped the man's arse. In a restaurant. The bastard's friends couldn't see it, but anyone at the bar could have. Shane slid his gaze to the right—yeah, the bartender had definitely noticed. But the worst part was, Shane's own balls tightened in response.

He shook his head and tore his gaze away. He shouldn't be watching her. He should be watching everyone else. Transitions—coming and going, arriving somewhere and leaving, getting to and from the car, the house, whatever venue—were when most attacks happened.

Shane scanned the patrons again, eyed the street again,

watching for any tells. Anyone acting just a little…inappro-
priate to the situation.

He didn't spot anything and proceeded out the door ahead
of Max. She ignored him, saying a last volley of goodbyes to
the group of men and gracing Gadget with a long heated look.
Which made Shane want to laugh. Or barf. Or hit something.

Then she turned and headed in the direction of her apartment. Her jacket had been left at the hotel coat check, so her
curves were on full display as she marched along in her three-
inch heels. He hoped she was at least cold.

Shane had no choice but to follow.

CHAPTER 24

EVEN AS HE STEWED, Shane alternated between scanning the people on the street and watching the swing of Max's hips. He practically prayed for the psycho that had targeted Max's models to show himself. This would be a choice time, with Shane feeling downright desperate to take somebody out.

The minute they got in the elevator to her apartment, he ripped at his bow tie and crushed it in his hand. She glared at him, then crossed her arms and cocked a hip. He didn't know what *she* had to be annoyed about. She'd had her fun—at his expense and at her risk, which he didn't appreciate at all.

As soon as they entered the apartment, she practically slammed her keys on the credenza along with her bag.

He snorted. "Uh-huh. You don't get to act up now."

"Excuse me?"

"You got what you wanted—a night out, a wee escape." His tone was snide, but he didn't care. He was ticked at her flagrant disregard for safety and angry at himself, too, for putting up with it. "What's with all the frustration—you couldn't seal the deal?"

"I can seal a deal just fine," she snapped. "My problem is *you*."

"Oh, poor thing." He smiled meanly. "I'm hampering your style?"

"Yes. You are. I could feel you watching me—staring—all night."

"It's my *job* to watch. A job that's dangerous enough without a stupid move like you pulled tonight." A flash of something—pain or hurt?—crossed her face, and then was gone a second later. He shook his head, disgusted. "Just because you need to get your rocks off."

She scowled.

He couldn't seem to stop and took a step toward her. "What—that jerk feeling you up wasn't enough? You need more?"

Max's nostrils flared and her eyes blazed, but she didn't back away.

"You need a real man, Max?" He stepped in even closer, his body only inches from hers. "Someone who can actually satisfy you for once?"

A throaty sound of frustration, desire, and need—a moan that held so much—escaped her. That kicked Shane into pure instinct mode. He grabbed her—hands on her face and behind her head—and kissed her. Hot, hungry, and desperate himself.

The next minute he let go and stepped back, somewhat shocked at what he'd done.

Max's chest heaved. Her eyes blazed and her lips looked ripe and wet. "Don't you dare stop," she said and launched herself against him so hard he stumbled.

They kissed and pawed like maniacs—so fast and jumbled he barely knew where he stopped and she began.

She was up on her toes, practically climbing him, her hands in his hair. She tasted amazing and smelled even better, but he couldn't think rationally about it because she was on fire in his arms. She ground her hips against him, but couldn't get purchase in her heels and dress, so he grabbed her arse and pulled her in tight. He yanked her dress up with no heed to designer price tags. The minute her legs were free, she hoisted herself up and wrapped her legs around him.

He spun and braced her against the wall, grinding against her while she rocked. She threw her head back and exposed the column of her throat. Such soft and hot skin there, he thought, as he licked and kissed his way down to her breasts, but he was impeded by the top of her dress.

He reached behind himself and pulled off one of her heels and then the other, then lifted her again. As soon as he'd deposited her standing on the bench, he ordered. "Lose the dress."

"Zipper," she said, half turning.

He pushed aside her silky dark hair, slid the zipper down, and bit her shoulder. He felt a surge of power as her knees dipped in pleasure. She shifted one shoulder and then the other and the dress pooled at her feet.

Jaysus. The woman wore a matching bustier, panty and garter belt set—all black and lacy and accentuating curves that were every bit as luscious as he'd imagined.

And no wonder the woman was so hot to trot tonight. She'd been walking around in underthings that must have made her feel sexy with every step.

He strained behind his fly. Already incredibly turned on, the sight of her body—so feckin' gorgeous—turned things up even more. He kissed his way down her back, and as he did, his hands stroked down her legs. Quick flips and the trailers of the garter hung free. He slid the stockings down, caressing her the whole way, still tasting her—her lower spine, her hips, the top hollow of her arse over the lace.

She'd braced herself against the wall and now crushed the expensive dress under her feet. "Shane," she said—and it sounded very needy.

He spun her around to work on her front. He managed to lose his jacket, letting it drop to the floor with a whoosh, and unbuckle his belt. He pulled at the panties and let them snap back as he scooped a lush breast out of her demi-cup. He sucked the nipple into his mouth and there her knees went again.

Her hands were all over him, and she wasn't quiet—gasping and moaning at his every move, making him feel like a king. She sunk down and lifted his wallet. The wallet hit the floor with a smack and a bounce, but above his head he heard a crinkle noise.

Yes, was his single thought as he snatched her up and moved. He went only as far as the carpeted area of the living room and laid her down, as carefully as he could manage in his haste.

Shane pulled hard at the front placket of his shirt. Studs went flying and bounced on carpet and marble alike. He ripped out his earpiece, peeled out of his shirt and threw it all to the side. Then he pulled off his shoes and dropped to his knees. He made quick work of his zipper, and as soon as his pants and boxers passed his hips, she sat up and slid the condom on him with deft fingers. One hand stayed there and squeezed, the other pulled at his shoulder.

"*Now,*" she said.

"No doubts?" he asked, though it about killed him to pause.

"No. *Now,*" she repeated.

Shane surged forward and she laid back—dear God, the panties were crotchless. He shoved into her with a "Jaysus, Max," and she gasped.

"More," she demanded, so he shifted to lay prone, bracing himself on his forearms near her head. He crushed her breasts with his chest and invaded her mouth with his tongue, as he pumped in and out, searching for the rhythm that would suit them both.

Her hands grasped his head and her legs pulled up. When her breath came fast, he knew he had it and began to move more deliberately. Her heels pressed into his arse, and even if she hadn't been spurring him on, he wouldn't have been able to stop.

She made a noise, the sexiest not quite moan, not quite scream noise that told him clearly that she was close—so close. He pushed even harder, even faster, and felt her fingernails dig into his shoulders. "Yes, love, for me now," he said and sucked her bottom lip into his mouth.

"Oh," she said again with that sexy noise, and then she was coming—pulsing around him so hard he wanted to weep as he exploded. It went on and on and he did, too, savoring every bit of her coming undone around him.

When they finally came to rest they were both panting and sweaty. He dropped his head down beside hers.

He kissed her on the neck and made to rise off of her. She clamped her legs around him. "Not yet," she murmured and stroked a hand down his back.

He levered up to look at her. "Don't worry, lass. We're not done by a long shot. But I haven't checked the apartment yet." She was a danger, he thought, truly—if he couldn't do his job, if he lost his head like he just had.

"I'm pretty sure they'd have taken their shot while we were involved," she said.

"Surely," he said, "but I'd like to be able to concentrate only on you."

"That was you *not* concentrating?" She smiled, a brilliant, sexy look. "By all means then."

He gave her one last something-to-look-forward-to kiss and jumped up. Kitchen first, where he discarded the condom and cleaned himself quickly. She'd moved to a kneeling position and was working on tucking a breast back into her corset when he strode by.

"It's gorgeous—you're gorgeous—but maybe you should take it off instead," he said as he strode by.

"Mmmm, maybe I will," she murmured.

Already so attuned to this apartment and its smells and noises, he knew—almost one hundred percent—that no one lurked in the shadows. Still he forced himself to walk away from her and do this one thing, to be certain that she'd be safe.

To ensure that he could see to her pleasure all night. Satisfy her so thoroughly that there'd be no more outings like the one he'd suffered through this evening.

Instead, if she felt needy—she'd look to him.

CHAPTER 25

MAX HADN'T DECIDED whether to remain in her sexy pieces or strip down before Shane was back. He pulled her immediately into his arms and kissed her. It took mere seconds and the kiss turned hungry, heating her right back up. She pressed tighter against him. He pulled away and unhooked her corset, eyes devouring her breasts as they fell free.

"I like all this," he said, setting it aside. "I like what's underneath more."

"I like this, too," she said, and smoothed her hands over the light hair on his chest, and downward. He was so fit, so big, so tan—he moved seamlessly, with surety, and he definitely knew what he was about when it came to women.

She slipped a hand lower, into his pants—pants he'd pulled up to prowl around her apartment. She wanted them off and used the other hand to work on that.

In moments they were both naked and she pushed him backward, toward the bedroom. They missed the hall and banged into the wall. She used that leverage to lean hard into him. He raised a knee, gripping her hips, and she moved against his leg. He kissed her hard, then spun them both, pushing her against the wall so that he could get at her breasts.

Around and around they went until they practically fell through the doorway of her bedroom. He scooped her up and deposited her on the bed.

He hesitated, his brows knitting together. "This one?" he asked. They were in the master, and he knew she often slept in the guest room.

She crooked a finger. "I think we'll need the space."

He opened her nightstand drawer, reached in, and threw a handful of condoms on the coverlet. He smiled, and *wow*, the man had the sexiest smile.

He said, "I think you've got the right of it."

———

Later, when their lust had been sated and their temperatures had cooled, Max lay stretched out naked next to Shane. She watched him under heavy lids, admiring his gorgeous physique. He knew exactly what to do with that stunning body, too.

But she had something she needed to say. She rolled to her side to face him.

"I'm sorry," Max said.

Shane turned his head, one eyebrow raised in question.

"About putting you in danger earlier."

"There is that," Shane stretched his arms above his head.

She nodded. "I didn't mean to put you in harm's way."

"Aye. Pulling a stunt like that risks a lot. You, your guard, the bystanders around you…"

"I hadn't thought it through. I just was so desperate to get the hell out of there."

"I get that," Shane said. He stared at the ceiling, his jaw tight. "But your feelings can't count. You are a target. Period. You're at risk every second until this is over."

He turned his head toward her and she saw real fear in his dark eyes before he focused on the ceiling once more. "I'd do anything to keep you safe," he said, with that tick in his jaw going. "But if you evade your guard…"

She waited, sensing there was more.

"People do die on our watch, Max," he said. "On *my* watch." He turned his head again, pain in his eyes.

She took a shaky breath. Oh, poor Shane.

He said, "Lives end because of stupid decisions."

"Tell me," she said, quietly.

He shut his eyes and heaved a sigh. "I lost a client. Recently. Carrie Sorrelle. Young girl who'd been witness to a big drug deal. She was waiting to testify but didn't really believe she was in danger. She was always trying to get around us, escape her guard and go party."

"And she got around you?"

He nodded his head. "By locking me in. Took me only seconds, but in that time she was gunned down. And I couldn't save her."

Max put her hand over his heart. "I'm so sorry."

He sighed again. "So am I."

"It's not your fault," she said.

"Tell that to her father," he said. Then he grasped her hand and squeezed as he pinned her with a hard look. "Do you see though? This is serious business. With dire consequences. Never again, okay?"

She nodded. "I promise."

He released her hand and her gaze.

She didn't want to be attacked—of course she didn't. And she certainly didn't want to die. But the thought that her impetuous, idiot move might have caused him harm—either physical or emotional? That was somehow even harder to swallow.

After a few moments, Shane said, "Try to remember that all this *will* come to an end."

Max felt a little lurch. She wanted this mess over with more than anything, but that also meant he wouldn't be in her bed any longer.

And what the heck? She'd broken her own personal code, yet she was keen to keep breaking it? Immediately she squashed that line of thought. She was not going there right now, and he needed a distraction.

So she reached out a hand and twirled a finger around his hipbone. Near enough to get a twitch from him. "*All* of it?"

A low rumble came from Shane's chest. His eyes lit with desire. "The perks of this job *could* continue indefinitely."

"Excellent," Max said, and gave him a sexy smile. She continued the wanderings over his skin with her finger—his hipbone, the ridges of his stomach—but she was too tired to do much more than that.

She already suspected that permanently slaking her desire for Shane would be impossible. Their coupling tonight had been anything but satisfying. It'd been wickedly incendiary. Fanning the flames of her need for him. Oh yeah, they'd reached crescendos, but the knowledge of how he felt, how he made her feel? She wanted more, more, more.

She shut her eyes thinking back, getting warm all over again. Then she chuckled.

"What are you laughing about?" he asked.

"Your tuxedo shirt studs. I'm not sure we'll find them all in that shag carpet."

One of his shoulders lifted in a carefree shrug. "I can't believe *you* stepped all over a St. Laurent."

She chuckled, scooted closer to him, and threw a leg over his thighs, her arm over his chest and her head on his upturned bicep. "It was worth it."

His large hand immediately settled on her hip.

Max sighed.

Shane said, "Are you regretting this?"

"No," she said. "That was a sigh of contentment." Then she got worried again. "You?"

"No. It *was* worth it."

"Worth the Laurent and the silver studs or...?"

"Worth everything," Shane said and smoothed his hand from her hip to her knee.

She smiled, suddenly very relieved. It had mattered, somehow. Whether he really wanted to be here with her, or whether he'd just wanted some.

His hand slid back up and his finger circled her tattoo. "Why an elephant?" he asked.

"I wanted something symbolic when I started Ivory," she said. "The elephant represents all the things I wanted to channel: strength and tenacity, stability and reliability, and power and dignity, too. The Hindu god Ganesha—the elephant-headed one—is the god of luck, fortune, and protection. He's a blessing on all new projects."

Shane smiled. "Hence *Ivory* Management."

"Right. Not only does Ivory polish beautifully, it's not easily damaged or destroyed. And, did you know that an African elephant's tusks continue to grow throughout their lifetime?"

"No," Shane smiled. "You obviously chose well."

She'd made it pretty enough to wear forever, too, as the elephant head was encircled in a ring of lush flowers.

But Max didn't care to discuss her company. She had something more pressing on her mind. "Can you stay here? All night?"

"I'm your security detail, remember?"

She flicked his nipple with her nail. "I meant, in my bed."

Shane caught her hand in his and pressed it into his chest. "I thought you'd never ask."

CHAPTER 26

ONE NIGHT, although it was still full dark outside, his dad had woken. He'd seen him standing there, watching.

"Like what you see, boy? Huh?"

His eyes tore from the smooth skin he'd been admiring to his father's haggard face. His body had frozen in place, knowing this could be bad, really bad.

"Maybe it's time you had a little taste of your own, eh?"

The woman had woken, shaking her head a little. Her name was Cherie. She was young, younger than dad's usual. And so, so very pretty. She'd had pink sparkly painted toes and fingernails and mouth. She was naked, but there were still sparkles on her skin—maybe from makeup or from the outfit she'd been wearing. It had shined magnificently on stage, casting little reflections around the club and on all the men's faces. He'd been watching those sparkles catch the moonlight as she breathed in sleep.

"Whaddaya think, sweetheart?" his father asked her. "You game to make my boy here a man?"

"How old are you?" she asked, turning on her side, with her hand propping up her head to look at him.

He didn't answer, and she chuckled.

"He's old enough," his father said and slapped her rear.

She yelped, but giggled. His father got out of the bed, and she scooted over and patted the mattress.

He didn't want to do what his father wanted. But he did want to see what she felt like.

Finally, he took a step forward and knelt on the mattress. She giggled again.

She bade him lay down next to her, and he did, but he could feel his father's eyes on him.

"Nerves. You'll get over those," his dad said. "Don't worry, son. She knows what she's doing." He went to the dresser and tap, tap, tapped his pack of cigarettes on his palm.

She placed her hand on his chest and then moved it down, over his belly, and lower. He felt panicked, his heart beating like a jackrabbit.

His dad lit one up and watched him through narrow eyes and an exhale of smoke.

She scooted closer and his eyes went wide. That beautiful, glorious breast pressed against his chest. This was his chance.

He raised a hand, shaking, and pressed it to her breast. It was warm, so warm. He remembered being surprised, because she'd looked cool in the moonlight. She covered his hand with her own and squeezed. She felt firm and full and almost exactly like what he'd imagined.

He shuddered with the pleasure of it. He smoothed his hand over that pale mound, softer even than it looked. He dared to trace her nipple and watched in amazement as the little bud at the center peaked.

He was in pure heaven, until she ruined it. She scooted up, her chest at his eye level. "Suck on it," she said. "Hard as you like."

He balked, rearing back into the pillow even though he was still laying flat.

His dad chuckled. "You won't hurt her. She likes it. It helps her get ready."

He didn't want to get her ready. He didn't want it in his mouth. He wanted to see it, he wanted to feel it.

He jumped then as her hand cupped his privates.

"It's him needs to get ready," she told his father.

"What the fuck?" his dad asked. "You got a goddamn feast an inch from your lips and you won't eat?" He put his hands on his hips and his face got red.

He wanted to do what he was supposed to. To please his father. And even Cherie.

His dad made it look so easy. So did his older brother, who was always out but occasionally brought girls home. He hadn't had to be made a man. He knew where things were supposed to go. How it was supposed to work.

But he didn't want that. He didn't want to be inside her. Not in her or her mouth. And he didn't want any parts of her inside his mouth either. He wanted to feel her with his hands. Although he knew it didn't make sense, he wanted to close his eyes and pretend he was feeling her body from the inside.

"You fucking pansy," Dad had yelled. "I show you how it's done every goddamn night. You think I do this for me? No! I do it for you. And you can't even get it up? Christ, you're a disappointment."

He shook his head, then his chin came up and he wore a hopeful expression. "What do you need, huh? Should we put on a tape? Which one is your favorite?"

He'd shaken his head hard. He loved the tapes, the women, but not for this.

"I see you watching, boy. Hovering in the doorway, your eyes glued to the screen. You can't fool me."

Cherie interrupted. "Just leave us alone, Hank," she'd cooed. "Lemme figure out what he likes. It's probably all your bellowing that's given him performance anxiety. Nobody wants an audience their first time."

"Fine." His dad left, and he heard him go straight to the refrigerator, and then the unmistakable snap of a beer can top. He slammed out the front door to the rickety porch, but didn't go down the steps.

"What do you need, sweetheart? Come here."

He looked out the window and saw the glow of red, the lightening sky.

Cherie tried, but he knew it was too late.

All he could think about was his dad coming back in. Seeing whatever he would see. A particularly nasty scar? A big, ugly birthmark? A tattoo his father hadn't noticed during the hurried pawing in the night?

Or worst of all—stretch marks. His father hated those more than anything else. Now that he was older, he knew it had to do with his mom.

All he could think about were the things he didn't want to see, but would have to, when his dad pointed them out. And so he couldn't do what she wanted. What his dad wanted. He just couldn't.

CHAPTER 27

MAX AND SHANE holed up on Monday, much like they'd done on Sunday. The confines of the apartment and enforced togetherness that had so tortured Max last week now felt ideal for exploring their newly sexual relationship. They lounged late in bed, nibbled as much on each other as meals, and laughed as much as they touched.

In the afternoon, Armand came over to spell Shane, who headed home to spend some time with the twins and trade out his clothes with fresh ones. Max wondered what his place looked like, whether the kids would give him a hard time, and whether he'd regret leaving them later.

With Shane in her bed, it'd been easy to cast aside for a time the reasons he was there in the first place. However with Armand standing sentry, she began to fret. She considered a nap, but wasn't sure her unease would allow her to truly rest. So she turned to work—something she should have been doing all day, anyway.

Max worked diligently for a few hours: plowing through emails, addressing a number of items over the phone, and reviewing and e-signing numerous documents. When a woman owned her own business, there was rarely a day truly free of the office. And the curtailed schedules didn't mean there wasn't plenty of other stuff to do.

Finally she showered, taking extra care as she shaved. She tilted her head back under the water and considered what she and Shane might get up to upon his return. Maybe she should put dinner in the oven, set the table with candles and greet him in lingerie. Or better yet, she'd greet him naked and never think of food again.

Two problems with those scenarios. One, a man like him needed sustenance. Two, Armand was in the house.

Honestly though, she was just looking forward to Shane's company again. She was pretty sure they could share dinner and hit the hay early without any nooky, and she'd *still* fall asleep with a smile on her face simply because he was near.

What was with her?

Just as she was drying off, her cell phone rang. She padded out to the bed where she'd tossed it.

"Hey," she said in greeting to Miranda.

"Head's up," Miranda said. "We're coming to you tonight."

Max groaned. There went her down and dirty with Shane or even her cuddle on the couch. Ladies night in was every Monday at Aggie and Cora's. "How is it Monday already? And why not at their place?"

"They don't want you exposed any more than necessary," Miranda said, "and neither do I."

"That's sweet, but I could really use an outing. I'm coming to hate my own four walls." Except with Shane entertaining her, she did have a new appreciation for her ceiling *and* her shag carpet.

"Pretty sure you won't sway the Wise Ones with that argument," Miranda said, "but go ask your shadow."

"He's not here."

"You aren't alone, are you?"

"No," Max explained, "he called in a replacement so he could go check on his kids."

"Kids? Plural? Is he married, and I didn't know it?"

Max swapped her towel for a robe, put Miranda on

speaker, and brushed out her hair while she explained about the twins and their reaction to her—which Miranda got a kick out of.

"He obviously had a very bad taste in his mouth after you canned him," Miranda said. "Have you two talked about that night he stormed your office?"

"Ummm," Max said. "We haven't been doing a lot of talking."

Miranda gasped. "You're sleeping with him? Oh my God!"

Max laughed. "I couldn't help it. I didn't *want* to help it. The attraction's been building and finally we just combusted."

"But your *rules*," Miranda said.

"Don't remind me. I'm trying not to think about that part," Max said, and then told Miranda everything—well everything she needed to know anyway.

"What were you thinking leaving the event alone?" Miranda sounded so stern, it might as well have been Aggie or Cora scolding her.

"Obviously, I wasn't."

"And you obviously still weren't thinking when you jumped him either."

"Definitely not. But for the record, he jumped first. And it was soooo hot."

———

Max had decided not to push it and just let Miranda and the Wise Ones come to them. She had, however, called Shane to tell him to take his time. Not only would Armand be here, Aggie could surely dismember any assailant with her sharp tongue.

To that end, she'd hoped to save Shane from bearing the brunt of the Wise One's attention. And hell, she'd hoped to save herself from a little embarrassment. He'd enjoyed the last time a little too much.

Unfortunately, Shane arrived before they did.

"You're early," she said.

Handsome as could be in jeans and a pullover and the ever-present earpiece, he winked. "Wouldn't miss this dinner for anything."

"Hah," she said. "You'll live to regret that."

She returned to setting the table while Shane consulted with Armand. In minutes it was just the two of them. Shane came up behind her, put his big hands on her hips, and planted his lips where her neck met her shoulder. "I missed you," he said in between kisses.

She smiled and pushed her hips back into him. "Mmmmm. I can tell," she said, the hard evidence clear.

She spun, looped her arms around his neck and locked her lips to his. Instantly they were on fire, but he pushed her away.

"Old ladies are always prompt," she said. "But we have time for a quickie."

"No, you minx," he said. "I need to do my sweep."

"Armand just did one."

"Need to do my own." She surged on tiptoes, and he took the bait—until he didn't. "*And* I'm not having your grand-mother and great aunt arrive with the both of us smelling like sex."

She pouted, and he gave her one quick kiss before walking away.

She finished setting the table, retrieved a bag of M&M's from the kitchen cupboard, and poured them into a decorative bowl.

When she'd set them in the center of the table, Shane said. "Dessert first?"

"Tradition," she explained. "Aggie and Cora call Miranda and me *M and M*, or sometimes *The M's*. And so at every gathering, they insist on the candy."

"Sweet," he said.

"And dangerous," she said.

"Your spreading arse, again?"

"Exactly," she said.

"It's perfection," he said, but just as he reached for it, the doorbell rang. Shane rolled his eyes. "That idiot security guard downstairs is supposed to call up."

"I already told him they were coming and what time, and he's known them for years," Max said.

"Extra precaution. I want him escorting them into the elevator and standing there until it's on its way," Shane said, frustration evident in his tone. "No extra passengers. No surprises."

This time Shane joined them for dinner and conversation flowed easily. Miranda talked about her weekend away with Eddie in the Poconos, and Aggie shared gossip about their neighbors—most of whom the M's knew well.

And Cora grilled Shane, albeit in her gentle way. She asked questions about his career, his upbringing in Ireland, and the minute she discovered there were children in his life—his niece and nephew, too.

Max found it suspicious that Aggie didn't ask any pointed questions. Instead, she got up from the table during dessert—not only M&M's but also cheesecake from Juniors in Brooklyn—which was *well* worth an extra hour of cardio or even a spreading backside—and disappeared.

After a while, Miranda looked at Max with raised eyebrows. Max said, "Excuse me," and set off down the hallway.

Instead of finding Aggie in the hall bathroom, she discovered her exiting the master bedroom.

She put her hands on her hips. "Everything all right?"

"Hmmpf," was the non-answer she got as Aggie brushed past.

Max shook her head and followed. Maybe she'd needed something from Max's bathroom that wasn't in the guest bath, but who knew with Aggie.

"Time to go," Aggie announced, and she didn't head for the dining area but for the foyer.

"You haven't finished your coffee, Agatha," Cora said. "And I haven't finished my tea."

"Too bad," Aggie said and wriggled into her coat.

Cora huffed, but followed her sister to the foyer.

"Miranda, you too," ordered Aggie.

"I'll stay and help Max clean up," Miranda said.

"No you won't," Aggie said.

Miranda gave Max a look and raised her hands in a whatever-this-is-I'm-not-getting-in-the-middle-of-it gesture. They all joined the Wise Ones in the foyer, and Shane held Cora's coat for her.

"What in the world, Aggie?" Max asked, sensing as she said it that she probably should just keep her mouth shut and let them go.

Aggie said, "Far be it from me to stand between two people dying to hop into bed together."

"Gram!" Max scolded, while Miranda said, "Aggie!"

"Don't act so shocked. We may be old, but we're not dead yet. It's clear as plastic wrap that you two are all full of the lust. Am I right, Cora?"

Max wanted to die on the spot when Cora nodded. Oh dear, God. It was easy to pass off Aggie as *oobatz*, but when Cora was on board, too....

Shane said, "Mrs. Stern—"

"Don't you Mrs. Stern me. It's Aggie to you." She glared at him. "Your bag is in our girl's bedroom and your overnight kit is on her vanity. You better not get so distracted in her bed that you forget that you're meant to be protecting her with your life, or you'll be answering to me."

"Yes, ma'am." Apparently Shane was smart enough to leave it at that.

Miranda laughed out loud before clamping a hand over her mouth. She didn't bother to put her coat on, only opened the door. "I can't *wait* to tell Eddie this one," she said as she darted out.

"*Madonna!*" Max muttered.

"No one ever died from mortification," Cora said. "So I'm going to say my piece, too."

Max groaned. "Please don't."

Cora patted her on the arm. "Don't sabotage yourself, darling. He's not like your father. Luckily, most men aren't." Then she turned to go.

Max didn't escort them to the elevator. She only closed the door behind them and pressed her hands to her burning cheeks.

"Do I need to know what that means?" Shane asked.

She shook her head and shut her eyes, unable to even look at him. "*I* don't even know what that means."

CHAPTER 28

HE'D FOUND A note on Tuesday, with a threat that really scared him. So he had to do it. He had to tell her to come tonight.

Something bad was about to happen…and given the events of the last few weeks, probably something really, really bad. Because once he got really angry, he got violent. There was no stopping him.

He thought the first time was just a fit of rage on his behalf, but it seemed a routine had developed. He knew because of the last two what was coming tonight. And he wasn't sure it was necessary.

In many ways it was a blessing to have someone who always had his back, someone who fought to make the world right for him when he'd been wronged. But the level of violence was… He squeezed his eyes shut tight. He didn't want to think about that part.

To some degree, he was grateful that he'd probably never have to see her again. Pleased that she'd never again be able to trick the world with her deceit. She didn't deserve the life she was leading—and left to her own devices, she'd destroy that life all on her own. So disgusting, so insane. He'd been avoiding her, afraid he'd say something that showed how he really felt about her choices, her weaknesses.

He'd written her off already, yet tonight meant he'd be truly free of her sooner rather than later. And she'd get her just desserts a little early. That was all.

But it was so much more complicated than that. Anxiety and fear had him completely on edge. He'd bitten the inside of his cheek raw with the worrying, and there was a long day to go, too.

It was all his fault. If only he could stop getting so attached. Invariably there was such disappointment. It was excruciating every time.

There was only one who'd been steady, who held herself above all others. She was a goddess, truly… She would *never* disappoint him. But she was hard to get close to. Always holding him at arm's length. Maybe that was for the best. Maybe that distance was safer for all involved.

Yes, after tonight, he should just concentrate on her. Not allow himself to get sucked in to another woman, no matter how enticing.

If tonight happened…well, it *would* happen, he was sure of that. After tonight, he *wouldn't* choose another girl. He simply had to avoid that, to refrain. Because if he kept on like this, eventually he would be caught.

They'd be caught…

Because he wasn't exactly innocent either. He'd assisted, kind of. And occasionally, he'd seen. Just glimpses, rather like a picture stuck in his mind. Sometimes he knew—without knowing how he actually knew.

He shuddered now, thinking ahead. Wondering what he might remember tomorrow. Wondering how bad it'd be.

CHAPTER 29

THE LOBBY OF Ivory Management was empty and dark this late in the evening, and Shane flipped the switch near the elevators.

Max said, "Don't bother. We won't be here long." They were there only to retrieve her laptop.

"Excellent," Shane said. Because he'd been dying this evening, watching her work the crowd at an intimate fashion show. All he could think about was peeling off that skirt, maybe keeping on the heels. She'd felt the same, he knew, given the heated looks she'd slid him. The quicker this stop at the office was, the quicker they'd be home and free to do as they desired.

Another thought lurked under the surface tonight. It was crazy, but he'd wished he could be at her side, instead of off in a corner. Someday, she'd be safe again. And then, who knew...

Shane cut off that line of thought with a shake of his head and followed Max into her office. The lights of the city illuminated the space, blinking neon casting a red and blue glow intermittently.

She stopped midway across the room. "It's beautiful, isn't it?"

Shane came up behind her and swept her hair to one side, tucking it over her shoulder so that he could place his lips on her neck. "Aye." And it was, but it was nothing compared to her.

"Mmmm," she murmured and leaned her head so he could have better access.

Her one-shouldered top meant he had plenty of real estate to work with, and he kissed his way down to her shoulder. His hands traced across her back.

When she hummed some more and pressed her rear against his groin, it was his turn to groan. He was already hard of course—no surprise, given he'd been watching her for hours, just biding his time until they could be alone.

Shane grabbed her hips, pulling her even closer against him, then slid his hands around her front, dipping low, but not too low. Then he teased his way along her tummy, up to trace under her breasts, along her ribs. He nibbled up the curve of her neck and behind her ear.

Her hands wrapped back, to squeeze his arse, her breasts thrusting out. That temptation was great, and he moved to caress under her chin, one hand sliding down her neck, over her chest and into her shirt, until he held the weight of one breast in his hand and could play her nipple with that thumb. His other hand kept a tight lock on her hip, and he rubbed against her just enough.

He intended to tease, to make her wet with wanting, so that by the time they got home, she'd be so fiery hot that—

It didn't take anywhere near that long. Max twisted her head to kiss him, hot and deep. Without breaking the kiss, she spun and braced both hands on his chest to walk him backward. When his legs hit the table, she practically climbed up him, forcing him to recline. He slid his hands up her legs, taking her skirt along with it.

She yanked his shirt out of his pants, frantically working his buttons. He had his holster on, and she left it, content apparently just to smooth her hands up and down his chest and stomach.

"Max—this isn't the best place," he attempted, even though God knew he didn't want her to stop.

"No one's here," she said, a desperate look on her face.

Shane knew sex was an outlet for her. And she had so much pent up stress and worry and fear waiting for the murderer to strike again. So he let this happen, promising himself that he'd give her what she needed and yet keep half his attention on their surroundings.

Max stripped off her top. Her demi-cup bra held her up like a bountiful feast. She made quick work of his belt buckle, then shifted and knelt on one knee. She brought the other leg up, strappy heel and all, and slipped it through one leg of her panties. She moved again, and this time knelt on the other side, while she braced one foot on the table. She took her time rolling the panties ever so slowly down that leg. Shane had one hand holding behind her knee, and he used the other to gently rub her where it really counted. She was practically dripping, and it was all he could do not to hoist her up and fasten his mouth there and make her scream.

But he sensed that she wanted to be the aggressor here in her office, where she was always, always in charge. Here, where she needed to reclaim some control.

He watched her eyes. She loved this, the fact that he could both see and touch her most intimate self, and yet she was still above him and in control—sore knee be damned. She moved back and forth, asking for more. He slipped his finger in and out of her while his thumb worked a bit of magic. She threw her head back, her hair dipping behind her shoulders.

Jaysus, she was glorious.

She didn't let herself come, though he knew she was close.

"Your pants," she said. "Now."

He gave her one last long stroke, and pushed his pants down as far as he could manage. She took the opportunity to come back to both knees. He shifted to untie a shoe, intending to ditch the pants entirely, but she said, "That's far enough."

His movement would be limited, but as she scooted forward and then lowered herself onto him, he found he didn't care.

He surged up, but she raised herself, shook her head and smiled wickedly. He groaned. She was going to make this slow and torturous, when he'd assumed she'd wanted hard and fast. With both hands propped on his chest, she slid herself just over his head, and God save him, squeezed with her inner muscles.

"Sweet Holy..." he thought he said, but it was all sensation now, narrowed down to this one gloriously torturous joining.

She slid up, the cool office air replacing warm wet, and then repeated the trick.

Shane's eyes rolled back in his head and he squeezed just above her knees—probably harder than he should, for something to grab onto. He forced himself to soak in every detail, the divine expression of pleasure on her face, eyes half-lidded with desire. The sway of her full breasts with their distended dark nipples, the strands of midnight hair that had gotten caught on her generous red lips. The deep inward curve of her waist and smooth flair of her lush hips.

The lights from the street glowed and sometimes flashed. She was cast in reds and blues, and a bright white light shone on her left hip. Right on that small tattoo—an elephant head in profile, flowers tucked in all around it. A hidden treasure, so unexpected.

Max sank lower, and lower by increments.

"Yes," he said, and palmed the globes of her arse, so soft and strong and full. He levered up to suck on a pert nipple, pulling hard.

She made a mewing sound and rocked hard. Shane moved to the other breast and teased the cleft between her sweet cheeks. Faster and faster, until she cried out. As her orgasm pulsed around him, he found his release as well.

He collapsed, clunking his head against the table and realized his earpiece had come off at some point.

She chuckled, still breathing hard and fell on top of him. "Oh damn," she murmured, without any real vehemence.

"You've broken the last of your rules tonight, haven't you, lass?" He pulled her hair to one side and stroked his fingers from her temple backward.

"Mmmm-hmmm. I'm not even sorry though," she said.

"Good, I'm—"

Just then there was a sound from the hallway. A creak. Shane spotted a movement, a shadow only, and Max gasped.

Shane practically threw her to the side. He was up and out the door, pants yanked up and zipped, and his gun in his hand immediately after.

He tore out the door and down the hall. The aggressor was running, too—he'd abandoned stealth and had fled. He'd headed opposite to the elevator bank, down the wing toward the stairwell.

Shane heard the slam of the heavy metal door. A few steps more and he plowed through it. He peered over the railing even as he took four stairs at a time. Feet pounded below.

"Stop," Shane called, even though he knew it would do no good. Shane knew there was no other way, he'd have to jump. Because if this guy hit the street, he'd lose him for good. Maybe they'd get surveillance video, but he wasn't willing to take the risk. This was their shot at snagging this guy.

And that was why he'd left Max—he wanted this done, for her sake, for all these women. But even as he ran, he was mentally kicking himself. He knew better than to leave a target—that was his whole job for God's sake, protecting the target, getting her out of harm's way. *Not* chasing down an assailant.

As soon as he hit the midway point in the second flight he grabbed the rail with his left, holding the gun in his right, and swung himself over the side with enough momentum to pass over the railing below—just barely. He missed landing on the assailant, who was a few steps further down, but it was enough to startle the guy and cause him to stumble. He recovered, but by then Shane was on him.

Shane yanked his shoulder and slammed him against the wall. He registered the build, the clothing, the face even before he'd leveled the gun at him.

Cam.

And all Shane could think was *what the …*

His brain skittered with possibilities.

"I'm sorry, I'm sorry," Cam sputtered, staring at the gun like it was a three-headed monster.

"What were you doing?" Shane said, adrenaline and the echo of the stairwell making it sound more like a yell.

"Nothing, I swear." Cam looked panicked. "I didn't mean to see!"

"Why were you here?"

Max's heels had been clicking away, trotting down the steps, making Shane want to scream.

"Max! Stop!" he yelled.

She didn't, of course. He could hear her still coming, and she was just hitting the landing above. "Stay right there," Shane barked. "*Don't* come any closer!"

He hadn't taken his eyes off Cam—a distraction like another person approaching would be the perfect time for the aggressor to strike or take off. Shane could see Max's feet coming down this flight, painted red toes with the black criss-crossing straps of her heels out of his peripheral vision.

Hallelujah, she finally stopped, near the top of the flight they were on. Probably it was the sight of him holding a gun to Cam's forehead more than his directive, but at least she'd actually halted.

"Answer the question," Shane said.

Cam's eyes darted from Max back to Shane. He looked like he was about to piss himself.

When he didn't speak, Shane lowered the gun from head height to chest height and tried again. "No one's supposed to be here after hours. "

"I wasn't!" Cam finally burst out. "I only stopped in because I forgot to leave Samara's Gucci contract on Max's desk and I knew she wanted to review it before they met tomorrow. I knew she'd never find it where I left it, it's in a folder, in my office." He managed to take a breath. "I was going to just leave it on her desk and go."

He didn't have any papers, nor were there any in the hall-way, but Shane also knew Cam's office was past Max's. So he'd come upon Max and Shane before he'd even gotten that far.

Cam said, "I didn't mean to see—" He looked away. "I thought it was better to just let you two—" He waved a hand instead of saying the words.

Max took another step down, and Shane warned, "Maaax."

Max said, "Cam, I'm so so sorry."

Shane could see that she was all put back together. His own shirt still hung open, held in place by his holster. His belt was also still undone, as was the top button of his pants. At least his fly was up.

"I..." Cam said. "I can't even." His expression was wounded, and he wouldn't meet her eyes. He shook his head.

Shane thought he might have seen the glisten of tears in his eyes.

"Shane, please," she said. "Put away the gun!"

Shane took a step back and lowered the gun a few more inches, but wasn't quite ready to let his guard totally down.

"Why the *hell* did you run?" Shane asked.

"Because you chased me!"

———

In the end, they'd let Cam go. Shane had talked to security, and they vouched that Cam had left earlier and come in shortly after they had. So his story appeared to be true. Still, Shane felt uneasy. Or maybe queasy was more apt. He kept wondering if there were minutes unaccounted for. Just how long had Cam watched?

Max, it seemed, had other concerns. In the cab ride home, she said, "I feel awful. I let Cam down."

"How so?" Shane asked, and pulled her tighter against him.

"I broke my cardinal rule. I always swore I'd never sleep with anyone I work with."

Shane tensed, but she wasn't done.

"And I broke it six ways to Sunday," she said, misery in her voice. "I had sex *in* my office. Of all places. With the door *open*."

She sounded disgusted, and it pissed Shane off.

"Your rules—broken or not—are none of Cam's business," Shane said through gritted teeth. "Neither is who you choose to sleep with."

"He's important to my work. Important to me as a friend. Cam holds me in the highest esteem, and he's wholly invested in Ivory. I let him down."

Shane didn't give a rat's ass about Cam's feelings, so they spent the rest of the ride in silence.

Max wasn't the only one kicking herself. Shane would love to take out all his frustrations in the ring. Hell, if he could, he'd pound himself.

By the time they got home to Max's apartment, he'd worked up a right head of steam. He shut and locked the door, and then did his site check, sweeping through the rooms, almost hoping there'd be somebody hiding in a closet so he could bust their dial.

"Clear," he said when he returned to the front door. For once, she'd waited there, and had actually sat down on the bench. She'd leaned her head back and had shut her eyes—so content, thinking he'd be smart enough to keep her safe. Blast it.

She opened her eyes and said, "I was the one who pushed things to the next level tonight. It wasn't your fault."

"Like hell it wasn't!" Shane said and stalked away from her.

"Shane—" She followed and put a hand on his arm, but he moved away again.

"Any other job," he said, "and we would've had a team of agents as gatekeepers and backups, but we're spread too thin. Any other job, and I'd never have been distracted. Feckin' naked and vulnerable getting my brains blown to sweet heaven by the asset for anyone to see!" He threw his hands wide.

"Any other job and I would have remained to *protect you— the asset*. Like I should have!" That one killed him the most. Dear God, what if something had happened to her?

He turned away from her and rubbed his jaw. "I should have called security downstairs, called the police, looped in my command. Not given chase, for God's sake, leaving you half-dressed and alone in your office—a wide open target."

But Shane would have had to either fix his earpiece or use the phone. Both would have wasted valuable time—almost surely letting the aggressor get away. And the desire to end this thing, to make Max safe for good was so strong, that he'd gone for it.

"I don't know about that," she said. "But thankfully, it was only Cam."

"Only Cam." He made a harsh sound in his throat. "And what if there'd been someone else there lurking, just waiting for the right moment to attack you?"

Shane wanted to beat his head against the wall and scream. Max had messed with his mind big time—and the worst part was, he loved it. Loved every second of being with her. From mad, risky sex in the office, to watching her run a photo shoot, to sitting with her as she laughed at something on the TV, all curled up on the couch in fuzzy socks and short shorts. He was a goner, he knew, and the thought of one single hair on her beautiful head harmed?

No. He had to get his head on straight and finish this job.

"I'd almost welcome the face to face," she said. "Even if I was hurt. If we could stop him and end this."

"Don't ever say such a thing," he said. "Jaysus, Max, I can't see you hurt. Thinking about it makes me…" He flexed his fingers, but there weren't words. "And if something happened to you because of my negligence?"

"Shhh," she said, and put a finger to his lips. "None of this could be anyone's fault but a madman. But I know what you mean." Her eyes glistened with unshed tears. "When you ran after him, I was so scared that something would happen to you, that you'd be hurt, or, or…"

She looked so upset, he couldn't help himself. He gathered her into his chest and held her tight.

CHAPTER 30

THAT BITCH. That soul-sucking devil-woman. He had never liked her, he'd never trusted her. He'd tried to tell the kid that he shouldn't either—but did he listen, no? Just like he never listened. No matter how many times he told him to protect himself. To stop getting so caught up. To stop giving these crazy witches all that power over him. To stop thinking they were such goddesses.

He paced across the small room and back, purposefully slamming into the wall at both ends.

Christ. If there was one thing his upbringing had taught him: women weren't to be trusted. They were lying, conniving, tricky... they *never* were what they seemed.

He stopped suddenly in the middle of the room, fisted his hands and flexed every muscle in his body. As he tilted his head to the ceiling, he let out a growl of pure rage.

He resumed his pacing. Thankfully, he'd already decided tonight was the night to rid him of Miss Skin and Bones. It'd feel *good*, after what he'd just learned. It'd be good for everybody involved.

That wouldn't be the end of it though. More work to do. The Goddess was next. Not only had she marred her body—with that stupid, ugly little mark. All this time, the bitch had hidden it. Saying one thing and doing another. The slut. At the work table no less. With *him*.

No wonder the kid was beside himself. He'd thought he'd known everything. But you never did with women.

Because they were so distracting, so enticing. Your body did the thinking—and next thing you knew, you were buried to the hilt in a train wreck.

As for the tattoo itself? He didn't care as much as the little man did. But it was his job to watch out for him. His job to make things right, keep the kid from heading into serious depression.

Did he mind? Hell no—he loved using his hands for something worthwhile. It was like a public service—you just couldn't broadcast it was all. He was *proud* to do it. But man, lately the kid had been on a roll. From one obsession to another.

Because that dumb ass Farm Girl had twisted the gut hard. The minute she'd started asking about abortion—well, who could blame the kid after all he'd endured?

Apparently he'd snapped, loosening a couple of marbles again. Usually he could get back on track. The downfall of his all-time favorite would hit the kid hard, too. He had it bad for her—had for years and years. Kept her on such a high pedestal—way beyond the others—that she may as well have been prancing around in space. He couldn't deny the kid had excellent taste—nice piece, that one—except for her smart mouth.

But she'd gone and fucked it up.

And she'd gone and fucked *him*. Of all people to break her precious rules with? It *had* to be him.

Poor kid. A knock-out punch for sure.

She'd be harder to get to. She kept things closer to the vest than these young girls. She was smarter—or at least he'd thought so. The ink and all that lust seemed to be making her stupid.

Plus, *he* seemed to have appointed himself her own personal watchdog. Was he gonna have to lace his kibble or chain him or send in a rodent as a diversionary tactic or what? There was always a way. He'd have to think on it.

In the meantime, he was very much looking forward to tonight. It was time to show the world what Skin and Bones was really made of. Or not made of, hah.

CHAPTER 31

SHANE ESCORTED MAX to the office early on Thursday. One of the newer models, hired just before all the chaos, had a second shoot scheduled with Damien at 8:00 a.m., and Max wanted the chance to review her earlier digitals in preparation.

Although Ivory was not exactly business as usual, to some degree the show must go on. As far as Max was concerned, it wasn't fair to hold off the young model indefinitely. The girl couldn't score any gigs if they didn't get her a decent start on a portfolio.

At least, Shane thought, he considered the two floors of Ivory one of their safer locations.

Shane knew Max was jonesing to have a regular day at the office. Her bright eyes and wide smile despite rising early made that clear. He figured that it'd been so long since anything had been normal, she was probably just happy to feel busy and see other people, too.

The commute was easy this early and they arrived at her office well before seven o'clock. Shane spoke with the morning guard.

Max tapped her foot. "Come on," she said, "I've got so much I want to accomplish this morning."

"You're the first one from your group here this morning, Ms. Ricci," the guard told her.

"Thanks, Desmond. Just the way I like it."

"You all have a good day now."

They hit the turnstiles and then the elevators and flipped on the lights when they hit her lobby.

"Oh, I want to go down to the studio and crank the heat up before I get too distracted."

"Let me check this floor first. Wait here," Shane told Max.

She said, "Desmond just said nobody's here."

"When I confirm that with my own eyes," Shane said, "*then* nobody will be here."

"Fine. Make it snappy, O'Rourke." She crossed her arms over her chest.

Everything looked as it should, and they proceeded to Max's executive suite. She dropped her bag and unloaded some papers, then booted up her computer.

"Okay, let's go," she said.

They went down the elevator together, and again, Shane ordered her to wait in the vestibule.

Shane went through each room methodically, starting at one end and working his way down the hallway. He chuckled as he passed Max, who was once again tapping her foot impatiently.

"What's funny?" she asked.

"Nothing," he replied.

The large studio where they did the photo shoots was next, and he pushed open the door. He hadn't taken two steps in when he saw the lights—and the woman.

A dark-haired female on her knees in a child-like pose, with her arms wrapped around her middle. She was illuminated by lights—all circled around her but her face was turned toward the wall. He couldn't tell whether she was alive or dead. Even as he swore—sensing the worst—he began to pray.

In seconds, he'd crossed the room and was dialing 911. He

felt for a pulse on the woman's neck, but as soon as he leaned over and could see the face, he knew.

It was Lillian Wilkins. And she was definitely dead.

"Fuck," Shane swore again.

Emergency answered. He gave the address and the nature of the emergency. He stood, but couldn't tear his eyes away.

Lillian's eyes were open and looked to him full of fear. Her nose was bloodied, one eyebrow was cut. But the worst part was her mouth. It had a black tape X. A big one, from cheekbone to chin in both directions. And the plastic—she had plastic wrappers and a mess of food—stuffed in her mouth, her jaw pushed wide.

This was one sick—

He needed to return to Max. Right now.

"We need Detective Danny Iocavelli," he told the dispatcher, interrupting her next question. He spun turning his back on the gruesome scene just as the door banged open.

"What's taking so—"

"Don't look," he ordered and charged toward her, aiming to block her view and hustle her out of the room.

But it was too late. Her face had gone ashen and she screamed, "Noooo!"

Max tried to rush forward, but Shane caught her. She beat on him but he forcibly turned her around so that she couldn't see more. She didn't need any more disturbing visuals in her head.

"Let me go! Let me go to her!"

"It's too late, honey," Shane said. "She's gone."

He carried her from the room, and pressed her back against the wall in the hallway, his body against her front.

"No, no, no," she moaned, grabbing fistfuls of his shirt and sobbing into his chest.

CHAPTER 32

ONCE MAX AND SHANE had been cleared to leave the office by Detective Iocavelli and the investigative team, they'd headed home to her apartment. The office—in fact the whole building—had been shut down for the time being.

Max had gone through the gamut today—horror, grief, anger. Shane wasn't sure where she stood at this point. As soon as they entered the apartment, she sank onto the foyer bench and leaned her head back against the wall, eyes shut.

"Max?" Shane asked.

She waved a hand at him. "Just go. Do your check."

Shane felt a tug of concern, but his first priority was keeping her safe. When he returned, she hadn't moved. He squatted in front of her and put his hands on her hips, his forearms along her legs.

"What do you need?" he asked.

She sighed heavily. "A nap. I just…don't want to think for a while."

"Done," he said. He slipped off her heels, pulled her phone from her bag, and grasped her hands to pull her to her feet.

Shane led her to her bedroom. "You want to get into something more comfortable?"

She nodded and went into the closet. She came out in leggings and a sweatshirt, and then went directly into the bathroom. He heard water running.

He didn't know Lillian as well as Max did. He hadn't hired

her, hadn't had plans for her future. But he did feel responsible. Frustration, disbelief, and grief churned inside him. He could only imagine how she felt.

And he'd give anything if he knew what in the world to do to ease her pain.

He turned down the covers and waited. When Max came out, her eyes were still red and puffy, but her face was scrubbed clean of makeup. She looked so much younger, so vulnerable, that Shane wanted to wrap her up and hold her tight and safe until all this disappeared. Maybe longer.

She took one look at the bed and shook her head. She went to the other room—to the same daybed he'd found her sleeping in that first night. She grabbed a big throw off the end and lay down on top of the comforter.

"Join me?" she asked.

At this point, there was nothing he wouldn't do, so he kicked off his shoes, shrugged out of his blazer, and removed his holster—laying it on the side table within reach. He climbed over her to the wall side, and pulled her in to spoon against his front. He folded a pillow over, and she adjusted hers to be able to hug it.

He noticed some tissues tucked into her sleeve. She'd probably learned that trick from the Wise Ones. One of his grandmothers used to do the same with her hanky.

Shane stroked her hair. She shuddered but eventually her body relaxed and she slept.

He simply held her and considered things. Ways to make push come to shove. Ways to make a killer come out of hiding, to mess up. Everybody'd had enough of this guy's sick games. Shane and Joe had women on their team—beautiful ones, even. They'd be willing to pose as bait—but other than choosing Max's agency, no one knew what really set this guy off. Why now? Why these particular girls? Had he chosen them recently or had he been stalking them for a while?

Max tensed in her sleep, and Shane pulled her tighter and pressed a kiss to her hair.

She sighed and his thoughts turned inward again. There was his other worry. He'd been trying to just enjoy, to not think too far ahead, but the truth was, he didn't want to walk away when Max no longer needed his protection. The fact was that to some degree he'd always had a thing for her. But now that he'd spent real time with her? Now that they'd been intimate? Now that he'd discovered that they matched up well, and dammit, he actually, really, truly enjoyed this woman's company?

He didn't want to give her up. Period.

But he didn't want to be just some guy she'd conquered and was currently playing with. And he certainly didn't want to be there because she was paying him.

He wanted to be her steady man. To actually date her, as in take her to dinner, or to a club to dance, or for a stroll through the park on a warm night, or to get gelato after visiting an art gallery. The *normal* stuff.

He wanted—if it got serious—to get to know her crazy grandmother and aunt, and Miranda and Eddie better, as well as let her get to know the twins, and Joe and Tricia, and Mrs. Costa, too.

When Max woke, she turned over and snuggled into his chest. "Thank you," she said. "I slept easier with you here."

Shane knew that sleep was a form of emotional defense—that she'd needed a respite and blocking it out with sleep was it.

"Why this room?" he asked.

She shrugged a shoulder. "It's cozier, less exposed. Feels safe. I don't know why."

Because, Shane thought, it was private. She reserved it only for herself. She didn't invite men to this room—except for him.

"And yet you wanted me to join you?"

"You make me feel safe, too."

That was good, Shane thought. Dare he hope that she was letting him in? That she felt as he did? That she might be willing to see where this went—after?

———

Max had zero appetite after the events of the day. Shane was trying to convince her to eat something, to keep her strength up.

"For what?" She'd snapped at him.

"For come what may," he replied.

"That's supposed to make me feel better?" she asked. Then held up a hand in apology. She knew he meant well, she just wasn't ready. "Don't worry about me. Please. You just eat."

He didn't look happy about it, but he turned and began to rummage through her fridge. With a man to feed these last couple of weeks, she had stocked up. She just didn't know at this point what was in there.

Just then Max's house phone rang, and it indicated it was the guard from downstairs.

"There's a Detective Iocavelli here to see you," he said.

Immediately Max felt a combination of fear and hope.

Would the police interrogate her some more—ask more questions she didn't have the answers to? Or would the detective have something concrete this time? Something to nail this bastard.

Iocavelli greeted her, then the men did that men-hug-back-slap-thing.

Shane said, "Tell us you've got good news."

Iocavelli grimaced.

Max wrapped her arms around herself. More long haul then.

"Come sit," she told him, and they settled around the kitchen table while Shane made a single cup of coffee for Iocavelli.

"He's an addict," Shane explained.

"Goes with the job," the detective said.

He took the first sip the second it was handed to him, and said, "The night guard, Keenan Smith, was drugged."

"What?" Max asked, incredulous.

Shane swore softly.

"Yeah," Iocavelli said. "He said he suddenly felt funny, worried he was having a heart attack without the pain. Laid his head on the desk, thinking it might help. By the time he tried to get up, he couldn't and fell. He lay behind the desk for hours. He was too mortified to tell the next shift. He'd soiled himself."

"Security cameras?"

"A guy came through at 11:47 p.m. Hat, hoodie, bandana, gloves, head down. Didn't pause at the desk, jumped the turnstile and went directly to the fourth floor. Hooded the cameras in the hall there."

Shane rubbed a hand over his scruff. "Not exactly a split-second crime of passion."

Iocavelli shook his head. "Victim came through at midnight. Slinky dress, long coat open in the front, heels. She glanced at the desk and slipped under the turnstile."

Max frowned. "A rendezvous." She had uncomfortable ideas about that.

"Yeah, looks like."

"What about the earlier tapes?" Shane asked.

"As in who slipped the guard a roofie?" Iocavelli asked. "Here's where it gets interesting."

Max didn't find any of this interesting, entertaining or fascinating, but detectives were surely a different breed.

Iocavelli continued, "We got Damien Closse—"

Max sucked in her breath too fast, too loud.

"Hang on there," Iocavelli said. "Damien left around seven—right when Keenan happened to wander off to the john. Damien went around behind the desk and took a good look at the screen. We can't see his hands." He continued, "Then we got Cameron Bender on his way out. He says something to Keenan, returns in a few with a coffee for the guy. They chat a minute and he leaves."

"Cam often gets the night guys coffee," Max said. There was no way, just no way…

"True," Iocavelli said. "We've got the same scenario on other tapes. And then a half hour later, we've also got a food delivery from the local Pho takeout place."

"The timing could have worked for any of those," Shane said.

"Yeah," Iocavelli said. "We don't have tox back yet, but any of the so-called date rape drugs would have had poor unsuspecting Keenan laid out flat before eleven o'clock."

"We're talking to the restaurant people of course, but Closse and Bender are looking better." He slugged the remainder of his coffee. "We've also got calls to Lillian's phone from both of them."

That didn't surprise Max either. Cam would have called all the models at some point or another and often regularly, and Damien, if he was having an affair with Lillian, certainly would have called her… She just wished Iocavelli wouldn't call them by their last names like that. She understood that they were suspects, but impersonalizing them like a file card made those possibilities real. If not to her, then to the detective.

Max rubbed her temples. She'd been a last name only to the detective, too, for a while. What had changed? Did he know that she and Shane were sleeping together? Had Shane given a statement verifying her all-night-every-night-with-him alibi?

Oh, who cared. She just wanted this over. She wanted her models safe. She wanted the sicko responsible behind bars. She wanted normalcy.

What she didn't want was her friend Cam or her co-worker Damien to be a psychotic murderer.

Shane reminded Iocavelli about the night he'd chased down Cam in the stairwell.

The detective said, "Just because his story that night checked out, doesn't mean we won't revisit it. Nobody gets a free pass."

Max placed her hands on the table and looked at Iocavelli. "There's no way Cam would be meeting Lillian for a tryst. He's gay. Out and flaming." She saw Shane nod, out of the corner of her eye. "As for Damien, he's slept with other models. I've had to have a chat with him about keeping it in his pants—but it's always mutual as far as I know. You could argue sexual harassment, but a lot of them do just as much for his career as he does for theirs. And murder," she gulped, "is a whole different stratosphere."

Shane said, "From what I saw at that shoot, she had it bad for Closse."

Iocavelli only said, "We've talked to her friends. They'd been screwing for a while. Friends said it was clear Closse wasn't looking for anything more than sex, but she didn't care."

Max blew out a breath, and with it a silent prayer for all of them.

"What do you need from us?" Shane asked.

Iocavelli shrugged. "Just wanted to let you know where we stood. I may have questions later for Ms. Ricci here."

Again, Max thought that something had changed if he was being this forthcoming. Maybe it was simply that he now felt he had viable suspects.

"Then again," Iocavelli said as he stood, "we may just get a confession."

Oh, God, Max thought, as her heart hit the floor. Both Damien and Cam were in custody.

CHAPTER 33

IOCAVELLI HAD TOLD them the office would be off limits at least another day. Max had flinched at that, but Shane knew she no longer cared about the loss of productivity. She'd said she was having a hard time even imagining going back to that studio—ever. And then there was the hard fact that two of her staff were being interrogated for murder.

They slept once more in the guest room in the small trundle bed. They weren't intimate, and although he always wanted her, Shane was glad for it. She needed to be held. She needed rest.

Although Max slept fitfully, she seemed to find comfort in turning to him every time she woke. That, in turn, somehow comforted Shane.

First thing in the morning, Max went to her home office nook and sent out a message to the entire Ivory staff. They'd honor any outside appointments—Shane's team was scheduled for coverage anyway and would remain so until the police officially charged someone—but the office was officially in mourning and would be closed entirely today and throughout the weekend.

"What about you?" Shane had asked.

Max wrapped her arms around herself and shook her head.

"Come here," he said, and pulled her up out of her chair. He held her and rubbed her back.

She shuddered, but little by little she settled into him. And eventually, she raised her face to his.

"Kiss it away," she said.

Shane kissed her gently, taking his time, cupping her head with his hand.

She kissed him back and her hands explored his back, then his sides, and wandered up his chest.

They took it slow at first. Soon, however, he scooped her up and carried her to the big bedroom. She stood next to the bed and stripped off her clothes. She kept her eyes on him, watching him take her in.

"Let's shower," she murmured, and turned her back on him.

He could no more tear his eyes from her generous, sexy backside than he could keep himself from rising to the occasion.

Shane discarded his clothes on the way.

Their lovemaking was slow and languid. All warm water, steamy mirrors, and wet mouths. Max was as sexy as ever—he'd never tire of this woman—and yet he could see the desperation in her eyes.

Shane tried not to think about it, but it almost felt as if she had begun saying goodbye.

————

They got the call a few hours later, and Max put the phone on speaker so that Shane could hear.

"Closse is in lock up," Detective Iocavelli said. "He's been formally charged."

"Dear God," Max said and covered her mouth with both hands.

Shane wrapped his arm around her and rubbed her arms. "He confessed?" Shane asked.

"Hell, no. This one's pleading not-guilty the whole way," Iocavelli said. "He admits to having an affair with Lillian Wilkens and with Gia Serra, but he swears he never harmed a hair on their heads besides a bit of rough sex."

"What about Helena?" Max asked.

"Claims he'd only met her the once," the detective said.

Max frowned. That seemed right. They hadn't even had her hair done yet. She wouldn't have had a shoot with Damien until later.

Iocavelli couldn't hear her wheels turning though. He said, "We found a key to Serra's apartment in his place. Boyfriend says they'd almost broken up over her affair with Closse. She'd promised to break it off with him, and he'd promised to tour less frequently." Iocavelli recited facts like he was reading off a grocery list. "Closse has priors for battery and disturbing the peace. Like the others, Willkens doesn't appear to be sexually violated, but we'll know better after the full M.E.'s report. Closse's prints are all over Lillian's apartment, and they lifted a good one from a granola bar wrapper with the body."

Shane squeezed her hand, just about the time she started to fear her stomach wouldn't hold through this horrid conversation.

Iocavelli said, "Must have been getting sloppy because one of his prints was also found on the gaffer's tape used on Willkens. And he's got more access to those colored sheets than anyone else."

Max squeezed her eyes shut—as if that would shut out his words.

"So Cam's been cleared?" Shane asked.

"Yeah. Sent him home," Iocavelli took a noisy slurp of

something—probably coffee. "Speaking of, you can head home, too. Ms. Ricci there no longer needs your services."

Max looked up at Shane. His jaw was tight, but he simply said to his cousin, "Thanks, man."

"Thank you, Detective," Max added.

"Yeah, sure. I'll be in touch," Iocavelli said.

Max hung up and set the phone on the coffee table.

"Damien?" She sank down onto the couch. "How is it even possible?"

Shane just shook his head.

"I just can't believe it's actually over," she said. She didn't feel any different. She didn't feel relieved or celebratory or anything. Everything she felt was heavy, uneasy. Utter shock and disbelief about Damien. Horror for what Cam had surely gone through in the last twenty-four hours. Grief for the models and their loved ones.

"Well, it is," Shane said.

And there was that, too. She was...still scared. Fearful in a different way. Because now Shane would leave. She'd gotten used to having him around. Used to having company, feeling cared for and protected. Safe. Even cherished.

How had he done that? In such a short time? Gotten under her skin? Made her think she needed him?

She didn't need anyone, goddammit. She never had. And she sure wasn't about to start.

Max sat up straight and slapped her hands on her thighs. "Well, back to reality. You should probably pack up."

Shane flinched, and she felt something in her own chest seize. She averted her eyes and stood up.

He stood as well. "Max, just because—"

"Surely Anna and Niall are ready to have you back," Max said in a rush.

Because she couldn't do it—and she couldn't let him do it

either. Just because it'd been good—so good—between them, didn't mean they couldn't just walk away. There was no sense dragging it on, ruining it with jealousies or fights, tainting it with eventual boredom.

She had a business to run—and rules to put back in place now that running it was possible again.

And he had other clients to take on, not to mention a serious deficit in terms of time owed to his twin charges.

All good things came to an end. It didn't—couldn't—matter that she hurt through and through.

CHAPTER 34

NO, NO, NO! His head screamed, replaying the sordid scene like it was yesterday.

Max was his be all end all. She'd been everything to him. The absolute pinnacle of perfection. The sexiest, most sensual, most perfectly proportioned woman he'd ever seen—her body simply made for gorgeous clothing, her attitude and strength enhancing her physical attributes. And for years—years, she'd kept that status.

Except it had all been a lie.

Her skin—it was marred. By her choice. Freckles were god's gift, even moles, when graced with the right placement.

But a tattoo? Ink pushed so deep inside the skin by a needle that it would never, never go away? A gross display that would fade and stretch and become even uglier as the years went on?

It was beyond him—especially from her. The women he used to know and love long ago? They didn't care about their bodies, or about much. Surface beauty was the only thing that mattered to them—a means to an end. He'd been so disappointed when he'd realized they were all the same.

But Max? Max loved her body. She treated it well. She ate carefully, she exercised smartly, she used all the right creams and products, got enough sleep, usually anyway. She never went overboard with gimmicky treatments. All things in moderation, she'd often said.

Permanent body art was *not* moderate. It was heinous. And it was forever.

He felt so betrayed. He'd put his trust in her. He'd believed in her. He'd held her up as the standard for all others.

He felt ill, as if he'd been physically hurt and now was reacting. In fact—

He ran to the bathroom and retched.

When he was spent and lay his cheek on the cold tile of the floor he began to cry. Because her betrayal went even deeper. What she'd *done*. With *him…There* in her sanctuary.

In *his*.

She'd broken her word… Broken her rules and her standards…

Straight up broken Cam's heart.

CHAPTER 35

MAX TOOK CAM out for a celebratory meal, though she felt anything but. He was obviously still shaken, too. "You can't imagine what it's like to be grilled by the police, Max," he'd said. "It was bad enough in an interrogation room. I was petrified they'd throw me in a cell."

It made Max tense, as all she could think of was Damien, behind bars himself. According to Iocavelli, they'd found their serial killer. She was just having a really hard time believing it. Sure Damien could be a grade-A jerk. Arrogant and oftentimes rude. But...a twisted psychopath? A sick murderer?

Goosebumps prickled whenever she thought about it. All the more terrifying precisely because it was so incomprehensible.

Max spent a few days buried in work and burying her head. She didn't even notice a difference between weekday and weekend. It was fairly easy to keep busy during the day with all her models scrambling to make up lost appointments and lost time.

But it was no good at night. She didn't feel like herself. If she was being frank with herself, she missed Shane.

On Monday evening, with no Wise Ones dinner scheduled because Aggie and Cora were spending a few days in the country, she decided that maybe a night out was the answer. Miranda couldn't join her, but that was perhaps just as well.

She enhanced her eye makeup, brushed her teeth, and fluffed her hair.

In her closet, she surveyed the skirts first. "No, no, no..." she murmured. She fingered a black jersey knit wrap dress, then shook her head. "Sorry, Jersey," she said, "not feeling you."

Max moved on to the pants. "Ah, you'll do," she told her favorite tight leather pants.

She chose a low cut blouse with a necklace that ended just between her breasts. Heels, of course.

Back to the mirror for deep red lipstick, and she was ready. On the outside at least.

Max headed for Twenty. Nearby, familiar, and nice, it was one of her favorite local places. As she settled at the bar, however, all she could think of was the night she'd been here with Shane in tow. The heat of his stare searing her even as she'd flirted with those other men.

"You lost your shadow," the bartender Samuel said.

"I did," she said. "Bodyguards tend to disappear like smoke when the danger's gone."

"Saw it on the news. That's good they caught the guy," he said. "What'll it be?"

Nothing sounded good, actually, so she chose something light. A glass of Sauvignon Blanc.

Someone slid into the seat next to her. "Should I be hurt you didn't call?"

It was the man whose rear she'd felt up, that night, just to stick it to Shane. And maybe he *should* be hurt, because she'd forgotten all about him, and had forgotten his name, as well.

She forced herself to smile widely. "I've been busy. Don't hold it against me," she said.

"I couldn't hold anything against a woman as beautiful as you," he said.

"Sir," Samuel said, "what can I get for you?"

Max said, "It's on me, Samuel." She winked at her stool mate. "My apology."

Time to get reacquainted. If she got into him, well then, she could count on getting past missing Shane. If she couldn't...

———

Shane and the twins had finished dinner. Niall was on dishes, Anna was setting out snacks and filling water bottles for them to take to school tomorrow.

Shane wiped the table, then picked up and dropped the mail. He opened the cupboard and closed it. He considered catching up on some paperwork, but the truth was, he couldn't settle to any one task. His mind kept returning to Max.

He didn't like the way they had left things. Okay fine—he didn't care for the way she'd booted him out the first second she could. There was more to it than simply sending him home to the twins. More to it than getting back to work, or even taking some time alone.

He kept thinking of Cora's parting shot that night that Aggie had snooped and found his things in Max's bedroom. Max had claimed she didn't know what Cora had meant by the warning, but it wasn't such a stretch to figure out. Shane had never heard Max talk about her father, or her mother for that matter. Seemingly they'd split or been otherwise unfit, and Aggie and her husband had raised Max, along with Great Aunt Cora it seemed. Max had been scarred, whether she wanted to admit it or not.

Shane didn't give a feck about her history, or her fears.

The fact was—he *missed* her in his life. He *hurt* at her instantaneous dismissal. He *ached* to see her, to *hold* her, to make *love* to her.

Jaysus. He'd fallen hard.

And he believed—no, he *knew*—the feeling was mutual. Now that they weren't working together, there was no reason they shouldn't be together. Surely whatever her other concerns were could be talked through, or would ease with time and trust.

And as for her habit of playing the field? That didn't worry him. He liked her just the way she was. It's what had drawn him in the first place. Max was flirty and sensual. Sexy and demanding and unapologetic. She could be all that with one man.

She *had* been all that with him these last few weeks. She hadn't tired of him, hadn't needed anyone else—and she wouldn't. Because he was the *right* one. They were good together—really, phenomenally great together, in fact.

Shane grabbed his wallet from the counter, snagged his leather coat off the hook, and opened the front door.

"*Where* are you going?" Anna demanded.

"Sorry—I just decided I," he shook his head, "need to go out for a while."

"To?" Anna said, as Niall came up behind her. Both of them eyeing him up with suspicion, and once more he felt his sister Janet's presence. She'd been almost a mother to him when he was young, doling out a swat or a kiss, depending on what he deserved. Heck, if she'd been around to witness his moping the last few days, she'd have been the first to give him a push right out the door.

Shane grinned. "I'm going to get my girl."

"It's about time," Anna said.

"Amen to that," Niall agreed.

Shane laughed. These apples definitely hadn't fallen far from their tree. "I won't be late."

The twins exchanged a look. "We won't wait up," Anna said.

———

Shane didn't even consider calling ahead to let Max know he was headed over. He refused to give her a chance to say no or time to make excuses. He wanted to see her face, gauge her reaction. Besides, he felt good about this.

So good that he had the cabbie stop when he saw a bodega with fresh bouquets outside. He could walk the rest of the way. If he was going to properly court Max, he may as well start now. Granted, he would have preferred a florist, he thought, choosing a mostly fresh grouping. He shook his head but went in and paid, sure she'd know his options were limited at this hour. It was the thought that counted, right?

Shane was three blocks from her place when he realized he was about to pass Twenty. The place he'd watched Max flirt for hours, getting both so angry and so hot for her, that he'd lost his head entirely. Antagonized her and baited her. Planted a kiss on her that would have melted Greenland. But she'd kissed him back measure for measure. That had been the beginning, and what a beginning it had been.

Shane grinned.

He glanced through the window as he passed. He did a double take and stopped dead in his tracks.

Max was in there. *With* feckin' Inspector Gadget.

The guy helped her into her coat, his mouth close to her ear. Whatever he said made her laugh.

He was so shocked, it took a minute for him to process, then Shane's heart exploded into sharp fragments—the points laced with humiliation. Anger shot his temperature high. His hands clenched into fists, and the foulest string of curses burst from his lips.

Gadget snaked his arm around Max, and they headed for the door.

Black Widow was back. And she hadn't wasted any time.

Apparently he wasn't the right man for her after all. He'd only been the most convenient one. His stomach turned with a sick twist.

He clenched the flowers in his hand and then threw them twenty feet to the garbage can at the corner. He heard them bounce off the side, but his legs were already moving of their own accord. He was across the street in seconds flat. He didn't want to be seen. Not by the bartender, not by that jerk, and definitely not by her.

In fact, he didn't want to lay eyes on her either—not ever again.

CHAPTER 36

MAX HAD TRIED Shane numerous times. Maybe her vague messages didn't seem urgent enough, because he hadn't called her back.

Maybe she should just be bold instead and leave a message that said, "I miss you, can we talk?"

Or maybe she should just be herself and text him. *I'm slipping into bed naked. Use your key and surprise me...*

Maybe she was delusional, and he didn't want anything to do with her.

That last morning, she'd sensed that he'd been hesitant to leave, that he'd been willing to see where this—they—might go...

She'd thought that *she'd* been the one to balk and say a hasty goodbye.

But who knew? It could be he was relieved. That he'd taken the handy exit pass she'd handed him, and gladly.

Still—she couldn't go on like this. It was driving her mad. She had to know: was there a chance at a future with Shane or not?

So she'd decided to deliver the last check she owed to O'Rourke Security to him personally. She'd talked to the secretary and found out Shane was in the office and should be until five p.m. She'd abandoned work and run home to freshen up and sexy up. She wore a body hugging skirt and high heels and a loose off-the-shoulder top. Dangling earrings and bangle bracelets. Her favorite sexy perfume and her favorite trolling lipstick.

But the only man she wanted to pick up was Shane. He'd ruined her for other men.

She'd realized that the other night when the man at Twenty hadn't done if for her—because there was *nothing* wrong with that guy. He was handsome, successful, charming, and engaging. He obviously wanted her, and yet beyond insisting he'd escort her home via cab for safety's sake, he hadn't pushed. Before Shane? He'd have been a very good time.

Now however, Shane's was the only attention she craved. Shane's was the only body she desired. Shane's were the only arms she wanted to hold her all night.

Shane, Shane, Shane...

Dammit.

Just what in the world was she going to do if he'd been avoiding her on purpose? If he wasn't willing to...just see... where they might end up.

Max's musings had gotten her all the way here, and now she stood right outside the door to the O'Rourke offices. She wiped her sweaty palms on her coat—a new Stella McCartney no less—and took a deep breath.

She reached for the doorknob but jumped when it suddenly swung open.

Shane. Her heart gave a little leap. She was both elated to see him and worried he didn't want to see her.

Indeed, his face registered surprise and pleasure for only a split second, and then became closed and—and what? Suspicious? Distrustful? Whatever that look was, it wasn't good.

"Hi," she said.

He raised an eyebrow.

"I came to—"

"I was just leaving," he interrupted. "Dawn will help you." He angled his body to the side and extended an arm toward the woman at the desk.

Max raised her chin. She didn't know what his problem was, and she wasn't about to turn tail and slink off—not yet anyway.

Max planted herself firmly in the doorway. "You're the only one who can help me."

Shane snorted—actually snorted—and said, "Yeah, right."

"Let's continue this in private," Max said. She stormed past him and his admin Dawn whose eyes had bugged out. Max dropped her bag with a thunk in the center of Shane's desk. She turned around, crossed her arms and glared at him.

He glared back, stalked forward, and slammed the door behind him.

She didn't waste time. "What was that comment supposed to mean exactly?"

He looked at her like she was crazy. "It meant, you and I both know just about any man can service you."

"How dare you?" Max's blood boiled.

"No, Max," he said, taking a step into her personal space, staring her down. "How dare *you*. You're going to strut in here like you could be special to me? Like I'm special to you?"

He looked her over, disgust plain as day on his face now. The feeling was mutual, but still she tried, "I thought—"

But he was on a roll, his eyes blazing. "You don't *do* special. Do you? You couldn't even wait a week."

Max had considered a lot of outcomes to this visit, but never this. She was so angry, so hurt and shocked.

She grabbed her purse. She didn't need this. She'd never taken crap from anyone, she'd never let anyone malign her. She wasn't about to start now. Normally, she could yell and sling insults with the best of them—but she didn't understand the origins of this battle. It was too much of a turnabout from where they'd left off, and apparently she didn't have all the facts.

Max walked tall and held her chin high. She dropped Ivory's big, fat check on Dawn's desk blotter. "Please see that *Joe* gets this," she said.

Dawn—who'd obviously heard every loud, charged word she and Shane had spoken—nodded mutely.

"Thank you," Max said. She walked out and didn't once look back.

If only it was that easy for her bruised heart.

————

"He didn't even give me a chance," Max said, sniffing. She sat tucked up into her couch in leggings and a sweatshirt, an empty cup—she never let herself buy a whole pint—of premium ice cream on the coffee table. When the ice cream hadn't done it, she'd called Miranda.

Miranda handed her another tissue. "Something must have happened to turn him sour."

"Oh something happened all right," Max said.

Miranda raised her eyebrows.

Max sighed. "I went to Twenty the other night and from what Shane said—or didn't say exactly—I'm gathering he saw me with this guy."

"Oh Max, you didn't," Miranda said.

Max pursed her lips. "Et, tu? Should I call you Brute?"

"Oh, come on," Miranda said. "It's your M.O. And you know damn well I love you regardless, so just tell me." She squeezed Max's hand.

Max squeezed back. "Well, nothing happened. I didn't sleep with the guy. I didn't do anything more than flirt. But I did go there on purpose, as a test." She pulled the blanket up higher on her chest. "I'd been obsessing over Shane. I thought if I got out there and someone else could do it for me, everything was fine. I was still me. I wasn't ruined forever." Max caught Miranda trying not to laugh. "This is *not* funny."

"Sorry," she said and did laugh. "You're just so dramatic. Go on."

Max sighed, with dramatics. "I figured if I found a willing playmate and couldn't get into it? Well then I'd know. I'd have to do something about Shane."

"Oh, sweetie, you do know that settling down with one guy isn't the worst thing in the world, right? Look at how happy Eddie and I are."

"You aren't me," Max complained. "I'm no good at this."

"How would you know? You've never tried it."

Max grimaced. "True."

"What do you want out of it?" Miranda asked. "Are you thinking marriage and babies and growing old—" She stopped short when she saw Max's face.

"I was thinking of *committing* to seeing him. You know, exclusively. That alone would have been a pretty big step for me."

Miranda patted Max's knee. "All right, so now what?"

Max shrugged. "I'll mope tonight and then pour myself into work and try to move on."

"You could try again," Miranda said. "Give him a few days to calm down. Then maybe he'll listen rather than jumping to conclusions."

"I don't think so. For one, why am I going to push a relationship with someone who so easily thinks the worst of me? And for another, he might well be right."

"Max," Miranda said sternly, "Just because you haven't done a long-term relationship doesn't mean you can't."

"I—"

"Let me finish." Miranda swatted Max's leg. "You *are* the kind of person who *can*. Once you make a commitment you stick to it. Look at your dedication to making a go of Ivory, to all your models and staff. Look at all you did to keep them safe and working while all the craziness was going on. God, we thought you might even be in jeopardy and you wouldn't leave them."

Max picked at the fuzz on the afghan, but Miranda wasn't done.

"Look at your devotion to your family—to Aggie, even though she drives you nuts half the time." Miranda said, "Look at me. You've been my rock for years."

"I have been a good friend, haven't I?" Max smiled.

"The best," Miranda said. "And you'll be a good significant other, too. My advice? Go for it. Men have their pride. If Shane saw you flirting with that guy? He's definitely nursing a big wound. But I saw the way he looks at you—before you were even intimate. He likes you—*really* likes you."

"You think?" Max asked and felt a little unfurling in her chest. Was that hope? Was she crazy?

"I don't just think so. I *know*," Miranda said. "Besides, if he shuts you down again, you'll be no worse off than you are now." She smiled. "If he doesn't…"

Lord, Max thought. Being shut down again would hurt. There wouldn't be a bandage big enough.

But a committed relationship? Now that was truly terrifying.

CHAPTER 37

MAX DECIDED TO bite the bullet and ask Cora exactly what she'd meant with her cryptic comment about Shane not being like her father. The sisters were home from the country house, so she stopped at Aggie's penthouse, bearing some matzoh soup from the Wise One's favorite Jewish deli.

"To what do we owe this surprise visit, dear?" Cora said.

Aggie said, "Don't press a gift horse. She brought soup—that means she wants something and therefore we're better off not asking."

Max couldn't help but roll her eyes. "Have you already eaten?"

As it turned out they had, but they forced some soup on Max even though she hadn't much appetite. Nonetheless it bolstered her. She'd left her platform heels at the door and now shifted her feet onto the kitchen chair. As if a yoga sit would keep her grounded for this.

"I wanted to talk to you both." Max turned to face Cora who sat at the end of the table. "You said that Shane isn't like my dad."

"Uh-oh," Aggie said. "She sabotaged it, just like you said she would, and that looker up and left her."

Max winced. "Not exactly. But we'll leave it at that."

Aggie rolled her eyes. Cora clasped her hands together on

the table and fixed Max with an understanding look. She said, "I've long worried that you'd think all men are leavers."

"Despite the fact that your grandfather who *raised* you—" Aggie shot Max a stern look "—wasn't a leaver. He was as steadfast as they come."

Grandpa Giovanni was the best. She missed him still. They all did. Max asked, "Is that a word? A leaver?"

"It may not be a word," Aggie said, "but it's a thing."

Cora didn't let Max or Aggie drag her off track. "From the start, your father was always chasing something. The next adventure, the next woman, the next job."

"Job, ha," Aggie added. "Scheme is more like it."

"He never outgrew it and it was clear he never would," Cora said. "The day he came home with a pregnant girl, your grandparents *knew* they'd be raising that baby."

Aggie said, "Best day of our lives. We got a do-over. And we got you."

Max's heart swelled with love for her grandparents, Aggie and Grandpa Giovanni, God rest his steadfast soul. "You've never said much about my mother."

Aggie flipped her hand in a motion of disgust. "Bosh," she said, "there's nothing to say."

"The truth is, dear," Cora said, "none of us really got a chance to get to know her. The pair of them were always out and about even while Carina was pregnant. And she had eyes only for your father. Wherever Giovanni Junior went, Carina went. Period. When Gianni decided soon after you were born to head to Europe to round up investors for—goodness, I don't even remember what, do you, Aggie?"

Aggie wore a puss of an expression and waved her hand. "It's not important now."

Cora nodded. "True enough. The point is, when your

father left, your mother went with him. And we all just let them."

Cora included herself in the 'we' because she and Aggie had always been a team, and Aggie's marriage hadn't changed that. Great Aunt Cora had been just as much a part of Max's upbringing as her grandparents.

"Huh," Max said. She crushed a cracker into bits over her bowl. "So my mother wasn't so much a leaver as a follower? Or a romantic schmoe?"

"A follower and a schmoe," Aggie said.

"A romantic as well," Cora said. "Either way, it wasn't a very promising combination, especially in conjunction with her devotion to your father."

"Wow, this is a lot to digest." Max rubbed her temples. "Sooooo," she said, "I'm actually more like him than her."

"Good lord, child." Cora reared back. "Is that what you think? We thought your lifestyle meant you'd somehow decided that all men were leavers and they were only good for one thing. That you weren't willing to get close enough to allow yourself to be abandoned by another man, like your father abandoned you."

Max cringed. She hated that the Wise Ones even thought about her sex life.

"Uh, no," she said. "I kinda figured I just didn't have any staying power in my genes."

"Maxine," Aggie said and slapped the table for emphasis. "You are *nothing* like either of your parents."

———

Max had been keeping busy. Today for instance, she'd attended two outdoor shoots, one fitting and one consult with a trusted stylist. She needed the stylist to reign in her errant model fast. Otherwise the woman would end up in the worst-dressed pages of this year's most popular weekly magazine—bad for the model, but also bad for Ivory.

She was just settling at her desk in the office when Cam walked in. She flinched—every single time he entered since the office had reopened. Because he had to walk right past the table where he'd seen her poised over Shane—in flagrante delicto.

Which was exactly why one did not do the dirty at the office.

Especially when one's partner was going to turn out to be a real schmendrik.

The damn image was seared in her brain forever, and so was the regret.

She slumped back in her chair. "Please make an appointment with Serge, that interior decorator I like," Max told Cam.

"For?" Cam asked. He was nothing if not nosy. He held one hand behind his back but perched on the chair facing her desk.

"This office," she said.

He looked around the room, his eyes skipping past the table. Yep, ugh, she definitely needed a hauler for the table. Then Serge and his magic would wipe out any remaining memories with a fresh look.

"How are things going out there?" she asked.

Cam shrugged. He was surprisingly tight-lipped these days.

"Not back to normal yet, then." Max sighed. "Things don't feel right to me either," she said. "It's like heavy turbulence on a flight, except even though it's okay now, my stomach just won't settle, and I'm still gripping the arms of the chair." She leaned forward. "How about you?"

"I know just how you feel," he said.

"You haven't heard anything more about Damien, have you?" she asked, both wanting to know and not wanting to.

"No…you?" Cam looked uncomfortable. He probably didn't really want more information either.

She shook her head and swallowed hard. "I still just can't wrap my head around it."

Cam's lips pressed tight. "It's…just impossible." He shut his eyes for a long moment then shook himself a bit—rather like a dog shaking off the rain. He leaned forward and produced a slim gift-wrapped box from behind his back. "On a happier note, though," Cam said. He smiled, although it didn't reach his eyes.

Max could relate. It'd be a long time, until she did much more than move through the motions.

"What's this?" she asked.

"Patience, patience," Cam said.

She read the tiny note card. *Thanks for pulling out all the stops to keep us safe. Forever yours, all of us at Ivory.*

"Awwww," she said and pulled the ribbon.

Inside, Max found a gift certificate. One week at the Bodhi in California—the same place Gia had told Max she was going to and then didn't. Not that Cam or anyone else in the office would know that.

"Oh my, God. They shouldn't have," Max exclaimed.

"Don't fuss. Just rejuvenate. You need it. Pronto."

Normally she planned far in advance to get away. Given everything that had happened lately though, a retreat would do her worlds of good.

Cam reached out as if to squeeze her hand, but instead

placed his palm on her desk. "Put that bumpy flight behind you once and for all."

He was absolutely right. She should go as soon as possible. No, she *would*.

"It's too much, but I love it." She was so touched that her eyes got a little teary. "Cam, were you behind this?"

"Of course. I'm behind everything around here," he said.

CHAPTER 38

SHANE AND A few others from his team had spent most of the day guarding a visiting dignitary during a speech at the UN, and then had escorted him and his wife to LaGuardia airport for a small charter flight. He was glad for it. He'd been on that assignment ever since he'd stopped working for Max, and it was a boring one—meaning he had way too much time to stew.

The kids had after-school programs to attend, so he hit Dub's gym. He'd needed it bad. He willed his anger into his fists, forcing out that negative energy little by little with every slam to the bag.

The last time Max had booted him—out of her company and modeling rather than out of her personal life and her bed—he'd been young. Still wild, still full of pent up energy, righteousness, arrogance and yeah—even ignorance. He couldn't say hitting a fight club now wasn't tempting, but he was a guardian now, a father for all intents and purposes, and he couldn't go and do stupid crap like that any longer.

He'd hoped to pick up a decent round in the ring, but so far the place was unusually quiet. The bag it was then, he thought, as he grunted through another set.

He was still thinking—and trying not to think—about Max.

Nobody made him as crazy as she did. She was so god-damned gorgeous, so vivacious, so sexy. He missed her laugh, her walk, her smart, sassy mouth. He missed the way she talked to her clothing when she chose an outfit, the way her brow knit when she concentrated on work. The way she moved, the way she touched him, the way her voice caught just before she came.

Damn. He needed to be thinking about what he *didn't* like about Max. The way she'd dismissed him so easily the minute the job was over, how casually she'd turned to someone else.

He hit the bag again—so hard he felt the jar of it in his brain.

Max was the one person who could always make him lose his head and say the most god-awful things. True or not, some things just shouldn't be said out loud. If he'd had even a lick of sense, he would have just heard her out at his office, kept his pie hole shut, and hustled her out the door fast so he never had to think about her again.

Instead, here he was kicking himself over his unchecked gob. And wondering—like a true sucker—why she'd come.

He could just hear his sister, "Well, ye wee idjit, if ye'd shut yer own trap long enough to hear her out, you'd know, wouldn't ya?"

He shook his head. Janet had never left Ireland, not even on holiday, and had an accent as thick as the foam on a perfect Guinness. Rather she'd had. Would it have eased if he'd have brought her over here like he'd promised?

He missed his sister something fierce. As did the twins, he knew. Perhaps this summer they should take a vacation home. Or maybe, like cousin Danny as a kid, he ought to send them to the extended family for the bulk of the summer break. Would it do them good, or bring the horror of their mother's death rushing back?

He leaned his head against the bag. So much to worry about now that he had the kids. Like a blooming idiot he'd even started to think he might end up with a partner in Max, someone to share the worries with or bounce thoughts of off. Yeah right. She'd never even darkened his door.

Shane straightened and rolled his shoulders. He was spent and dripping. It'd have to be enough for today. Maybe he'd stop on the way home and see if Danny was at the precinct. His cousin might be able to give him some advice.

Right then, Shane heard his cell ring from the bench nearby. He sprinted over, in case it was Anna or Niall—or maybe Max. Shane snatched it up and checked the display. None of the above, but Joe rated as well.

"What's up?" Shane asked.

"Good news," his Uncle said.

"Yeah?" Shane asked. Like… Max had rented a billboard at Yankee Stadium that said *I was an idiot, Shane, will you be mine*? Fat chance.

Joe said, "That lawyer called. Sorrelle dropped the lawsuit."

"*Yes*." Shane raised his face heavenward and pumped a fist.

He'd always feel he failed Carrie Sorrelle, but O'Rourke Security was safe from ruin, and thanks to Max, just happened to be flush, too.

"That's great news," Shane said. That was really, really great news.

———

As far as Shane was concerned, his cousin Danny looked like total crap. His cousin was so pale that even his many freckles seemed faded, so Shane pushed and cajoled until Danny agreed to leave his desk for a while for some fresh air and a bite at the nearest pub.

Once they'd ordered and Shane broached the subject of the twins summering across the pond, his cousin had laughed in his face. "What makes you think I'd know? I don't have kids."

"No," Shane said, "but surely you remember what it's like to leave your friends and family here every year and then turn around and leave the other half there."

"Eh, it was fine. You get back into whichever routine quick enough. Sometimes it sucked, but in the long run?" Danny lifted a hand. "Family's important."

Shane explained his worry that being home would dredge up bad memories for the twins.

"Why don't you just ask 'em?" Danny said.

Shane barked out a laugh. "Hadn't even thought of that. Thanks."

Danny looked at him sideways. "Is this really what you wanted to pick my brain about?"

"Yeah," Shane said.

"Uh-huh," Danny said. "How's it going with that sexy client of yours?"

"Not my client anymore," Shane said. "As you well know."

"You're still seeing her though, right?"

Shane winced. He'd been that obvious, huh? "Nope. Moved on."

"No shit?" Danny shook his head. "Huh. I thought she was pretty into you."

Embarrassingly, so had he. And that really stung. Yet, he'd known who and how she was. Just because he'd deluded himself into thinking...whatever. Shane said, "She's not one to stick around."

"Sorry to hear it, man."

Shane shrugged again and signaled for another round. "How's the case against Closse coming?"

Danny scrunched up his face. "Mmm."

"What does that mean?"

Danny flipped a hand out, annoyed, as if he were swatting a fly. "I don't even know," Danny said. He took a healthy swig of beer, then set the pint glass down and spun it around and around on the bar, staring at it. Finally he shook his head. "On paper, it looks pretty neat overall, nice and tidy. All sewn up. My chief likes him, the D.A. likes him, the media has this guy buried."

"But?" Shane asked, watching his cousin closely.

He was still shaking his head. "Something just doesn't *feel* right."

"And you trust your gut, most of the time, yeah?" Shane asked.

"In this line of work? Oh, yeah," Danny said. "No different from yours, I'm sure."

It was true, Shane often went with a hunch or suspicion. Instinct was rarely wrong, in fact. He looked at Danny. "Shite."

"Uh-huh," Danny said. He raised his glass. "Here's to hoping I'm wrong."

CHAPTER 39

SHANE HAD SEEN the twins briefly for an early dinner, but the happy hour with Danny had diminished his window of time with them. Then, he'd rushed out for an assignment—escorting a CEO and his wife to an evening soiree nearby. Now, it was nearly one a.m. and he was heading home on foot.

Sometimes the hours got to him, but with school tuition for two, he felt he needed to take all the work he could. The twins handled it better than he did, it seemed. Besides having each other, they were rather independent, and Mrs. Costa, Joe, and Tricia made all the difference. But at some juncture, he'd really have to stop taking protective assignments and do more of the team management. Likely when Joe stepped further aside—but Shane would never push that. As far as Shane was concerned, O'Rourke Security would always be Joe's more than his.

Shane blew out a breath and crossed Columbus Avenue near the twins' favorite diner for pancakes. Maybe they'd go this weekend. Or hey—maybe they'd do breakfast for dinner tomorrow. They'd like that. Pancakes and milkshakes. Not exactly a meal of champions, but it'd make for some wide smiles.

Less than a week ago he would have been thinking about inviting Max, easing her into their lives without freaking her out. He glanced at the diner ruefully. Wasn't gonna happen. Not ever.

In the glass of the restaurant windows, Shane saw a shadowy figure crossing the avenue, walking fast, almost bearing down. He tensed. Except for the occasional car zipping past, splashing through yesterday's puddles, the street was deserted.

He shifted his shoulders and decided to keep to the avenue, rather than turn onto 61st Street where he lived.

He turned his head, gaze searching and saw no one. Had the guy darted into a doorway—to go into an apartment, or to hide? His ears picked up nothing. And *yet*—

Shane sensed he was now a target, the same way he knew when an opponent in the ring was contemplating a cheap shot. Experience sure, but largely just pure instinct. And here Shane was looking ripe for a mugging, like some pansy decked out in his expensive tux.

He weighed his options and hooked a right at the next corner, picking up speed as soon as he did. At the first stoop that offered a basement entrance, he ducked down on the far side and sunk into the shadows. Although the corner he'd rounded was also rather dark, he had a good view.

If he wasn't the target, the assailant would walk on. No harm done, other than Shane feeling a bit needlessly paranoid. If he *was* the target…well, Shane wouldn't be handing over his wallet and watch like a good little victim. Hell, with all the anger and frustration he had built up lately, he'd relish a little hands-on. He was confident he could take just about anyone—unless they simply shot him point blank.

Shane felt his jaw tick at that thought. Because then what for the twins?

A figure came into view. He'd rounded the corner tight to

the wall. Head erect, chest forward, the guy practically swaggered with belligerence. Medium build, knit cap pulled low, and a boxy jacket that could easily hide weapons.

The man's steps faltered as he realized his target was no longer in view. *No doubt now,* Shane thought, *definitely after me.*

The guy bobbed his head and pushed his fists down and back in a gesture of extreme frustration. Shane heard a low growl and choice swear. The guy spun and ran back the way he'd come.

Shane leapt out—stumbling over a metal trash can, that banged and rolled. He lost precious seconds navigating it. By the time he reached the corner, the dude was already across the block and darting onto the next street.

Blast it. Shane put his hands on his hips, the adrenaline making him breathe hard. He had hoped to at least catch a good look as the guy passed under a streetlight.

———

Shane stood at the counter, shoulders hunched, staring at the brown liquid in the coffee pot increasing ever so slightly with the hisses and burbles. He'd slept poorly, and he'd woken in a cold sweat from a dream that was disjointed and non-sensical but disturbing nonetheless. Between Danny admitting that something didn't feel right about the Ivory murders investigation and someone aiming for Shane with ill intent late night...

The creeping feeling of dread that hung over him sure hadn't dissipated with the morning's light.

There was no way the two events could be related, and yet the timing boded ill. Many Irish were known to be superstitious. Shane wouldn't admit to believing in curses or magic. But fate? Perhaps. Omens and signs? A wee bit.

So much of it went back to simply listening to your gut or trusting your instincts, hence an omen or a sign could be a very practical thing.

He couldn't imagine that someone would have been gunning for him specifically last night—more likely he'd been convenient. A lone man, out on the street in the middle of the night on a weekday. He also couldn't see any reason why someone following him would be related to Ivory. He wasn't even working for Max anymore. So again, more likely the two things were completely random.

He rubbed his hand across his chin, as much scratching his morning beard as trying to wake himself up. What really bothered him, he thought, was that there was something vaguely familiar about the figure he'd encountered on his way home. He sure couldn't put a finger on anything specific, though. Probably the guy reminded him of someone else.

As soon as he'd hustled the kids off to school, Shane rang his cousin.

"Miss me already?" Danny answered.

"You wish somebody did," Shane said, but the truth was he wanted to be in the loop regularly on the Ivory murders. No matter that he'd sworn he was finished with that place once and for all.

Danny chuckled. "Nah," he said, "I don't wish this job of mine on any woman."

They'd talked about it once or twice, and Shane knew that Danny often watched his brothers in blue struggle in their marriages. Worthwhile work, but it definitely took a toll—on one's partner as well.

"What's up?"

"I was just thinking," Shane began.

"Uh-oh," Danny teased.

"Screw you, too," Shane said, though he grinned. "Seriously though, are you going to mention to Maxine Ricci that you have that feeling?"

"What feeling?"

"Come on," Shane said, immediately frustrated.

"I'm serious," Danny said. "Half the time I'm supposed to keep even hard facts quiet. You think I'm gonna call her about a *feeling* I can't substantiate? One that no one agrees with me on? No."

Shane practically threw his mug in the sink. "Then what will you do?"

Danny gave a heavy sigh. "Keep working it like I always do."

"*And* keep me informed if anything comes up," Shane said.

"What, did you earn a badge overnight?" Danny joshed. But in the end he said he would.

The conversation hadn't eased Shane's mind in the least. Danny's feeling might not warrant a bodyguard, but at the very least she should be warned to watch her back. And if Danny wasn't willing to tell her that, Shane would.

He wished he could just turn everything he'd felt and experienced with Max off—simple as flipping switches on an electrical box.

The area that controlled desire? *Click. Off.*

Admiration? *Click. Gone.*

Connection? Poof.

Hurt? Vanquished.

And the most pressing issue at the moment: that continued urge to protect her? *Click. Off.*

But it didn't work that way. He needed to know that Max

was okay and safe. He rubbed that achy spot in his jaw again. He shouldn't care, but he did.

Shane tried Max's cell phone. She didn't answer, and he decided not to leave a message. He showered, shaved, and tried again with no luck. He made the short commute to his office, then gave her cell one more try. No dice. She could be busy, or she could be ignoring him.

He called her office line, but she must have set call-forwarding because Cam answered instead. He sounded like he was outside, huffing around lots of street noise. Maybe not though. There was an announcement of some sort in the background.

"How's she doing?" Shane asked raising his voice to be heard. He tensed, waiting to hear the answer.

"She's working too much, as always," Cam said. "But that's always her go to. She'll be fine."

She'll be *fine*, Shane thought. *Cam, too, will be fine, I'll be fine, we'll all be just feckin' fine.*

"Don't worry about her," Cam said. "You know I'll watch over her."

"Thanks, man," Shane said. "Have her call me."

———

Max poked around her private cabin at the Bodhi. She was still marveling at the fact that her staff had gifted her with this trip, that she'd actually booked a flight straightaway, and that she'd willingly dumped her phone in a little safe near the front desk during check in—safe from theft but safe from distracting her, too—and walked away.

Abandoning work was a move so very unlike her. But she'd needed the time off. She hadn't even realized how desperately.

Max hadn't really taken time to grieve, either, and thought

both nature and meditation might help. Although she loved her work, no matter how stressful sometimes, things had changed. It now held minefields of distress and sorrow. Every time an opportunity came up that would have been perfect for Gia (like this place), she felt a heavy weight on her chest. Whenever she sent one of the newer models out to a go-see or a fitting, she thought *Helena won't have this chance,* and she had to shut her eyes and brace herself for a moment. When Lillian's latest pictures showed up in Vanity Fair, paired with an article about violence against women? She'd locked her office door, sank to a stool and cried.

They were all punches to the gut. Failures on her part. She hadn't seen, she hadn't suspected, she hadn't done enough…

It wasn't just that though. She needed the space to think—to decide what, if anything, to do about Shane. And it was impossible to think reasonably in the spaces where she'd recently spent so much time lusting after him, making love to him, flirting and laughing and arguing with him. Both her work and her home held too many memories.

Missing someone was unlike her, too. All the more reason to be sure of her feelings before she took action.

She was seriously contemplating what Miranda had said. That she could explain her actions to Shane, tell him how she felt about him, ask if he'd be willing to give her another chance and date her—only her.

Miranda would tell her she had nothing to lose.

Aggie would sniff and raise her chin in the air and tell her to live her life any which way she wanted to.

Cora would tell her to follow her heart.

The thought of committing to one person felt monumental, yet that was where her heart seemed to point at this moment. If, of course, Shane would still have her.

When Max prowled through the fridge for the second time, she acknowledged that it was simply going to take some time to adjust to the freedom from pressing obligations, the noise and go-go-go of the city, the siren call of her cell phone. Wine would've helped move things along, but here there was only bottled water, cucumber water, sparkling water, various herbal teas...

This place was whatever you wanted it to be. Most models came to lose weight and improve their health. They chose only water and the full-on cleanse program. Max shuddered. She was not a model and thankfully wasn't here for a physical transformation. Cleanses made Max feel wrung out rather than rejuvenated. Instead, she'd requested healthy meals full of grains and vegetables, clean smoothies with fruit and powders, plenty of roughage, legumes and seeds. Rather than go to the common dining area, most of Max's meals would be delivered to her door.

Max simply didn't care to be social this trip. She'd go to the spa for beauty and wellness treatments, but she'd avoid the group expeditions and classes. There were maps and guides in the cabin so that she could navigate the trails and waterways solo, or she might do some yoga down by the water. Solitude was preferable for her goals. She was here for some space to rest, heal, and rebalance, for some much-needed mental and emotional clarity.

"Patience, patience," Cam would tell her.

She smiled. She'd take a leisurely hot bath, making use of the bubbles and candles she'd seen near the jetted tub, she decided.

And then she'd wrap herself in the thick robe, open the doors wide, and sit outside in a deep chair to watch the sunset with a cup of tea. Or maybe she'd put on leggings and a sweatshirt and wander to the end of the dock and let her feet trail in the water as dark fell. It was warmer here in California overall, but the nights were cool.

Either way, she wouldn't put any pressure on herself to figure anything out tonight.

She'd give herself the gift of time. Time to do nothing but think. Maybe tomorrow, she'd find her way to some answers.

CHAPTER 40

SHANE GOT IT, he really did. He wasn't exactly thrilled with Max either. What they'd had together had obviously meant nothing to her. Then he'd pissed her off when he'd laid into her at his office. So she'd tossed him to the curb like the stub of a cigarette—spent and worthless—and kept on walking.

Still, did the words *I need to talk to you about something important* mean nothing? She hadn't responded to the message he'd left with Cam, the numerous missed calls, the messages or texts he'd left. And the longer Max didn't respond, the more ticked off he got.

Still, he couldn't give it up until he'd spoken with her. He'd seen crazy things in his line of work. Insane people. Unbelievable situations. Life was…bizarre. And often terrifying.

Annoyed as he was, he couldn't bear the thought of something happening to Max—especially if she hadn't even been given a head's up. No matter how messed up things now were—or weren't—between them.

Max usually went to work early to make use of the quiet morning hours. So he let Joe know he'd be in late and headed for Ivory Management's offices. If he planted himself in front of her, she'd be forced to hear him out. He'd explain Danny's 'feeling,' tell her to watch her back, and then leave. All business.

The guys at the desk greeted him warmly. "Hey, Mr. O'Rourke. How you been?"

Besides having his mangled pride handed to him like roadkill by a heartless enchantress? "All good, Desmond. How's the baby?"

Desmond smiled broadly. Shane hadn't engaged much personally as he preferred everyone remain focused in protective situations, but he did keep an ear to the ground. And he wasn't working with Ivory anymore.

"I don't believe Ms. Ricci is in yet, but go on up."

Shane's keycard had never been inactivated. He'd make a point to tell Max that she should call down and have all of O'Rourke's agents' passes revoked.

The minute he stepped into Ivory's fourth floor lobby he was hit with a rush of memory. Max planting herself between him and the elevator, Max swishing her hips down the hallway even as she gave orders. Max sliding against him in her office.

The longing was so intense that he had to shut his eyes for a moment and concentrate through a breath. He had it bad. He'd been fooling himself big time. Blast it all to hell. It'd be far harder to walk away—and to recover—than he'd been admitting.

Shane was early enough that Max's receptionist, Susan, wasn't in yet. Just as well since he probably wore the expression of a depressed, lovesick fool. He continued on to Max's office with the intention of waiting until one or the other of them arrived. Or maybe he'd see if Cam was in.

Walking down Ivory's lushly carpeted, wide corridor, Shane recalled first coming here to tell Max he'd take the job. His concern about whether his seedy fighting past in underground fight clubs was common knowledge at Ivory. Had Cam's brother told Cam? Had Cam told Max? He still didn't know...

Shane's legs slowed as his brain caught up, until he stopped dead in the hallway. His memory narrowed down to walking behind Cam—the stature, the build.

Then, on Cam's brother, so long ago, half lit in that rank basement. Same build, opposite styles. Twins physically—but only when they were standing still with their eyes and mouths shut. The minute they moved or spoke—they couldn't be more different. It wasn't just the clothes or the hairstyle, the glasses or lack thereof. Instead it was in the movement, in the attitude.

Cam was a gay male living in New York City. He wasn't the least bit hesitant about showing his feminine side or his penchant for dramatics. His brother had a cocky swagger and an attitude that shouted angry belligerence.

Weren't those exactly the words he'd used to mentally describe his assailant last night?

And there'd been that nagging feeling that something had been familiar...

Shane reached out with one hand, bracing himself against the wall.

Holy Mary, mother of... Could Cam's brother have followed him last night with ill intent? Could Cam's brother somehow be involved with...

Shane couldn't even finish that thought.

He heard a noise behind him and spun—braced for the worst.

But it was only Susan, or Sue-Sue as Cam called her. Shane had been so deep in thought he hadn't heard the elevator doors. She crossed the common area toward her desk. Her trendy shoes were silent on the carpet but he'd heard her shopping bag banging against her leg with each step. She juggled that, her lunch tote, her purse and a coffee.

Shane cleared his throat as he approached, in hopes of

avoiding coffee ending up all over the cream rug. She looked up at the sound.

"Morning, Susan," Shane said. "Just wanted you to know I'm here. I'll wait in Max's office until she arrives." He'd use the time to call Danny.

"You'll be waiting a long time," she said as she unloaded her things onto her desk. "Max is in California."

Shane's eyebrows hit his hairline. "California?" He'd just seen her—when had that been?

"We all pitched in and got her a certificate to the Bodhi."

"That's great," he managed. He knew of it. Models talked about it like it was heaven on earth—a place of miracles, a.k.a. career jumpstarts and second chances.

"I know, right? What I wouldn't give to experience it," she said looking all starry-eyed.

"When did she leave? When will she be back?"

"Yesterday. She's booked Wednesday to Wednesday, but I don't know what time her flights are. She might not make it in here until Thursday."

So, she'd been in the air on a plane yesterday, and likely there wasn't much service near the retreat. But there would have been at the airport. Surely she'd gotten *some* of his messages—and had chosen to ignore them, or him. Shane ran a hand through his hair.

Plan B then. Shane said, "I'm going to see if Cam's in." But how exactly did he ask a guy if his brother was...what even?

Susan's normally sunny expression turned sour. "He isn't. He texted me early this morning. No notice, just said he desperately needed to get away for a few days. Well guess what?" She gestured to her shopping bag and raised her chin in defiance. "If no one's here running this show, I'm actually *taking* my lunch hour."

Cam usually relished the chance to boss everyone around. Not to mention, any opportunity to prove himself invaluable to Max. What would make him up and leave unexpectedly *while* Max was away?

That low-level feeling of uneasiness Shane had woken with suddenly became a full-blown sense of foreboding. He had to talk to Danny and fast.

———

"Something's off, man." Shane loomed over Danny, who'd leaned back in his desk chair in the bull pen of the station and listened intently to all that Shane had learned between last night and this morning.

"You seriously think that someone was following you last night? That that someone was Cam's brother? And that he meant to do harm?"

"I do," Shane said. He made to move—to pace, to work out some frustration—but the desks and chairs were jammed together in this place like elbows to ribs in an Irish pub during the Six Nations Rugby Championship. How did Danny stand it?

"And somehow you think that it connects to the Ivory murders?" Danny scowled but Shane knew it was more a look of displeasure at the possibility, than any annoyance at Shane himself.

"No idea how, but yeah."

Danny leaned forward. He gestured with his hands, even with his elbows on the desk. "I just can't see why Cam not going to work is such a big deal. Human nature, right? When the cat's away the mice will play."

"Not this guy." Shane shook his head and dropped into one of the wooden chairs that faced Danny's desk. "Cam's the type to make himself invaluable, and he's a bit of a know-it-all. He'd love to play Max for a few days and order everyone around, to make decisions that might influence careers. He adores Max, always has. So I don't think he'd just up and leave her in the lurch. He—"

"All right, all right," Danny said testily. "I get it."

"I can't tell you how it all relates, only that I have that *feeling.*"

Danny rolled his eyes. "Great."

"You yourself said—"

Danny held up a hand. "I'm only worried that now there's two of us working off instinct alone," he said.

"What's Max—or even Cam—have to say about his brother?" Danny asked.

"She won't take my calls." Shane rubbed his jaw.

"You fucked it up that bad?"

"*She* messed it up, I just reacted to it." Shane still got angry when he thought about Gadget and his stretchy arms snaking around Max's shoulders, when he thought about Max so cavalierly jumping into the sack with someone else, when he thought about her waltzing into his office like he'd—

Dammit, he needed to *stop* thinking about it. "I've never talked to Cam about his brother."

Danny typed furiously.

"What are you doing?"

"Cam's parents were both noted deceased, but there was a brother listed in the CLEAR database. Not a lotta info on him though. Some people are like that. If they don't own anything and get paid in cash, they can easily stay largely under the radar." He clicked and muttered. "Let me..."

Shane had of course explained about meeting Cam's brother—only once, at the fight club. That if they weren't identical twins, there'd been a time warp. Or an accidental separation at the hospital. Because they looked alike, but acted nothing alike. Perhaps their upbringings were different. Maybe their parents split up and each took one kid. Maybe that would explain why Cam never spoke of his brother—not that Shane could remember anyway.

Shane's mind was spinning with possibilities. "What are the chances that Closse is innocent? That Cam is following Max out to California?"

Danny raised not one, but two eyebrows. "That limb you're walking out on strong enough to hold, ya think?"

Shane shook his head. "I don't know. Just—nothing makes any sense, you know?"

"I do," Danny said, hitting a few keys and glancing at his screen.

"Are you able to check flights?" Shane asked.

"No," Danny said, "I wish."

Shane pulled out his phone. "Maybe the receptionist at Ivory has more information than she told me."

Danny's mind was obviously hard at work churning over new thoughts as well, because he asked Shane, "You think Cam is capable of violence, maybe in conjunction with his brother? The kind these girls encountered?"

Shane thought for a moment. He couldn't picture Cam being physical at all. Nothing beyond classes at the gym or rollerblading or some light jogging. And the man adored women. Women were his best friends, his tribe. Cam could get snippy and out of sorts, but he seemed to get over it fast. Cam cared about his women friends, and Shane thought that Cam was a loyal sort. He couldn't imagine…

But his brother? Shane thought back to the fight club—so many years ago, but he remembered that night well enough because his two worlds had seemed to collide. He'd been sure that Cam would have been shredded in that ring—but it hadn't been Cam. It'd been his brother, who'd been damn near itching to brawl. He'd gotten right in Shane's face, and would have gladly taken the first swing...

Shane knew that Cam had had a crush on him years ago, and since Shane had reappeared on protective duty, Cam had made a couple of innuendos. Shane had assumed that Cam was just being a flirt, that he knew that Shane wasn't interested.

But what if he'd held out hope, and was hurt that Shane had gotten together with Max? What if seeing them together—naked and literally joined together—had so upset Cam that he'd mentioned it to his brother? What if the brother was the type to exact a little revenge—just for fun? It would explain him following Shane...

But what about the girls? How would—

"Helloooo?" Danny waved a hand in front of Shane's face.

"Sorry," Shane said. "What?"

Danny huffed out a breath in exasperation. "Cam capable of violence, you think?"

"No," Shane said, completely sure of that at least. "But his brother? Yeah."

CHAPTER 41

CAM WISHED WHOLEHEARTEDLY he was at the Bodhi under different circumstances. He'd always wanted to see what it was all about, and he relished the chance to watch the changes in the women. To see them transform. Gorgeous creatures already, made more and more stunning by treating their bodies right. Oh, it was just....

But no—he mustn't be seen, especially by Max. Besides, he was having a hard time staying present. Not only did he cringe away from the thought of seeing Max, he also feared what was to come.

Once upon a time he would have enjoyed nothing more than watching her. For years, he had. Of course, it'd been sweet torture because unlike most women he'd come to love, he'd never been able to watch her unclothed, to truly see her body, her curves, her skin. That had only made her all the more enticing, however. It meant she held herself above, that she was off-limits, unlike the masses. Her profession didn't lend itself to prancing around half naked or being photographed in the buff. As a woman business owner, she dressed the part. Always so fashionable—her instincts were dead on, her choices so perfect for her body type—and yet she never showed too much skin, never looked slutty.

He'd envied the men who she'd allowed in, who'd been able to see and touch her. He'd always thought of her many conquests as lucky. As if her beauty was *meant* to be appreciated...

But it'd all twisted in his mind now. A once beautiful vision had been tainted and dirty.

Ever since…well, she disgusted him now. He felt bile rise up in his throat every time he pictured her hip, that tramp stamp marring that once-gorgeous skin.

He'd never have expected it from Max, of all people. She was, he'd thought, so far above these other women. He'd built a pedestal so tall. A high rise, in fact.

She'd fallen stories and stories to the dirty city gutters below.

No—he didn't want to think of her any longer. He didn't want to be here. He was scared and upset, unsettled and full of dread. He just wanted this awful, acid feeling in his throat to go away.

It wouldn't be long now. He could feel it.

Ronnie would make it go away. Ronnie had a way of righting things. He thought of himself as Cam's protector, his avenger. It was like having your own superhero, Cam supposed.

But he worried something fierce—if something happened to Ronnie… what in God's name would happen to him?

CHAPTER 42

ACCORDING TO DANNY, Cam's brother, Roy Bender, had priors. Lots and lots of priors. Arrests for assault, breaking and entering, disturbing the peace, and even pandering.

"Pandering what?" Shane asked.

"Women. Prostitues." Danny shook his head. "That charge was dropped, it looks like. It's all very interesting but there's nothing current. Nothing even close."

"Explain," Shane said through gritted teeth. He was ready to tear his hair out. He didn't have a fraction of Danny's patience and doggedness. He just wanted to go out and use his fists to pummel information out of somebody, anybody, related to this insanity.

"There are no credit cards, no address but his father's, no wife, no kids, no employment history and no further arrests," Danny said. "It's like he vanished."

"Well, he didn't, because I met him," Shane said. "Maybe he went to jail for a good long time," Shane said. Maybe he'd been on the straight and narrow simply because he hadn't had the opportunity to be bad. Maybe he'd recently gotten out.

"Nope. No incarcerations either," Danny said.

Shane had been at the precinct nearly two hours when Danny *finally* found something interesting.

"Holy shit," Danny said, his reddish eyebrows shooting toward the ceiling. "Dear old Dad was murdered."

Shane sat up ramrod straight. "Cam's father?"

Danny nodded, eyes still skimming the screen. "Cause of death was strangulation. Never solved."

"That's rough," Shane said.

"That's not the worst of it," Danny looked at Shane, his expression tight.

Shane braced himself.

"Post-mortem staging. His cock was cut off and stuffed in his mouth. Covered over with tape."

"*Jaysus.*" Shane felt the overwhelming need to cross himself—a habit he'd left behind years ago.

"Ask me the obvious question?" Danny said.

Shane truly didn't want to. "The tape," he said, swallowing hard. "Was it in the shape of an X?"

"Yep." Danny looked almost gleeful, whereas Shane thought he might throw up.

Danny continued, "But it wasn't gaffer's tape. Or even black. It was silver electrical."

Shane stood feeling like he was going to burst, like violence or fury or—yeah, the late breakfast he'd inhaled on the way over—was going to explode from his body.

"Still," Shane said.

Danny had finished the report he'd found. "No colored gel or anything mentioned, but there was a workman's light hung to shine directly on the handiwork."

"How come this wasn't found before?" Shane asked tightly. "When you were looking at both Closse and Bender?"

Danny shook his head. "Investigations are like diving down rabbit holes. You aim to cover the whole field, but sometimes the burrows are such a warren you get lost."

"Very eloquent," Shane said.

Danny shook his head. "I don't know, man. All the hard evidence tagged Closse for it pretty early. If that's all you look at, it *still* points to him." He rubbed his eyes. "We probably stopped looking as closely at Bender. And we sure as hell weren't looking for a look-alike brother." Danny leaned back in his chair. "I'm not any happier about it than you are, man," Danny said.

Shane didn't agree. Sure, Danny was the lead investigator on this one, but at least he'd told his supervisor that something didn't feel right to him. Not like he'd lose his job.

Shane, on the other hand, had real stakes in this thing. Max was on the other side of the country. A plane ride and two time zones away and not answering her phone, while a killer was at large. The woman he loved was in mortal danger and—

The woman he loved.

Shane bolted away from Danny's desk. He went to the water cooler, struggled to get out just one crappy paper cup. Instead the dispenser let loose and a stack dropped out and then rolled all over the floor. He scooped them up and tossed them all in the trash. He filled his palm with water and splashed it on his face once, then again. He braced his arms against the wall, hung his head and let water drip off his nose and chin as it would.

What a goddamned inconvenient time to realize you loved someone. He'd known it, somewhere deep down. Shite—no wonder it hurt so bad that she didn't feel the same.

Or did she? *What* had she come to say when she brought that last check? He'd give anything to know right now.

If he'd only stopped lashing out long enough to hear her out…just maybe she'd be home right now. She might even be safe and tucked into her single bed with him guarding her with his body, or leaning over her big table in the office, marking model's pictures with sloppy circles and stars, or giving some misguided stylist the what-for over the phone.

It didn't even matter now though. Whether she loved him, or might come to eventually—or simply didn't and never would—Shane loved her.

Shane spun and strode back to his cousin's desk. There had to be something Danny could do. Otherwise, he was taking matters into his own hands.

CHAPTER 43

MAX HAD DONE yoga at dawn on the dock. It was slightly chilly, and she'd had to work to loosen up, but it'd been invigorating. The air smelled so fresh, so crisp. And the water had come alive before her eyes, shifting from flat black to tinted red and then in no time at all, painted with gold. She'd considered snapping the scene with her phone, but knew it wouldn't do it justice. It would take a talented photographer like… Dammit, she thought, flinching. Damien Closse was in custody, his talents likely to never be utilized again. Her mind just refused to wrap around that fact. She let out a long breath. As soon as she returned, she'd have to start interviewing for a new in-house photographer. It wasn't fair to her models to wait.

The air warmed fast, and she shed her sweatshirt. Shockingly, she'd slept well, and she was looking forward to a hike after breakfast.

There was plenty of bottled water, however she didn't have any granola bars or nuts to take with her. She'd like to hike as long as possible and not be hampered by her stomach. She skirted her cabin and followed one of the many paths toward the cluster of main buildings. Due to her quest for solitude, she'd requested one of the more remote cabins, and the walk took Max over five minutes.

She drew deep breaths, enjoying the green. Living in New York year-round, she always forgot how much she missed being outdoors—really outdoors. She used to summer in upstate New York at her family's country house. Aggie had kept horses, and Max had loved to ride. She absolutely must book a trail ride here.

Max reached the clubhouse and headed for the desk, where another woman asked some questions. Max recognized her—an up-and-coming model from another agency. She'd had some small successes, but she must be up for something big, something breakout, if she was here.

Max wandered around as she waited. Her gaze kept landing on the safes behind the attendant, wood-faced in keeping with the natural theme, where her phone rested. That itch to check in was coming back. Like an addiction. She forced herself to look at the art on the walls and out the windows.

She caught a glimpse of a man heading toward the clubhouse. Not many men came here, but there were a few. This guy didn't seem like a model though. No matter that she hadn't seen his face—she could just tell. Probably a Hollywood producer. Nah, he moved like a thug. An actor, she decided. The guy had Cam's stature but dressed entirely differently. Track sweats and a hoodie. He'd probably just come from the gym. Whereas Cam would surely have worn Lycra, at least a little bit of Lycra. She smiled thinking of her friend.

"Ms. Ricci?" the woman at the desk called. "What can I help you with?"

Max asked about some protein-heavy snacks for energy during her hike, and the woman promised to have a selection sent over on her morning tray.

Max glanced at the bank of safes again, then back to the woman whose eyes were sympathetic. She probably saw people who nearly frothed at the mouth, Max decided with a wry twist of her lip. She turned that into a real smile.

"Thanks again," she said.

She turned and scanned the lobby. She'd been curious to see which actor was in residence, but oddly, he hadn't come in yet. Maybe there was a back entrance, or one directly to the dining area if you chose not to eat alone.

———

Max's tray arrived just as she'd come in from a swim. Chilled but refreshed, she took the time to get clean in a warm shower. She wandered in and out of the bathroom, squeezing out her hair and nibbling on the strawberry that had garnished her smoothie. The tray held a full basket of assorted protein bars, nut packs, and dried fruit, plus some flavored electrolyte packets to add to water.

She wrapped herself in the towel and gazed out at the lake, completely enchanted by this view. She grabbed a sports bra and underwear, dropped her towel and shimmied into them. Not a fan of bug bites, she put on a long-sleeved T-shirt and a pair of lightweight trek pants. Then, she set out tennis shoes and socks since she hadn't thought to bring hikers, and padded to the Adirondack chair outside in her bare feet to drink her breakfast.

Sun toasted her skin, so she slipped on her sunglasses, pushed up her sleeves, and stretched her legs out to prop her feet on a stool. This place was gorgeous.

After the smoothie was gone, she decided to sit a while— or rather she simply didn't bother moving. Leaning her head against the chair back, she watched the leaves sway and the occasional rippling of the lake in front of her. It was such a luxury to have no schedule, nothing to rush off to. She could see the allure of vacationing someplace like this as a couple. With Shane to lounge around lazily with? Making love whenever they pleased, eating casually, swimming or hiking and enjoying nature, cuddling up to take a nap or read a book…

Of course, first he'd have to apologize for jumping to conclusions and his rude words. And she'd have to explain her actions. That is, *if* she decided she'd wanted him for good… although, he'd have to want her for good, too…

She sighed. The making love part sure sounded good… lots of Shane sounded good, in fact.

But was she willing to forgo all other men? Indefinitely?

Could she hit Twenty and pass on the heavy-duty flirting? Could she refrain from giving some hottie her number at a party or club? Could she tell her few good with-benefits-friends, like Scott, that she was no longer available?

She breathed deep, testing the idea out. Surprisingly, the thought didn't give her agita.

Max smiled and wrapped her arms around herself.

She was nearly dozing when she heard a twig snap off to her right. Her eyes flew open and caught a flash of someone through the trees. She squinted behind her shades. Was someone hiding behind a tree? Or had it just been another guest on route to their own cabin, and he or she was now out of sight?

She'd thought her cabin was apart from the rest far enough to avoid foot traffic, but maybe not.

Max fought a ripple of unease. She'd believed herself completely alone. She'd been naked when she'd changed with the French doors and sheer curtains thrown open.

She snatched up her cup and headed inside. She threw a glance over her shoulder…

Surely it was nothing. Because she certainly saw nothing now—nothing but the pretty view.

And yet, she didn't *feel* like she was alone.

Max shut and locked the French doors and pulled the

sheers. She shook her head and went to the bathroom to brush her teeth. Unlike at home when she often spent a fair amount of time primping in the mirror, here she barely gave herself a glance, only quickly swiping on some lip gloss because it felt nice.

She pulled her hair into a low ponytail, grabbed a ball cap, and then pawed through the basket of snacks. She chose a small pack of nuts and a granola bar and shoved them in her pocket. She'd have to carry the bottle of water, since she hadn't thought to bring a small backpack.

Max set the basket of snacks aside in order to leave the tray outside for pick up.

That's when she saw it on the tray. A little note card on what appeared to be recycled paper with the Bodhi logo. It must have been tucked under the basket. She flipped it open.

Her chest seized at the words.

Call me asap. You are still in danger.
Detective Iocavelli

Max read it three times—as if she could make it say something different. Then she lunged for the front door and locked it, too, flipping the extra security lever. She spun, searching for her cell.

Mannaggia! Locked in the safe in the clubhouse.

The detective's phone number was below his name, so Max headed for the cabin phone and searched for directions on getting an outside line. But there didn't seem to be such a thing. Why hadn't the idiot who took this message alerted her right away? What if she hadn't found the note?

Then she sank to the bed, slamming her fists on the mattress beside her.

What did it mean? Had someone been working with

Damien Closse? Two insane partners in madness? Or had he escaped—or been released for some reason—from prison?

And if Iocavelli knew she was here and went to the trouble of getting that message to her—then he must believe she was in danger *here*.

Dear God—the movement she'd seen outside? Had someone been watching her? Waiting for an opportune moment to strike?

Unbidden images of each of the bodies—women she knew, women she'd mentored, women she'd cared for—flashed through her mind. Helena, so young, so bloody, on that outdated tile floor. Win laid out on the weight bench in the gym, beaten so badly only her ponytail looked familiar. Lillian curled over as if she were doing yoga, her beautiful black hair fanned out and surrounded by food and waste. And then Gia in her bed, her eyes and neck mutilated by a knife, which thank God Max hadn't seen for herself...

She swallowed as she thought of how someone might find her—what might be done to her body, what story an unbalanced killer might try to tell about her.

She was all alone in this little cabin. She'd requested solitude. She might not be found for days.

Or if she'd gone hiking before she'd seen the note? Maybe never.

She had to talk to Iocavelli and fast. But how to go about that?

Race to the clubhouse and demand her phone? She bit her lip—she'd have to leave the security of these walls to do that.

Call the clubhouse and request her phone be delivered? She was *not* inclined to open the door, to anyone...

Had the detective called Shane? Did he know? She thought of her staff, her models—oh no, how was she going to alert them without her goddamn phone? Could Shane call the troops back in to protect her team? Or was the danger only here—focused on her?

Max's breathing became rapid as she began to panic. She'd have to make a choice—and fast.

Max reached for the room phone and called the front desk. She didn't have to open the door. They could leave her phone outside. She'd simply wait until she was sure they were gone before snatching it inside. Right?

"This is Maxine Ricci. I need someone to open my safe and deliver my phone to my cabin right away."

The young woman said, "I'm sorry, that's not possible."

"Listen, I don't care what I agreed to or asked for. This is an emergency." Max imagined she heard that all the time, but hers really was an emergency.

"Ma'am, I apologize, but the only one who can get your phone out is you."

"Listen—"

But the girl plowed over her with a raised voice. "It's touch-pad security, remember? You must be present to open it."

Crap. That was right. The damn safe had a biometric scanner. It had taken a digital imprint of her finger.

She dropped her head in her hands. No choice then, she'd have to go to the clubhouse.

Max laced up her tennis shoes with shaky fingers. Should she walk as if nothing was wrong, to keep from alerting him, if he—whoever he was—was even here?

She blew out a breath. This was so nuts.

Maybe it was better to just flat out run.

CHAPTER 44

MAX HAD TO wait in line at the clubhouse, panting hard from running so fast. She kept looking around. This place had French doors thrown open everywhere—so much so it was nearly wall-less. She felt exposed in the worst way, and was never so relieved to lay hands on her phone.

As soon as it powered up, numerous alerts flashed. Little red circles showed twenty calls and even more texts. She went to the voicemail screen. A few that were work-related, two voicemails from Detective Iocavelli, and six from Shane.

Iocavelli had kept him in the loop then. He was worried about her. Her heart gave a little leap of joy, even as she logically told herself that wasn't important right now.

She glanced up, searching the lobby. Where to tuck aside to make a phone call? Max put the phone to her ear as she searched.

The dining room was full of people. Too noisy. The lobby definitely too open—she could be jumped from any direction. The bathroom?

No, she thought, she couldn't see out from there and a shudder rippled through her at the thought of being trapped like Helena.

Max kept searching. There was a little reading room. Lots of glass—just like everywhere else in this place, but only one was floor to ceiling, and those doors weren't open. She slipped into the corner of the reading room, her back pressed against two walls and kept her eyes trained on the outside.

She listened to her messages one by one. Iocavelli sounded serious, Shane tense. Both said nothing more than *Call as soon as you can, it's important.*

Quickly, Max scanned the texts. More of the same. And a couple from Shane that held promise of more. *I'm sorry for lashing out.* And *I miss you. Please, be safe.*

She'd have to think about those things later, because one message in particular caught her eye:

We had the wrong man.

What?! Meaning...

Damien Closse wasn't guilty. She felt a huge wash of relief and then realized that also meant a psycho killer was roaming the streets—or these paths—freely?

She dialed Iocavelli with trembling fingers.

He answered on the first ring. In lieu of a greeting, he asked, "Are you okay?"

"Other than being terrified at your messages, yes." She sounded snippy, but she didn't care. She was scared, which in turn made her angry. "What do you mean you had the wrong guy?"

"We believe Closse is innocent." She heard him blow out a hard breath. "We now think Bender—"

"Cam?" she asked incredulously.

"Listen," he said sharply. "Your man Cam apparently has an older brother who looks just like him. Except we can't find him."

"He's never mentioned a brother," she said.

"Shane has met him," he said.

Shane had met Cam's brother? Cam had a brother? She'd known Cam for *years*...

Iocavelli said, "We don't know if Cam's protecting his brother or working with his brother. But something's off there."

Max's brain was exploding. Cam? Somehow involved in murdering women? It was so unfathomable, so completely preposterous. She'd thought so when he'd been questioned. She still felt that way now.

Iocavelli said, "What we do know is that Cam jumped a plane only about fifteen hours behind you."

"No—he's running Ivory while I'm gone."

"No," Iocavelli said, his voice hard with frustration. "He's on the west coast. He told your receptionist that he was taking a few days off. She snooped, managed to access his email, and found his itinerary. Assuming he made the flight, he landed in Reno and likely rented a car. He could have picked up his brother on the way. They could even have flown together."

The actor she'd seen. He'd reminded her of Cam. She hadn't seen his face, but…

Combined with the movement she'd seen off the path outside her cabin? And the distinct feeling of being watched earlier? *Not* some actor. But a man here for her.

God help her.

"This brother…if he's the one…" Max was trying hard to make sense of this news, but nothing, nothing seemed to fit. "Maybe Cam is coming to protect me?" she managed.

"Like he protected your models?"

Max gulped hard. She started to sink down, to slide down this wall and hide behind the wing chair forever. But no—then she wouldn't be able to see out, to see what was coming. She forced herself to stand, locked her knees, and scanned the outside. The patio garden and paths that looped the clubhouse, the dense, lush vegetation and beyond. So beautiful earlier, so menacing now.

Iocavelli said, "I'm informing the police out there, but we are working largely on suspicion. We have very little solid information."

He paused and Max had the fleeting thought that he wasn't telling her everything. Did she want, or need, to know every detail?

The detective continued. "Shane is on his way. Once he lands, you'll be able to reach him and he'll meet you wherever."

Her knees went weak again at that. *Shane*. Ever her protector.

"You shouldn't wait though. You need to get out of there, without being followed. Can you do that?" he asked.

Could she? She had no idea how to evade someone, nor did she have a car.

"I'll figure something out. Where do I go? Does it matter?"

"Best thing would be the airport—to book the first flight out of there."

"What if I can't get a flight right away? How much time do I have?" she asked.

"I'm not sure," Iocavelli said. "The important thing is that you leave. Your chances are better if you aren't where you are expected to be."

"Okay," Max tried hard not to let her voice shake. Her *chances*...

———

Max had been so determined to relax that she hadn't even brought her laptop. She'd have to call the airline—

or airlines—and pray there would be something available soon.

Max remained nestled in the corner of the reading room, pressing her back hard against the wall, debating how to handle this craziness. Should she stay right here—or even go sit near the front desk—to call the airline? Because without a laptop, she'd have to deal with a real live agent. And that would likely be easier to do from her room where it was quiet. She could pack up at the same time...

But Detective Iocavelli said not to be alone.

Maybe she could have a staff member pack up for her and bring her things here...but what if she couldn't get a flight until tomorrow? Should she sleep alone in the room, or camp out on a chair at the airport?

God, this was nuts—and yet she had to take it seriously. She'd seen what had happened to her models—blessed life or gruesome death.

But still, one thing at a time. Max forced herself from the wall and back to the front desk. She'd taken a car service to get here. However the resort shuttle might be a better bet—safety in numbers.

"A shuttle will run whenever I need it to get me to the airport, correct?" she asked the young woman at the desk whose name tag read Sherri.

"Leaving so soon?" She effected a syrupy frown. "That's a shame. But yes, just give us a few hours notice."

"Is anyone else headed for—" Max fake coughed, thinking better of announcing her destination. "Sorry. Anyone else leaving soon?"

"Not that I know of, but no worries. The shuttle will go anytime you need it, even if you are the only guest."

That was exactly what Max was worried about.

She selected a chair in one corner—no glass behind her—and dialed the airline she'd flown in on. She waited on hold for ten minutes, then twenty, then thirty, before the recorded voice promised she was next in line.

Max chewed on a nail—something she hadn't done since before gel nails. She got up, she sat down, she sat on her hand, she gnawed some more. Finally, finally a real live person came on the line. She didn't know her frequent flyer number, and she had to answer obscure security question after obscure security question before she was finally able to explain that she needed a flight home, and fast.

"Let me see what we have available, ma'am," the agent said in a slow, measured tone that was completely at odds with Max's frantic request.

"The earliest flight with an available seat—"

The words stopped. Just disappeared. Max held her phone out, staring at it incredulously.

It had died.

"Noooo," she wailed, springing up. She pushed buttons, all to no avail. The screen was black, and it was staying that way.

She scrambled over to the desk. "Do you have a charger?" She thrust her phone out so the attendant could see it. "Please? That I can borrow? I'm desperate."

"I'm sorry, I don't," Sherri said, shaking her head.

Now she'd have no choice, she'd *have* to go to her room. Max glanced outside again and gulped hard. She turned back to the desk.

"Then I need an escort," Max said. "A male one. A big one." Now that she'd thought of it, she realized she should have done that coming *to* the clubhouse. Except how would she have known it was really a Bodhi staff member and not...

Max realized Sherri was staring at her with one eyebrow crooked question-mark style.

What to say? No, I'm not planning on molesting your co-worker, Sherri-with-an-i, but there may be a serial killer on your grounds so we should definitely make it public and incite some mass panic? She decided on, "I have a stalker, and I just found out he might be here."

Sherri looked skeptical, but Max didn't give a crap. She just needed that escort—one Sherri could vouch for—so she could pack up and meet Shane anywhere but here.

CHAPTER 45

RONNIE HIMSELF COULDN'T fathom what they did here other than eat rabbit food, bend themselves into pretzels, and scrub sand on their face—but hey, Cam knew his industry and he knew models. And Cam said that no woman could resist the place. That even those already beautiful simply glowed once they'd been there. It sounded to him like pure bull, but even the almighty Maxine Ricci had taken the bait, so maybe the kid had the right of it.

He grinned. Max wouldn't glow of course. She wouldn't even make it home. It'd been a pure stroke of luck, like winning the freedom lottery, that that womanizer Closse had been pegged.

No sense messing with that—*her* punishments would have to look like an accident or at least a random, unrelated crime—when what he really wanted to do was send a message to the world, on Cam's behalf, of course.

He slammed one hand into the other. She'd betrayed the poor kid—tricked him into thinking she was such a goddess. She was worse than all the others.

That so-called art on her hip? Cam felt it showed a complete disregard for beauty, for the glorious temple that was her body, and couldn't fathom why she would maim herself voluntarily like that.

Why pretty it up with fancy words? That tat marked her as the whore she was. They called 'em tramp stamps for a reason.

Ronnie cracked his knuckles and bounced on his toes. It used to be he had to protect Cam from bullies at school. A couple of Ronnie-style beatings and they'd learned to steer clear. And once—and only once—from his father. Cam had eventually found his own way in the world and it'd been a long time since he'd been needed. But now Ronnie had to protect him from these self-centered, self-destructive women.

Or was it more accurate to say he was protecting Cam from himself? Keeping him from spiraling into a depression so deep he'd never dig his way out. Helena's bullshit had flipped Cam's switch, really flipping him out. Things had gone from bad to worse. And now Max's betrayals were sinking the kid. Ronnie had never had to do this much damage control before—not in this kind of timeframe.

He supposed it didn't matter. He'd make this right for his little bro. He'd remove the fallen goddess, just like the others, so that Cam could stop obsessing. Time for the kid to move on. To try again.

As usual, it was Ronnie to the rescue.

CHAPTER 46

MAX WASN'T SURE which was worse—the mad, paranoid dash to her cabin with a lifeguard in tow who kept telling her to slow down, or the terror of being alone and stuck in her cabin. Because although she'd asked that boy—big but young—to stay, even offering to pay him, he'd refused claiming he'd lose his job. Sexual harassment and all that. She, however, was more worried about putting him, or anyone for that matter, in danger's way. So she'd let him go and then threw the bolt fast.

She triple-checked every lock on every shutter and every door. She made sure the seams of the curtains matched up so no one could see in. There were—thankfully—room-darkening shades in addition to the sheers, so she felt slightly less exposed.

She pulled out her luggage and gathered up all her cosmetics and shower items while her phone charged enough to handle a call.

Once connected and on hold, she put the phone on speaker and shoved her clothing into her suitcase. She was still waiting when there was nothing left to pack.

"This is Rayanne with customer service. Who am I speaking with please?"

Thank God, Max breathed. She bent to the phone—careful not to yank out the charger, switched off speaker, and told the agent her name and her needs.

After a few minutes playing question and answer, Rayanne

began the search. The first flight the agent had a seat on sounded great—until she realized that she could never get from here to the airport in time. It wasn't dark yet, but the hours were counting down. It was a long shot to think she could get a flight tonight. The agent put her on hold to check further.

Right then call waiting beeped, she shifted the phone to look—*Shane.*

She nearly wept with relief. He must be on the ground—maybe even taxiing to the gate, but his phone was on...

But dammit, she couldn't answer his call while she was on with the airline. No way could she risk getting disconnected again, and if the agent returned from the hold and she wasn't there...

Shane would have to wait. She'd call him back the minute she'd booked a flight.

The thought that he might feasibly be with her in a few hours bolstered her.

Did Shane already have a flight back? Or not? Would they be fleeing together? Or would this be over—somehow—and they could simply travel together, maybe nurse a cocktail at the airport bar or hold hands as they people watched?

Max shook her head. If she could get two seats, she'd book him a flight, too. If they could get one tonight, great. Tomorrow, fine. Even the next day.

If Shane was with her, she knew she'd be safe.

She didn't care if he already had a flight. She didn't care how much it cost. Even if there was—please God—no longer any reason to protect her, she'd convince him to stay with her, be with her...

She'd made up her mind.

All that was left was making up his.

Oh—and surviving this nightmare.

CHAPTER 47

RONNIE WAS SO frustrated. He was practically vibrating, needing to take action, sick of trying to hide behind trees and bushes and stay out of sight—especially when he didn't exactly fit the profile of this crazy place's clientele.

He slapped at a buzzing noise near his ear. He friggin' hated nature. He preferred the city. He'd rather dodge rats and cabs than flying bugs any day.

But it looked like his frustration was far from over. Something must have tipped that slut off. She'd run like a bat outta hell to the clubhouse, spent forever hiding in there, and then hustled back with a burly staff member at her side. She hadn't left her cabin since.

He'd pictured, you know, pushing her off a cliff or down a deep ravine—maybe snapping her neck first if the tumble didn't look like a sure thing. Or dragging her underwater during a swim and holding her there until she went limp for all time. Shit—if only he'd managed it this morning. By the time he'd crept close enough to slip into the water unnoticed, she'd been climbing back up the ladder at the end of her dock, grabbing a towel.

Fuck. It would be far harder to make it look like an accident in the cabin, even at night.

And sure as shit, she was clamped up tight in that little place. Shutters drawn, shades drawn, doors shut and surely locked. Unlike earlier when she'd had the doors thrown open, and he'd gotten a nearly unhampered view of her in her birthday suit. No wonder Cam had been so into her. The hussy had curves to rival any pinup girl, and the attitude to go with the body.

Dammit. He had to figure something out fast. Not only was it playing with danger to drag it out and keep lurking around like this, but Cam's distress was killing him. He couldn't stand it.

And Cam wouldn't really be well until Ms. Maxine Ricci was no longer. Until then the poor kid would suffer—torn between adoration and bone-deep betrayal. Ronnie shook his head. The kid *felt* so deeply.

It wasn't like that with Ronnie. He could take women or leave 'em as needed. He didn't need friends either. The only person that mattered was Cam. Because the kid needed him. Nearly always had, and probably always would.

CHAPTER 48

THE FACT THAT Max didn't answer made Shane insane with worry.

It was feasible that Danny hadn't reached her—that she simply wasn't on her phone. That she was sitting cross-legged in some small group session, chanting om, centering her being on simply being—completely oblivious to the danger awaiting her.

But it was just as possible that Cam and his brother had already found her, already hurt her. That he was too late.

Shane was out of his tiny airplane seat well before the ding. Earlier he'd shown his card and identification to the flight attendants upon entering and explained that he was trying to reach a client who was being threatened. He was the first one off the plane in San Francisco.

He called Danny next, who thank you Mother Mary, *had* actually spoken with Max.

"How is she?" Shane said, following the signs toward car rentals.

"How do you think?" Danny's Italian accent sounded harsh—a sure sign he felt stressed.

"Does she have a plan?" Shane asked.

"She must, by now. You didn't reach her?"

Shane's jaw ticked. "She's not answering."

He heard Danny swear on the other end of the line.

"I'm almost at car rental," Shane said.

"It's Enterprise, remember?" Danny asked. "I'll call you back as soon as I have anything."

"There's nothing new? Nothing since I left?" Shane had hoped for more.

"No man—it's crazy. There's zero. No trace of the brother."

Shane swore, incredulous, and they hung up. How was that possible? Shane had met the guy—seen him with his own eyes. The man had even said Cam was his brother. Hadn't he?

Shane stood at the back of the line, his jaw ticking, but only for a moment.

A man with a stomach that jutted out in front of him like a watermelon suspended inside his straining button-down shirt, came out from the back. "Shane O'Rourke?"

Shane stepped forward and managed a tight smile.

"Mr. O'Rourke, come with me please."

They proceeded to the man's tiny office in the back. All Shane had to do was show I.D., scribble his signature a couple times, and he was handed the rental agreement and keys to a 4-wheel drive truck, which was already waiting.

Danny had called ahead and booked the rental, then called again when Shane's flight had touched down. Ahhh, the power of the police.

Now if the rest of this operation would go as smoothly.

Shane took a minute to plug the address into his phone's navigation and connect Bluetooth. He'd need it, as he expected to be on the phone a large portion of the drive.

He was going north, toward Lakewood. About two and a half hours and he'd be with Max. Shane gripped the wheel. She'd better be okay, they'd better not be too late, she'd better be playing it safe...

He glanced at his watch—he'd deplaned and gotten the car

so fast that it hadn't been that long since he'd called last time, but he tried again anyway.

It rang and rang, and then went to voicemail. He hung up, gritting his teeth.

Next up was Joe, who answered right away.

"We're good," Joe said. "My buddy Frank should be there soon."

"She know he's coming?"

"Left her a message."

She'd be petrified by now, surely, and wouldn't take well to a surprise visitor. Shane hoped she got the word before he arrived. "Kids okay?" Shane asked.

"They're just fine, and Tricia's eating them up, so don't worry about us here at home. She's promised them soda bread tomorrow and invited Mrs. Costa." Joe chuckled.

Shane breathed a little sigh of relief on that score at least.

"Just go take care of your lass," Joe said.

Was she his? Shane wondered. She would be, someday, Shane vowed.

Just then the phone rang—Max, *thank God.*

"Are you all right?" he asked.

"Yes. About earlier this week, it wasn't what you thought."

Shane shut his eyes for a moment in relief and then remembered he was barreling down the highway.

He said, "Let's cover that ground later." They had to stay focused right now.

"I'm scared," she whispered.

"I know," Shane said, his heart squeezing painfully for her. "Hang in there. Joe has a buddy of his coming soon to guard you until I can get there. His name is Frank Ryan. Check his I.D. Make sure it's him before you let him in."

"Detective Iocavelli said I should get to the airport, where there's lots of people."

"Frank should be there in the next half hour. Wait for him to take you. Have him call me when you're en route. I'll meet you and take over."

"Okay."

———

Shane counted down the minutes until Joe's pal Frank should be with Max. Then, after another ten minutes grace period, he reconnected with Max.

"I'm okay," she answered.

And Shane heaved another sigh of relief. "Are you and Frank on the road?"

"He's not here yet," she said. "Maybe these back roads are taking longer than he thought?"

"Maybe. Let me call Joe. I'll get his number and find out what his E.T.A. is." Shane gritted his teeth. What he really wanted to ask was why the hell it was taking him so long.

"What about you? How far away are you?"

"About an hour and a half." Too long, he thought.

"Should I just get out of here and not wait?" she asked.

"Maybe." Transitions were dangerous, Shane thought. But so was remaining a sitting duck. "Let me see if I can reach Joe. If we know exactly when Frank is arriving, we can gauge better."

"Okay," she said, and she sounded like she was chewing on something.

"Hang in there," he said. And wished desperately there was something more comforting he could tell her.

"Just in case," Max said.

Shane said, "Don't. Don't do that."

"Let me," Max said. "I need to tell you how sorry I am. I was freaked out. Because I was...really, *really* into you. And really scared about what that meant. I've never stayed before. And I panicked."

Shane thought back to the serious brush off she'd given him the moment his protective services were no longer needed.

Max continued. "I only went to Twenty that night as a test. I figured going back to my usual would tell me one way or another if I needed just somebody, or needed *you*."

Shane held his breath. When she didn't say anything, he asked, "And?"

"You. Only you," Max whispered. "I let that guy escort me home, but I never once considered sleeping with him."

Shane felt a rush of pleasure. She wanted *him*. She'd only humored Gadget. She hadn't really been trolling, she'd been, for lack of a better word, testing. Testing her feelings for *him*.

"Good," he said, "that's good." His cheeks felt warm. Relief...and shame. He cleared his throat. "I'm sorry, too. I jumped to conclusions. Said stuff that was out of line. Somehow with you I seem to always..."

"Thank you," she said quietly. "Do you think you can trust me? Going forward?"

"I already did," he said. "Or at least I trusted that you felt the same way I did about us. That's why I was so shocked... so angry."

She made a small sound. Like she was hurting. Like she understood.

"I think we'll have to learn," he said. "To trust each other." He wasn't thinking of cheating necessarily, just...trusting each other to be careful. With each other's feelings, with their hearts.

"I'm still scared though," Max said. "I don't know how to do a real relationship."

He laughed. "Who's to say I know how either? We'll figure

it out together. I guess the most important thing will to be honest. To keep talking. A lot."

She shuddered out a breath. "I hope we can do that."

"Max," he said. "We will. I promise. I'm on the way. And we're going to get you out of there and safe. And then we'll end this once and for all. And start something good."

CHAPTER 49

SHANE DID REACH Joe, but his uncle hadn't heard from Frank either.

"I don't like it," Shane said.

"Don't jump the gun," Joe replied. "Let me try again to reach him."

"Give me the number as well, so I'll have it." Shane got the first six digits jotted down on the back of his rental paperwork, when Joe's voice vanished. Shane stared at the display, incredulous. Service had cut out.

Shane swore and slammed the palm of his hand on the wheel. Damn California hills.

His only consolation was that Joe was on it, and surely he or Frank would think to update Max.

After that, Shane didn't regain service for more than a couple of minutes at a time. No voicemails or texts showed up. The radio silence was making him crazed with worry.

He had the pedal pushed as far as he dared without flying off the road. He didn't give a crap about a ticket. Danny would fix it, and maybe he'd even end up with an officer or two to help in this bizarre situation. Shane drove another good thirty miles—each one ratcheting up his stress level further—before there was a signal steady enough to make a call.

Instead the phone rang almost immediately. Shane was torn—who did he want to hear from first? Max? Frank? Joe?

Shane glanced at the display. None of the above.

"I have news," Danny said right away. "Max called earlier with the name of Bender's therapist, thinking he might know more about Cam's family than anybody else did."

Shane could hear the tension in Danny's voice and braced himself.

"The guy didn't want to share much—client privacy and all that. But he loosened up a bit when I told him about the murders and the current situation and our search for the brother. I've requested a subpoena to access his records in full, but not sure we'll get it. In the meantime..." Danny paused.

A bolt of unease shot through Shane.

"There's no brother."

Shane's mind spun, but Danny didn't make him wait.

"Only an imaginary one."

"*What*?" That ticked Shane off. This wasn't a feckin' child's game. "That database you checked said there was a brother. Roy Bender. Did you forget about him?"

Danny said, "Roy Bender is presumed dead. Took a knife in a bar brawl when he was nineteen, ran off, fell down a ravine and was never seen again. There was no funeral or burial because they didn't find the body. Nobody was willing to risk their neck to find a no-good like him. Even his own father. But I spoke with the retired Chief of Police where they grew up. He has no doubt Roy is dead. The shrink confirmed the same."

"Then who the hell is murdering all these women? And who murdered their father?" Shane knew even as he asked that they were just words. There was only one person left who could have.

Danny heaved a heavy sigh. "Cam. It's Cam. He's got a serious case of Dissociative Identity Disorder. More commonly known as multiple—or split—personalities."

———

Max was beside herself. Another twenty minutes had passed, and no Frank. Nor any word of Frank from Shane or Joe. She sat in the cushy reading chair in her little bungalow, yet she was as uncomfortable as could be. Tense as all get-out, her neck and shoulders were so tight they were nearly cramped. Her ears strained for every little noise, and she jumped whenever she heard one. She got up repeatedly to try and peek around the edges of the curtain. Her stomach churned with fear. She should probably eat something but the granola bar she tried wouldn't go past the lump of fear in her throat.

She had loads of time before she had to be at the airport, but she was giving this bodyguard guy only ten more minutes...if he didn't show by then, she was calling the front desk—maybe asking for two people, a man and a woman, to come escort her—and getting the hell out of here one way or another.

Yes, she'd prefer to leave *with* Frank. He'd have had the same training and experience as Shane and his team, making him her safest bet in case of an actual attack, but she simply couldn't stand to wait much longer for the guy. And she'd surely have a coronary if she tried to hunker down here long enough for Shane to arrive.

She tucked her legs up and buried her head in her knees.

Max must have dozed—or maybe she'd simply shut down from pure stress—but she came awake at a crackling noise. She jerked her head up. Then she smelled it.

Smoke.

CHAPTER 50

MAX SHOVED ASIDE a curtain. Flames licked up from below and she figured it'd be no time at all before the thatched roof caught. She ran to the front door, flipped locks frantically and yanked. But it didn't open.

Had she missed something in her haste? She took a deep breath and carefully but quickly re-worked the locks. Yet when she pulled—the door only moved about half an inch.

Bastard. There were big rectangular wrought-iron handles on the outside. He—Cam's brother, or hell, maybe the pair of them—had wedged something in there.

Oh God...death by fire...not, not, not good. And the smoke was getting bad.

Max grabbed her phone and dialed 911, then hung up just as fast. God only knew how far the nearest emergency services were from this remote resort. She snatched up the room phone and punched zero. The second she heard a voice, she said, "My cabin's on fire! Come quick!" Then she dropped the handset and darted into the bathroom to grab a washcloth, which she slapped over her nose and mouth. Her eyes and throat were already starting to burn. They'd know what cabin had called, but could they get here in time to help her?

No exit from the bathroom—she'd wet towels and drape them over herself if she had to, but first she'd check all the doors and windows for a clear escape. She ran around the bed to the French doors that lead out to her little deck and the dock down to the lake. She yanked open the curtains and flipped locks. She pulled with all her might—and tumbled to her butt when they swung in freely.

Clear air rushed in as she scrambled to her feet. But…

It had to be a trap. He—they—didn't really want her to fry. They wanted her flushed out—in this direction.

Think, *think* Max.

She could go up. Put the chair on the bed, ram something through the ceiling and escape through the roof…somehow. But that would take time…She could wait for help, but staying put in a burning building was insane…

Already, she coughed and her eyes watered. She glanced left and right, and could see orange glowing around the edges of the windows. The one she'd checked first had become a solid wall of flame.

Max darted to the drawer near the tiny kitchenette area. She'd seen…yes! Silverware. The real stuff, not plastic. And a pen, too. She shoved the pen in one pocket of her pants, the fork in her other, and grasped the knife in her right hand. It wasn't exactly a steak knife, but if she could hit an eye or other vulnerable soft spot, it'd do. And it steadied her. With her left, she held the washcloth in place.

There was no time for alternatives. She had no choice but to go forward. If ever the term out of the frying pan and into the fire was appropriate, this was it.

———

Although his cell service seemed to hold, Shane had to pay close attention to the GPS to find the Bodhi, nestled as it was in the foothills of the Mendocino National forest. He also thought maybe it was best to break the news about Cam's psychosis to Max in person.

Finally, finally, Shane arrived. Luckily he'd thought to ask Max earlier to add him to her room, so there was no trouble when he pulled up to the security gate. Despite the urge to bust out of the truck and start hollering like a madman for her, he'd taken a minute to ask for a map of the grounds. The gate attendant used a marker to circle where they were now, the main buildings, and Max's cabin. Which meant that as soon as he'd jammed the truck's nose into a parking space and grabbed his phone, he was able to set out on foot toward Max's cabin.

He called her as he crossed the small parking lot, intending to let her know he was on site. He chose the path about fifty yards to the left of the main entrance. It would wind to the left, curve to the right, swing left again, and finally end ahead of the small lake. What was hard to tell was the actual distance. So often maps of this sort had no scale.

The sun was nearly set, the sky orange and red and fading fast. The campus, as the gate attendant had called it, was very quiet.

Max's phone rang a few times, then cut to voicemail. He left the briefest message. Shane tried again and quickened his pace even more. She could be on the line with Joe or Frank, but…his bad-feeling-o-meter was ticking upward.

When she didn't answer the second time, Shane broke into a run.

Wait—

Shane skidded to a stop. Something had caught his eye… what was it? Shane turned and retraced his steps.

There. The bright blue toe of a sneaker sticking out from under a copse of big leafy vegetation—a cross between plants and bushes. Shane bent and then surged into action. Because that shoe was attached to somebody—and Shane had a bad feeling he knew exactly who it was.

Shane called "Hey," and put a hand to the man's leg and shook it. No response. Shit. He reached under the bush, grabbed hold of both legs and pulled.

He was ready to bellow for help. He smelled smoke and figured there was a barbecue or a fire pit going, which meant people nearby.

Light track pants and a loose windbreaker... He grabbed the man's hips and yanked again—and swore.

Blunt force trauma to the temple. From who knew what weapon. And he'd definitely taken multiple blows. Was he...

Shane had instinctively felt for a pulse—yes! There it was. And his eyelids were fluttering.

Thank God. His mind was racing. He dialed 911 on his cell, then tucked it between his ear and his shoulder so he could unzip the guy's jacket. Sure enough—there was a holster... now empty.

This was definitely Joe's friend Frank.

And Cam—and his violent alter ego—now had a gun.

"Frank," Shane called squeezing his arm. "Hey, mate, wake up." He told the operator the particulars as quickly and concisely as possible. Frank had opened his eyes, grimaced and raised a hand to his head.

"Don't. Just relax," Shane told him.

Frank groaned.

Shane looked around and answered questions as best as he could, but the smell of smoke was getting stronger.

Frank's eyes widened. He smelled it, too. "That fucker," he said.

Shane began, "Frank—"

"Go," Frank said. "Go!"

Shane pressed the phone into Frank's hand and took off running toward the water—toward Max.

CHAPTER 51

MAX STEPPED OUT onto the deck, moving forward enough to clear the smoke. She blinked, trying to clear her eyes—which way?

She could gain seconds if she chose correctly, but it was nearly dark. She had to guess where he might be hiding. The path was to the left—near the front door. That would be expected. She cut right.

Just as she slipped into the landscaping, she was yanked from behind by her hair.

Pulled back and down, she slammed to the ground, her hip and elbow connecting painfully with the wooden decking.

"No you don't, bitch," said a voice she didn't recognize.

She struggled to breathe between the smoke and the shock. She saw a figure backlit by the raging fire with his arms raised above his head, ready to slam something—what? A pipe? A hammer?—into her.

She rolled left and clambered to her feet. She faced him. Miraculously she still held the knife—not that it would do any good against a pipe. Good God—

"Cam!" she said. No matter that Iocavelli had warned her Cam was involved, she simply couldn't believe her eyes.

But it *was* him. Or a twin—but if so, then where was Cam?

As calmly as she could manage, she said, "It's me, Max."

He lunged forward and swung the pipe with one arm in a wide arc—she jumped back, just missing being hit. The odd thought that he looked bigger than Cam skittered through her mind. Except—it *was* Cam, wasn't it?

"Stop it, Cam!" she shouted.

"It's your turn," he snarled. "And mine. Cam's not coming."

Max blinked. Not a brother. Definitely Cam—and yet not Cam. Somehow. He'd fractured or broken or lost his mind. She didn't know.

"Tell me why," she said. "Why are you doing this?"

"You betrayed him," he said. He held his weapon in one hand, cocked up like he was ready to use it at any second. He looked angry but oddly calm, like this was all in a day's work. Cam's face was always animated. Not-Cam looked hard and mean. His mouth set in a cruel sneer, his eyes bored into hers with purpose.

Max didn't know what to make of it, yet a different kind of fear gripped her.

"The other girls?"

He laughed. "Them, too. They never live up to his ideals."

She took another step back. Midway down the dock now. Her options were getting narrower and narrower.

He smiled—an evil twist of the mouth. He knew he had her cornered, and he was enjoying toying with her. Otherwise, she'd be beaten to a pulp already.

"You were the worst though. Never the idol he thought you were," Not-Cam said. "We finally saw proof of that, you tramp."

We, she thought. Was Cam still in there? Could she reach him?

"Cam—"

He swung again—she dodged it. But immediately he'd swung again. She scrambled back so fast she stumbled and fell. The pipe just caught her upper arm—and she cried out.

He raised the metal piece over his head. Down it arced.

Max rolled—into the water with a splash. Immediately, her tennis shoes and clothing weighed her down. She couldn't touch bottom, and instinctively stretched out her arms to swim. Diagonally, toward shore and away from the dock.

A heavy weight slammed onto her shoulder and back—he'd jumped on her! She went under fast and struggled not to gulp water.

Max got free for a second as he fell off. She thrust an arm out and hit him but nowhere near enough to do damage. She realized she'd lost the knife. The water was dark. She bobbed up just long enough to gulp air before he pushed her down again—both hands, all his weight.

Max thrashed and tried to twist free but couldn't. The dark shape of him loomed over her, blocking out what little light there was from above. Everything in her screamed *no*.

One foot connected with something—weeds. And a second later she touched mucky bottom. She pushed off and shoved at him at the same time.

She still wasn't free. She sobbed inside as more air escaped her—she couldn't hold on much longer.

Then suddenly—the weight was gone.

Max kicked and pulled. She broke the surface and gasped for air. A churn of water next to her. She coughed, swimming toward shore. It was only moments before she could stand—they'd been so close. She grabbed at the vegetation and hauled herself up.

Two heads broke the surface—

Shane.

Oh God…

She watched the struggle—barely able to tell what was

happening. She pushed her hair out of her face and swiped at her eyes so she could see. She looked around. She needed a weapon. She clambered up onto the dock. A pole or a... *Something.* Something to help.

The fire roared behind her—my God, where was help? Why was no one coming?

There—the pipe he'd wielded was on the dock. She hopped up, ran for it, and snatched it up. Not long enough to help from here. She ran back down the dock to enter from the bank where she could stand.

Suddenly, the struggle ceased. Shane pulled toward land dragging a limp body behind him by the shirt. Not-Cam was face down in the water.

Shane was upright now, water only waist high.

Max dropped the pipe and jumped back down, climbing through the bushes to get to him.

"Shane!"

He yanked the body up, feet only remaining in the water and let go.

She rushed him. He reached for her.

"You came."

"Of course I came." He shook the water out of his eyes. "God, I wish I'd been sooner."

She pulled back to look at him. He cupped her cheek.

"Are you all right?" They both said it in unison.

She grabbed him and held on. He wrapped her in his arms and squeezed.

Finally, finally—people appeared. There was shouting, and frantic activity. A water truck pulled up and the hose was yanked free and connected somewhere. They were focused on her cabin and hadn't seen them yet.

Max glanced at Cam. Unconscious, Max thought, he

looked like the Cam she loved once again. Her heart broke and a single sob escaped her.

Shane squeezed her hand. He seemed to want to say something, but instead looked down at the prone body practically underneath them. "I need something to secure him. And we have to let them know you aren't inside," he said, gesturing to the roaring bungalow.

He unbuckled his belt. She saw him glance at her waist, but she wasn't wearing a belt. She patted her pockets—only a fork. She shook her head. The fork had stayed in her pocket through all that.

"There," she said, pointing to the dock. There was a life ring with a long length of rope attached.

"That'll do."

Again, she ran to the dock and climbed up. The end attached to the post was just a clip. They'd have to just work around the buoy.

A crash sounded, and Max looked up. The bungalow's roof caved in. She turned back toward Shane, who was yanking on his wet belt, stuck in wet pants.

Suddenly, Not-Cam rolled and surged at Shane's knees. She yelled, but it was too late. Shane fell and twisted on the way down. His head slammed into the edge of the dock and bounced off.

"Nooo!" Max yelled, already running.

Not-Cam began kicking Shane's prone body, then bent to slam his fists into his face. Shane hadn't moved.

Max launched herself off the dock and into him—taking him down. The fork was in her hand, the other fisted in his shirt. Overhand she stabbed repeatedly—going for the Adam's apple, the neck. Cam pushed and hit her, but she didn't stop. She stabbed his eye and he roared and threw her off. She tumbled. He stood, ripped the fork out, and threw it to the ground. He pressed a hand to his face and took off running.

Max scrambled over to Shane. "Shane!" She patted his face as hard as she dared. "Please. Oh God." She pounded on his chest, filled now with an entirely different kind of fear. She couldn't lose him now. She wouldn't. She scooped handfuls of water and threw it on his face. His eyelids flickered.

"Shane, wake up!" she pleaded.

Finally, his eyes opened and he groaned. Max bent her head to his chest, gulping back sobs of relief, and sent up a prayer of thanks. She rose up and put a hand to his cheek, so happy to see his gorgeous eyes staring back at her.

Shane blinked a few times. Then he seemed to really come to and sat up, grasping her upper arms. "Max," he said. He looked around—past her, even as one hand moved to the left side of his head. "Shit. Move—" he said practically throwing her aside.

"No—" she said, "just stay."

He jumped to his feet. He cupped her face. "I have to finish this. Once and for all."

Then he took off. He called back over his shoulder. "Get help. Call the police."

Max yelled back. "If he turns back into Cam, don't hurt him!"

And yet she was far more worried about Shane. Not-Cam she'd be glad to see pummeled and behind bars. Her Cam... might be gone forever. If he was still in there somewhere, he would likely never be well or free.

Max swore and sent up a quick prayer—the only one she might have some control over—that she'd have a chance to love and be loved by Shane.

Then she ran toward the burning rubble and help.

———

Cam must be hurting because he wasn't running well. He stumbled and weaved through the brush. He stayed close to the water, crossed another dock, and continued into the dark vegetation.

Shane's own head throbbed with every footfall, but still he caught up easily and lunged to tackle Cam to the ground. They rolled, swinging.

Shane wondered which Cam he had, until he took one to the jaw, and alter ego smiled with sick glee. That was that then, and murdered women meant he didn't have to fight fair. He slammed a fist into Cam's already bloody eye with all the strength he had. Cam screamed and fought to stay conscious.

Shane righted himself. He kept a knee on Cam's chest, as he tried again to take off his belt.

But Cam lashed out and rolled. They both jumped to their feet. Facing off, they circled.

Cam's one good eye burned with hatred. Max needn't have worried—the Cam they knew wasn't here. His alter ego was still firmly in place. Shane wondered at this point if he'd taken over for good. Was that even possible?

Round and round they went. Cam feinted left and swung right. Shane easily evaded it and came in hard. Cam stumbled and yanked Frank's gun from the back of his pants. Shane didn't know how he'd managed to keep it on him, but he sure didn't want to find out if it would fire wet.

Shane raised his arms as if he was backing off, but really he shifted into a stance from which he could kick. His foot connected with Cam's wrist, catching it from the inside where it would bend.

Crack!

It had fired, but Cam's grip was wobbly and the bullet, Shane thought, hit the earth.

He rushed Cam—noting the rage on his battered face—and delivered a solid blow to Cam's temple.

He went down. And stayed down.

CHAPTER 52

IN THE WEE HOURS, when the police had released them to go get some sleep, Shane drove them to the nearest regular hotel. As soon as they entered their room, Shane apologized to Max.

He looked pained. "I just wanted you to know, I didn't mean to kill Cam."

She cupped his face and kissed him gently. "I know," she said.

Tears sprang to her eyes, and she cried. For Cam, who was a wonderful man when he was just Cam. For the pain he must have endured to have also become someone so sick and violent. For the women he'd killed, ripping them from their families, their bright futures. For Shane, who had to bear the burden of his death. For herself, even, who would likely always harbor guilt for not seeing the full picture in time to stop any of it.

Shane wrapped her in his arms and let her sob. He cried, too. Eventually, she was spent and shuddered out a breath.

Shane helped her scrub the smoky smell from her hair, and they made love—slow, serious, life-affirming love.

There would be time, Max knew, to talk about the details of them. A couple. But she wasn't worried. They were together. Solidly together. The details didn't matter. They'd sort it all out in due time.

They slept—but only for a few hours. Afterward, and

for days, they dealt with the police, Bodhi's management, a hospital visit to Frank Ryan who thankfully was going to be okay, their missed flights, buying some clothes for Max, and replacing her phone, which of course had burned in the bungalow.

Detective Iocavelli flew out. With a preliminary death certificate, he had been able to read Cam's therapist's file.

Danny explained to Shane and Max that Dissociative Identity Disorder resulted from serious abuse or intense trauma. By the time Cam started seeing the therapist, Cam was an adult. He talked very little about his childhood, but the therapist believed there were both significant abandonment issues regarding Cam's mother, trauma over her death, and ongoing abuse—largely verbal but possibly physical—from his father. His older brother was significantly older and fit the father's mold. He'd grown up near poverty, in a rural community, and likely stayed under the radar at school and otherwise.

"Ronnie," the therapist believed, had begun as a 'healthy or positive split.' Like an older brother should have been. He protected Cam: made Cam feel safe, loved, cared for, part of a family. It allowed him to be who he really was—a gay male with a penchant for fashion and makeup and an adoration of women's bodies—because he knew Ronnie had his back.

Danny said, "Nothing in the file, but I'd bet Cam—Ronnie, I mean—killed his father. Probably protecting Cam." Shane had already told Max about finding the information about Cam's dad's death and the tape over his mouth.

Max felt such sadness. She could only imagine that even then the tape had been symbolic…Verbal abuse? Sexual?

She'd never understand the cruelty people could exact on those they were supposed to love and care for…and now only God knew what awfulness young Cam had endured.

Shane said, "It's astounding that none of us saw it. Never had a clue."

"Not really," Danny said. "There aren't any slips, any tells, because they believe they are who they are. They don't even believe, they just *are*. So much so that even physicality is affected. Fully formed other people that sort of take up residence, pushing another personality out of the way. I've seen video of these sorts of cases. It's…" He shook his head giving up on trying to explain. "Besides, in this case, Ronnie may have been dormant for years. The psychologist believes there must have been a trigger event. Something that brought Ronnie back to the forefront."

Max struggled to understand, but it seemed per Danny's rough explanation, that when Ronnie came forward, Cam disappeared. But with all the access she'd given Cam to her files, it would have been easy for Ronnie to snoop and find out any information he needed. Could he even have enlisted Cam at times? It was impossible to figure. And they'd never really know.

She hugged herself. Shane wrapped his arm around her, tucking her into his chest.

Danny looked pained. He rubbed his face then looked right at Max. "I owe you an apology."

She shook her head.

"I do," he said. "I—we—screwed up big time. We pegged the wrong man. You nearly paid for that with your life."

"Thank you," Max said. She reached out and squeezed Danny's hand. "But you figured it out in time. Really, it was your warning that saved me."

"Hey—" Shane said, "I had a little something to do with it." He pointed to the stitches on the right side of his head. She already knew that Shane was really the one who'd figured out something with Cam wasn't right, that his suspicions about a brother had pushed Danny to dig harder. And God knew, if he hadn't flown out here…

"You, my hero, I'll thank later." Max twisted around to kiss him.

Shane grinned around her kiss. "I can't wait."

Danny said, "I'm outta here."

————

The minute they were free to go home, flights were booked for early the next morning and they shifted to a nicer hotel near the airport. Shane and Max both took scalding showers and ate their room service dinner in robes. They were largely talked out, but as Shane watched her twirl her fork in some angel hair pasta, he remembered.

"Not to take you back there again," Shane began, "but I've been wondering about something Danny said."

"What's that?" Max asked.

"The wounds to his neck and eye," Shane said. "How is it that you just happened to be carrying around a fork when you were attacked?"

Max laughed, then nearly choked. She shook her head as she worked to swallow, then wiped her mouth. "I hardly happened to be carrying around a fork. I armed myself," she said. "I had a knife and a pen, too—the only sharp objects I could find—but somehow the fork was the only one left. And I didn't care what the hell it was—when I saw him beating you to death when you were already unconscious, I just went nuts."

"You saved my life."

She raised her chin.

"You saved my life," he said laughing, "with a fork."

"Yes—I did! Now stop making fun of me," she said.

"Oh my, Kierney, you—"

"That word!" Max said scowling. "Stop calling me that."

Shane looked puzzled. "When did I—"

"Just stop. It's rude and I don't like it. Especially because I don't know what it—"

Shane leaned across the bed and kissed her on the lips. "Shush, lass." He swiped the tray of food they'd been sharing.

She pouted. She was still hungry, and now she was grumpy, too.

"Let me make it up to you." He grabbed her ankle and stretched her prone. Her robe rode up but it didn't matter because he untied it first thing. He dropped his own robe and it was quite clear he didn't care if she was mad or not.

"That's not fair," she said, even though her heartbeat had already kicked up a notch.

"What about this?" Shane said, and proceeded to wipe away any memory of her annoyance by lavishing delicious attention on every inch of her.

When she was practically incoherent, Shane pulled her arms above her head and held them there. He murmured, "I've only said that word to you once before."

She most emphatically did not want to think about a young, drunk angry Shane right now.

"You've had it wrong all this time," he said, and sucked hard on a nipple.

She gasped. "What?"

He attended to the other nipple until she could barely remember the discussion. Then he poised himself at her entrance. She positively quivered in anticipation.

"Ask me what it means," Shane said.

"No," she said.

He smiled and nudged her legs farther apart with his knees.

"I don't want to know," she said.

"I think you do," Shane said and pressed ever so gently against her.

"I don't," she said.

He shrugged a shoulder and made to get up.

"Okay, fine."

Shane took up position again. Max pulled on his hips. He didn't budge. Instead he gave her a wicked smile. "Not until you hear me out."

She'd have crossed her arms if she could have but he had them pinned once more. "I said fine."

He smiled, pleased, and kissed her softly on the mouth.

"For us Irish men," he said holding her eyes with his own, "a kierney, is the most crazy beautiful, wild lass you've ever seen. A siren you'd follow to the ends of the earth and back."

"Oh," Max said, her heart filling with joy.

"Yes, oh," Shane said, and then *finally*, he stopped talking.

Thank you for reading,
and I truly hope you enjoyed!

———————

— UNLIKELY SERIES —
Evil lurks in the most unlikely places...

UNHINGED
(Book 1)

Social worker Tori Radnor and wealthy businessman Aiden Miller team up, but as the desire between them increases, so do threats from an elusive villain. When bizarre taunts escalate into terrifying attacks, they must confront their worst fears—before it all becomes unhinged.

UNCOVERED
(Book 2)

To find a murderer, marine Eddie Mackey must enlist the help of Miranda Hill, the reluctant photojournalist who filmed his wife's last words. The investigation soon lands them both in a world of danger, and he must take on the role of protector. If only he knew how to protect his heart.

— RETRIEVAL, INC. SERIES —
Where everyday meets evil...

RUNAWAY
(Book 1)

Detective Mitch Saunders uncovers a disturbing link between his missing sister and one of his cold cases. Years ago, Laura Macnamara walked out her backdoor and simply disappeared. Runaway, or victim? Time to find out. Because Laura—now known as Charlie Hart—holds the key to his sister's safety. Except Charlie refuses to help him. Between her carefully guarded secrets and well-founded fears, too much is at stake to look back. Nor can she consider a future with Mitch—a man who will expose her to evil, if that's what it takes to bring his sister home. He leaves Charlie no choice but to run—again. Or is it already too late?

ACKNOWLEDGMENTS

It takes a village, indeed! And I sure rely on mine! Huge thanks go to:

Maureen Hansch, whose brilliant insights into my villain's psyche made it all come together for me. (Note to self: always walk on the beach with Maureen before starting a new manuscript!)

Diana Quincy, RoseAnn DeFranco, and AJ Scudiere, critique partners extraordinaire, and Eli Jackson Collier, the best fight scene guru.

Jen Hinger, Robyn Donovan, and Marco Conelli, for helping me nail various industry information, and my daughter for sharing key documents and videos from her AP Psychology class. So important to me to get it right! To that end, I must include Molly Sims with Tracy O'Conner for The Everyday Supermodel and Terry Hipp for Executive Protection, The Essentials. Out of all the research books I read, these two were the most valuable.

The real Lillian Willkens, who graciously let me borrow her name with no stipulations for good or evil!

My fab editing team who excels at seeing what I can't: Aquila Editing, Barbara Greenberg of BJG Publishing Services, Carol Agnew, and Jan Carol. What would I do without your expertise?

My family, friends, and writing pals, I'd be lost without your never-ending belief in me.

And last but never least, to my readers for your support, great reviews, and lovely notes! Your enthusiasm makes it all worth it!

Ever grateful...

JB SCHROEDER, a graduate of Penn State University's creative writing program and a book designer by trade, now crafts thrilling romantic suspense novels. Blessed with a loving family and friends, JB has no idea why her stories lean toward gritty, and her characters keep finding evil—but she wouldn't have it any other way.

JB loves to connect with readers and can be reached through her website:

www.jbschroederauthor.com

Made in the USA
Columbia, SC
06 November 2018